T0147531

Our Father Died

Our Father Died

CASTELLANO TURNER

authorHOUSE®

AuthorHouse™
1663 Liberty Drive
Bloomington, IN 47403
www.authorhouse.com
Phone: 1-800-839-8640

Published by AuthorHouse   11/26/2012

ISBN: 978-1-4772-8860-3 (sc)
ISBN: 978-1-4772-8858-0 (hc)
ISBN: 978-1-4772-8859-7 (e)

Library of Congress Control Number: 2012921246

For
Ezekiel and Kieran
Our Future

Table of Contents

CHAPTER 1:

The Day Our Father Died

It was January of 1989, nearly forty-four years after the day our father died. At the UCLA Medical Center the main waiting area for the families and friends of the sick straddled the long, wide walkway from the hospital proper to the parking garages. I sat, paced, and fitfully read a few pages from a book I had brought in my briefcase. I understood that this area was special, had a meaning, a role. I shared something with most of the people around me; I saw, in their faces, the semi-fixed stare of worry. We had a common purpose—wait and watch.

It was easy to tell the difference between kith and kin and volunteers who told us the good or bad news, whenever it came. Most were late middle-aged women, well-dressed and well-coiffed. But more than anything else, they looked out of place in the company of the distressed. They were nice, generous people, endeavoring to be pleasant. They were even chipper. I wondered whether this up-beat attitude was an intentional part of the service provided or whether it simply reflected why they were there. Why should they wear faces of distress or concern? They were helping the hospital and us, so had every right to feel good about themselves.

From time to time the telephone rang on the desk where a volunteer sat. Typically the message was for those waiting. The volunteer paged one of us and delivered a brief message or directive:

"Please go to the third floor waiting area."

"Surgery is scheduled for 2:30 PM and is expected to last two hours."

"The attending doctor will meet the family in the waiting area around 5 o'clock."

Sometimes the volunteer paged the family and handed the telephone to whoever approached. The doctor wanted to speak with a family member directly, or the family had left the phone number with others, so they could report quickly on the status of the sick.

Having delivered my sister Precious (*given name:* Preciosa Lolita Turner) to her room in the early morning, I sat nearby while two young doctors interviewed her for about an hour. The questions were presented as routinely as reading a bus schedule, but the content of the answers felt to me like peeling away the scab of half-healed wounds. I was amazed at the information my sister gave them without a hint of hesitation. I listened and wondered whether she wished I were not there. For my part, I couldn't tear myself away from what felt like the intimate conversation we had rarely shared. She had a hysterectomy eight years earlier. She had decided against the "radical" hysterectomy in order to avoid the life-long discipline of medicine to offset the loss of estrogen. Her right breast had been removed five years later. She had gone through several series of chemotherapy over the years. Although she reported everything as if she were applying for a job or answering a survey, I knew she was aware of the seriousness of the situation. I admired her strength and wondered whether I would be able to be similarly stoic when facing the critical operation she now faced.

As Precious was rolled away, a nurse told me I could wait in the main waiting area and I would be contacted by the early afternoon.

Precious had called me a few days earlier. My wife Barbara and I were on sabbatical leaves at the University of California San Francisco and lived in Alameda, an island east across the bay. I was immediately struck by the worry in Precious's voice. "I have some bad news," she began.

Gripping the receiver with both hands, I squeezed. Her doctor had discovered a growth in her abdominal area. "It's probably cancer again," she said. I had never heard her sound like that—not when her first breast cancer was diagnosed, not when she had the mastectomy. She was strong. Somehow she had always felt she would survive. Without her telling me, I knew she thought this was more serious.

In spite of the terror she must have felt, she was calling mainly because she was concerned about how our mother and sister would manage while she was in the hospital. She asked whether I was available to stay with them. I was pleased to be able to help and quickly made arrangements to go down to Los Angeles. The thought that this meant Precious would probably die didn't occur to me.

In the early afternoon a doctor still dressed in an operating room gown and cap paged me. When I identified myself, he pulled me aside, shook my hand, and assured himself of eye contact. He spoke quickly and with no sign of emotion.

"You are a relative of Lolita Turner?"

"Yes. I'm her brother," I responded, trying to be as crisp as he was.

"Let me explain what has happened and what is happening now. I was the primary surgeon. I began the operation. We understood it was exploratory. When we opened your sister up, we found her entire trunk cavity filled with tumors—undoubtedly ovarian cancer. This was as expected."

I lost my focus on him and felt my body weaken. I felt faint, but I held my attention on the words as if they were anchors to survive what was being said.

I regained focus while the doctor continued. "The standard procedure at most hospitals, when this is discovered, is simply to close the person up again and send them home to die. The prognosis is very poor. Here at UCLA the surgical oncology group takes an aggressive stance toward cancer. They were standing by when I walked away from your sister. They intend to continue the operation and remove everything they can."

With a question in his eyes, he slowed his pace; he seemed to get more in touch with what the implications would be for a brother, but he went on. "Your sister had talked with the oncology group and agreed that this was what should be done. Do you have any questions about this? This is the last time I'll be directly involved with your sister's case."

Is this what I was supposed to expect? I thought. *Had I been in denial? No, I wasn't expecting this. Some doctor walks into the waiting room and announces that my sister has a massive cancer in her body and is certain to die? Where is this coming from?* The scene was briefly unreal. Then

I realized from the doctor's body shift that he wanted to make this conversation brief.

I came back and finally asked impulsively, "When did they start? How long will the operation last?"

"It may take a while. They try to get as much out as they possibly can. It may be four more hours. Someone will contact you when it's over. If you wish, you can go to the waiting room on the tenth floor. After the operation she'll be in intensive care up there."

I was looking past him, into the distance. He noticed and moved his body and head slightly to put himself into my line of vision. His head tilted to the side. "Do you have any other questions?"

"No, I think I'll stay here for a while."

As the surgeon walked off I turned and slipped down into a leather chair nearby. It was softer than before. I felt as if I was sinking into it, falling slowly. Tears were in my eyes. The sadness I felt ran through my entire body. I was going to lose my sister? Precious was going to die? The space around my body felt like soft mud, and I was floating motionless, gasping through tears.

After several minutes I pulled myself up and back into the seat, squeezed the tears from my eyes, rubbed my face with both hands, and reached into my briefcase for a pad of lined paper and a ballpoint pen. I wrote at the top of the page: "The Day Our Father Died." Without forewarning came the feeling, the idea, the recognition that what was happening to Precious and my response to it were related to our father's death forty-four years earlier. The words, the sentences, the images were immediately available. I simply watched myself write the story of that distant day, as if I were witnessing it there in the waiting room.

Our father died in the early spring of 1945. When I try to think about that day, I feel as if I'm reaching back into a dream—watching blurry figures move about, reconstructing dialogue with small variations each time. Whatever the picture, however clear or vague, no matter the emotions present, I always know that everything important in my life began on that day. After forty-four years of remembering and reconstructing, of getting bits and pieces of new information—sometimes in a rush of a few hours or days and sometimes after years of waiting and pushing thoughts away—I'm prepared to look straight at that day and what happened.

In the late afternoon of that dark Chicago day in March of 1945 I was sitting on the ledge of the third floor hallway window, which opened onto the fire escape that cluttered up the front of the four-story red brick and dingy concrete building at 812 West 14th Street, where my family lived most of the time I was growing up. Over the course of ten years I spent more time on that fire escape than I spent anywhere else other than bed and my wood and pig iron row desk at the St. Joseph Mission School. At six years of age, I was barely beginning to be aware of where I was, who I was, and the world around me. That afternoon a teenage distant cousin, who was my mother's godchild, came to visit my mother. He had come many times before, but I didn't really know him. He joined me on the window ledge and with our pairs of shoes lined up together in a row on the steel grating of the fire escape, we talked about nothing, and he asked me often when I thought my mother would be home. Leroy had come to be referred to in the family as "crazy Leroy." He nervously and insistently asked me why my mother wasn't home. All I knew was that my mother was working, and when I came home in the afternoons, she was usually gone. He was weird, and on that day he annoyed me for the first time.

The day must have been close to the beginning of spring. I think so because every year Mr. Goldberg, the landlord of the building, locked the windows and nailed them shut for the winter when the weather became so cold the tenants complained of drafts from the hall. Then there was little daylight in the hall until the weather was warm enough that someone took the nails out and let the spring in. If it wasn't the first day of spring, it was close, because the window was open but Leroy and I were wearing jackets warm enough to hold off the bite of cold winds.

"You don't have a key, Castie?" Leroy asked abruptly.

"No. I had one, but I lost it," I answered, silently staring at the building across the street.

"When does your daddy come home?" began a series of questions trying to locate and set a time for the family's return.

Daddy? I thought to myself. "I don't know."

"How about Jimmy. Where is Jimmy?"

"Where is June? Why isn't June home?"

"How come you're here and nobody else is here?"

"Where is Precious? Didn't you go to school with Precious today? Where is Precious?"

"I don't know," I answered blandly to each question. "I just walked home after school and I been waitin' for somebody to come home so I can get in." I hoped he wouldn't ask me anything more or just leave me alone to look into the street. He did stop asking but he didn't leave.

After a short while we both turned our heads and looked down the stairs in response to the sound of footsteps. After a another minute a tall, dark-haired white man reached the bottom of the second floor landing and looked up at us at the window. I had never seen anyone like him in our building before. He was wearing a dark suit, a white shirt, and a dark tie. On top of that he wore a loosely hanging, dark, worn-thin overcoat or raincoat. As he climbed his eyes flitted back and forth between the two of us. We must have looked like an odd pair. Leroy was a small teenager (fifteen or sixteen) and probably assumed to be white. When the man looked at me he saw a milk chocolate colored boy with curly hair and patchy clothes—like many around that neighborhood who had been sent into the streets by families of hopeful migrants from the South and immigrants from Mexico.

"I'm looking for Mrs. Turner—Mrs. Loretta Turner," he said hesitantly while he quickly consulted a hand-sized spiral notebook. "Do you know where she lives?" he continued, letting his eyes move back and forth between us.

Leroy gestured at me but continued staring at the man. "That's his mother. She's my Nanan," said Leroy with the twang of Louisiana Creole clearest on the name he always used to address my mother.

"She's not home yet," I said, with my stare as fixed on the man as was Leroy's.

The man hesitated again, this time longer. He seemed to be considering what to do. Walking away from the hallway window and toward the stairs leading up, he passed by the three doors on the floor.

"Which one is your apartment?" he asked.

"That's the front door, where you are now. This one here is ours too," I answered quickly and pointed to the door near the window, "but we don't use it."

The man moved as if he would knock on the door, but then he saw us following his movements and walked slowly toward us.

"I guess I could wait a while," he said quietly, mostly to himself. He had a pleasant face, but he looked tired and a bit dispirited. Leaning against the window frame, he looked blankly past our shoulders and down into the street.

Leroy and I finally turned back toward the street. I was uneasy. So was Leroy. We took turns sneaking quick, nervous glances at the man. He didn't look at us for several minutes. The only thing below to hold any real attention was an occasional red electric streetcar rolling by noisily, banging the steel rails and clanking to warn cars and pedestrians out of its way.

Finally, the man focused on Leroy. "Are you going to be here until Mrs. Turner comes home?"

"Uh huh. I'll be here," answered Leroy, a bit excited but uncertain.

"Well, would you tell her something?" He waited only the second it took to make sure he had Leroy's attention and went on without waiting for a response. "Would you tell her police detective Dempsey from the Maxwell Street Police Station came to see her? I need to talk to her as soon as possible." While he said this he casually pulled out a wallet, which he opened to flash a silver badge with star points.

He stopped, seemed embarrassed, and said quietly to Leroy, "Tell her there was an accident, and Mr. Turner died this afternoon. He fell . . ."

"What?" I blurted out and stared at Leroy, as if to have him confirm that the man had said what he said.

"He fell . . ." the man continued, but he caught himself. Glancing uncertainly from one to the other, he tried again. "He fell at work. She needs to come over to the station on Maxwell Street when she gets home. Ok? Will you tell her that?"

"Jim dead?" Leroy couldn't answer until what he had heard sank in.

The man didn't answer. We both stared at him. He repeated, "Will you tell her that?"

"Yes, I'll tell her," said Leroy slowly, not quite attending as the man turned and walked down the stairs. We heard the policeman reach the ground floor and push open the noisy front door. Looking down to the sidewalk through the iron bars of the fire escape, we saw him turn to the right out of the building, walk down to the corner, and turn right onto Newberry Street heading toward Maxwell Street, only a block away. With his hands stuck deep into his coat pockets, he was gone.

Over the next hour, as the cloudy day turned to a dim grayness, we waited nervously. At first Leroy kept talking about what he would say to his Nanan, but then he fell silent. I said nothing but began to worry about my mother. Time was suspended, and we sat there staring into the street.

By the time we saw my mother turn the corner off Halsted Street and onto 14th Street we had made our way down to the window on the second-floor hall and had spent an hour looking away from each other and occasionally mumbling. We sprang when we saw her. Leroy was ahead of me, but I could hardly have tumbled down the stairs faster than I ran. We were racing to reach my mother, but I didn't want to reach her. I didn't want to tell her. I didn't want to say it. I slowed down, but Leroy sped ahead.

My mother yielded a tired smile when she noticed us running toward her. She was carrying a large brown-paper bag with both arms and probably thought we were rushing to relieve her of her burden. Even as he ran Leroy was yelling out "Nanan." He reached my mother half way to our building. I was a few steps behind him.

"Nanan! Nanan!" Grabbing for her right arm, Leroy begged for her attention. "Nanan, Jim is dead. Jim is dead, Nanan."

She kept walking, but her face turned into a stony mask of fear and despair, and she looked straight into my eyes. Leroy was talking, but my mother was looking straight at me. What was I supposed to do?

"Leroy, get away from me with your foolishness," she said with an insecure smile.

"Nanan, it's true. A policeman came and told us. He told me to tell you. Nanan, it's true!"

My mother's face fell again, but she continued to walk—even faster now, as if she needed to get away from Leroy, out of the street, and home as soon as possible. I had been staying slightly in front of them and I kept looking into my mother's face over my shoulder. Now she and Leroy passed me, and I trailed them to the front of our apartment building.

At the top of the five steps to the first floor landing stood Mrs. Wilson. She was a short, very heavy, dark-skinned woman, who never had anything but a sad look on her face. She seemed always to be laboring just to walk about. Because she lived on the first floor and because her apartment had a large window looking out onto 14th Street, she was aware of everything going on in the building and around it. She must have come to investigate the commotion Leroy and I had made going down the stairs followed by Leroy's shrill and insistent voice moving back down the street.

When my mother started up the short flight to the first floor, she hesitated. Leaning on the banister, she looked up and saw Mrs. Wilson.

"What's wrong?" Mrs. Wilson asked, more with a tone of interest than of concern.

"They say my husband is dead," my mother answered in a daze, but she began to pull herself up the stairs.

Mrs. Wilson responded with increased concern; she saw that my mother might faint there in the hall. "Come on inside and sit down for a minute," she said and ushered my mother into her dining room.

As my mother sat, Mrs. Wilson went on with a combination of compassion and inquisitiveness. "Lord have mercy! I'm so sorry. What happened?"

Finally my mother began to cry. Her tears came in a gush, but they were brief, as if she had found herself in a strange place and now needed to find a way out. She drank a little of the water Mrs. Wilson brought to her and appeared to recover. She finally answered Mrs. Wilson. "I don't know. I have to go and see about my children. Thank you. I'll be all right now."

The door had remained open, and Leroy and I stood looking in. When my mother came out, she turned and went up the stairs briskly to our door. Leroy finally took the bag, and my mother searched frantically through her purse until she located her key. She had stopped speaking in Mrs. Wilson's dining room. Leroy had been saying "Nanan" and asking questions, but she didn't respond.

"Nanan, what are you gonna do?" asked Leroy repeatedly in uncontrollable excitement. It was as if he needed to know what would happen next more than my mother needed to get control of the situation and her own feelings. She stared at him blankly but didn't answer. Her whole body seemed shrunken, as if a boulder were on her back. All she could do was to go to the kitchen, put down her purse and sit at the table.

She tried again to undo Leroy's news. She pulled up her body, looked squarely at Leroy, and said with a combination of bitterness and suspicion, "If this is some foolishness, Leroy . . ." She intended no end to the statement and was prepared for Leroy's interruption.

"Nanan! No, Nanan!" Leroy answered insistently. "A policeman came and told me to tell you. He said you was to come to the station on Maxwell Street. He told both of us." He gestured at me as if to get my backing for his report. Half standing and half sitting on one of the chairs, I was mute. I was a bystander too frightened to be active but unable to break away from the hold of what was happening. My mother looked at me as if she didn't want an answer, then as if she didn't expect an answer. After a few seconds her face took on a pained expression. She grabbed her mouth and nose, but the tears had already started running down her cheeks. For a few minutes even Leroy was quiet. We looked at my mother now bent over the table with her face in both hands. We looked at each other, embarrassed by our helplessness.

After several minutes my mother sat upright, reached for her purse, drew out a small handkerchief, dabbed her eyes and nose, and blew her nose. Even as she fought off the tears, she brought her focus back to Leroy and asked quietly, "You said it was a policeman that came? I'm supposed to go to the police station on Maxwell Street?"

"That's what he said, Nanan," answered Leroy, now somber.

My mother rose and began to put the items from the large paper sack in various places around the kitchen. At the door to the kitchen was an old red grocery-store icebox with "Coca-Cola" on all sides. As usual, the fifteen-pound block of ice that fit loosely into one side was half melted. She lifted the lid and placed a small package on top of the block of ice and some vegetables near the ice on the bottom of the box. She put the other items onto a shelf near the gas stove that occupied one corner of the kitchen. She folded the bag and placed it neatly with others just inside the pantry near the door that led to the back stairs, which were almost never used. While she did these things she said nothing, but her face was as frozen as the ice. Finally, she pulled her overcoat around her, picked up her purse from the table, and said "I'll be back soon as I can," and left.

Leroy followed her out, but I went into the living room. I felt empty and numb.

Later she sent the older children, June and Jimmy, to stay with friends on the other side of the city. I can only guess what burdens they carried with them on that long streetcar ride.

In the evening a number of adults were in the apartment comforting my mother, who had retreated to her bed in one of the two tiny bedrooms. I hesitated but finally went in. She was crying uncontrollably and rolling around on the edge of the bed. The adults in the room looked awkward and helpless, just standing around watching my mother's agony. Finally, my sister Precious approached the side of the bed in tears and implored our mother to stop crying. "Mama, don't cry! Mama, please don't cry! Please, Mama, don't!"

Without hesitation, I did the same. I pressed my face, wet with tears, into her arm and pleaded with our mother not to suffer, not to show us her pain.

She lay on the bed crying with her two youngest children, both kneeling at the side of the bed, in tears, wanting to share her pain and wanting it to stop. She pulled us into the bed with her. We cried until we were tired, and finally I must have fallen asleep, because I remember nothing more of that day.

The policeman who appeared while Leroy and I sat on the fire escape window ledge had spoken to me in the waiting area; he was replaced by the surgeon. He had some bad news to give to somebody. An unpleasant task. He needed to get through the relating of the story as if it were somehow routine, readily understandable by anyone who heard it, without too much pain. Before it was over, though, there was the same questioning expression, some doubt about whether this could be made so simple. The policeman had a premonition about the next forty-four years. He hesitated. Then he walked down the stairs and away from the future that began with his announcement. The surgeon walked away from the story that lay behind the cancer, away from the story of a woman and her four children left behind.

When I finished all I could write, I called my brother Jim, and we arranged to meet there in the waiting room in the late afternoon.

When Jim arrived, we walked outside into the sunny plaza that is the roof of the hospital's main garage. Sitting on one of the stone and concrete blocks decorating the large plaza, I related all the doctor had said. I was agitated and distraught but didn't cry. This time *I* was bringing bad news, and it was as if the only way I could get through it was by relating what I knew clearly and quickly, much as the surgeon had.

"They take an aggressive stance toward cancer here," I said as I ended my report, "but the prognosis is never good with late-stage ovarian cancer."

Jim looked at me in silence as I gave my report. When I ended with the poor prognosis, he looked away and said, "There is no stopping these things. No matter what you do, they keep coming back." Did he mean this was Precious's third cancer diagnosis? Or was he giving his own estimate of where this was leading?

We looked at each other grimly, as if we were unprepared to share our personal misery with each other. It felt like a wake, where people surmise the sentiments of everyone else present by the occasion itself. No one cries. People speak little, and only obliquely.

"I think we have to be careful how we tell Mom," I said. "I'm prepared to put as good a face on what the doctors say as possible. For now the operation is proceeding, and I'll let her know what the doctor tells me—but not the prognosis. I doubt they'll be able to tell me much in any case."

I was determined to stay on there until after the oncologist's report. We agreed to meet when I knew more from the doctor. Jim left, and I continued my vigil.

When I reread what I had begun in the waiting area, I realized that the most painful part was remembering my mother. How would I be able to tell her? What would she say? What could she do? The news about our father had turned her face into a mask of terror and despair. How would she react to the prospect of having her daughter die before her?

Somehow there was a mix-up between the volunteers in the main waiting area and the doctors coming out of surgery. I had moved to the waiting room upstairs, and the surgeon went looking for me downstairs. Finally we managed to find each other. Dr. Peterson was a small and remarkably young looking surgeon. We talked by the elevator. He was clearly tired and eager to get out of the hospital.

"I'm Dr. Peterson," he began. "I'm an associate of Dr. Montz. Dr. Montz tried to find you earlier. You are Lolita Turner's brother?"

"Yes," I responded, but my legs immediately felt weak again.

"Dr. Montz asked me to explain to you what we did and how things stand."

"Yes. Thank you," I said softly. A part of me wished he hadn't found me.

"There's not that much I can tell you now. Your sister was in surgery for six hours. We cut her up pretty badly. We were trying to get everything. The prognosis is better, if we get more of the tumor out. That's what took so long."

"Did you succeed? How's she doing?"

"We got all the visible tumors. It's difficult to say whether the cancer had metastasized to other areas we couldn't see. To be perfectly frank with you, it's very unlikely that everything will be cured with this surgery. Dr. Montz will talk with you sometime in the next few days about the follow-up treatments he recommends."

I tried to put on a courageous, business-like front. I asked when I could see her.

"As I said, we cut her up pretty badly. She'll be under heavy sedation, at least until late tomorrow. You should come and see her then and try to get an appointment with Dr. Montz. She'll be in a great deal of discomfort for the next few days. Don't expect too much of a response."

I thanked him for his efforts and for his consideration in waiting to tell me about the surgery. We parted with a handshake and smiles, but I hoped never to see him again.

When I arrived at Ma's house, where she and Precious had lived together for twenty-six years, she was in bed. I went in quietly, I kissed her and sat on the side of the bed. She cried but didn't ask me anything. Holding one of her hands, I simply sat with her for a while. Then I told her I had been at the hospital all day. I told her everything—except the prognosis. As far as the surgeons could tell they had gotten all of the cancer. They had done all they could for now, but there would be a need for treatment later.

Giving her the easiest and most palatable information, my emotional expression was muted, because I didn't want her to show me the full extent of her own distress. Sitting up in bed she cried more as I finished my report; she said nothing; then her head fell back limply into the pillow.

During the days that Precious was in the hospital and I slept on my mother's living room couch I was the messenger and the comforter, but I felt unable to care for my mother as I wanted. Was I afraid of her enormous need for comforting? Instead, I took care of chores and made some minor house repairs.

When I returned to the hospital the next day, I went about finding Dr. Montz first. I made an appointment and he appeared promptly. Like Dr. Peterson, he was younger in appearance than I had expected. He was a handsome man of medium height and muscular build. Sitting in his small office, we spoke for about half an hour across his cluttered desk. Given my experience the day before, his manner of giving his news was more comforting than I had expected.

"I would be pleased to answer any questions you have," he said, clearly wishing to engage.

I had thought about what the main issue was to be and, like the doctor, I didn't hesitate to go to it. "What's the prognosis?"

"Mr. Turner, your sister's condition is very serious. Her chances of surviving are substantially less than 50/50. But her chances are also substantially greater than zero."

I pressed him a bit on this point. "Can you be a bit more precise? What percentage of cases of this kind survive past five years?"

He clasped his hands in his lap, settled comfortably back into his swivel chair, and said, "That's hard to say. My own general guess would be around 20%. On the other hand, it's difficult to say whether your sister's case is more like the 20% who survived or like the 80% who did not. Do you see what I mean?"

"I think I do," I said. "The research hasn't identified very well what factors are associated with survival."

"Exactly."

The doctor was pleased that he had succeeded in clarifying this point. He went on to give what sounded like a standard speech. "We take the position that giving up will lead to no survivors. With intensive treatment and some luck, some of the people we treat here have many good years. There is something of a gamble, of course. The treatments themselves are likely to be very unpleasant. Sometimes patients get to the point when they wonder whether the suffering part of the treatment is worth the possibility of survival. Given the probabilities, it's difficult to disagree. The gamble is whether to suffer and hope for more time or simply give in, knowing your time is very limited indeed."

"My guess is that my sister will want to try whatever treatment is available and might work," I said with a sense of reintroducing the specific party into the discussion. Some mixture of fear and despair washed over me even as I said this.

"I think you're right," the doctor said. "Your sister is intelligent, reasonable, and courageous. She seems like a fighter. And we'll do everything we can."

The hard part was over. We both took cleansing breaths and sighed after the high probability of death could be acknowledged. I asked, "What are the next steps in the treatment?"

The doctor sounded confident as he answered. "I'm going to put her on a series of chemotherapy treatments. She'll be in the hospital for a week or ten days just healing enough to move about. Her first chemo treatment will be given two days before discharge. Learning what the treatments are like is important, and she'll have to get used to some uncomfortable side effects."

"Like what?" I asked, keeping my control by focusing on my role as the family member who will need to tell others.

He took the briefest of breaths as if he had anticipated the follow-up question, and without losing his rhythm, said, "The major problem will be a great deal of nausea and general physical discomfort. For the first few treatments she'll feel sick for two weeks after the treatments. She'll lose her hair. There may be some neurological problems, mostly loss of feeling and tingling in her extremities. She'll feel wretched for long stretches of time. Then there'll be a few weeks to rest before she has to come in for her next treatment."

"How long will this go on?" I asked with just the mildest accent on *this*, revealing my distress.

"Six to eight treatments," he said quickly. "One each month for six to eight months. It'll be difficult and very tiring for her. Each time after the first she'll come in the day before. This is for evaluation and preparation. We need to monitor how well she is tolerating the treatments. Sometimes we need to make adjustments, if the patient is reacting poorly. She'll have the treatment on the second day and usually be able to leave on the third day. It depends on her physical condition."

"And at the end of this six or eight month series?" I asked, breaking in as the doctor's voice began to trail off indefinitely. "Will you know whether she has been helped?"

The doctor became more alert at this question and began enthusiastically what seemed a new chapter in the story. "At the end of that time we'll have your sister in for what is referred to as 'second look' surgery. Basically, we have to go in to see what the effects of the chemotherapy have been. We would remove whatever looks like the recurrence of tumors, but we would also take samples from all over the abdominal cavity for biopsy. On the basis of this, further treatment may be prescribed—probably a second course of chemotherapy."

He focused on me again and directed the next statement squarely at me, with the mildest of challenges. "A great deal depends on how well your sister tolerates the treatments. If we're forced to reduce the intensity because it's doing her harm, then . . ." He hesitated, looked to the left, and continued, more removed. "Then it's difficult to say what her chances of survival would be. But if her body can stand the chemotherapy, she has a chance."

I withered in the face of the doctor's candor. Tears came to my eyes, but I quickly wiped them away.

The doctor leaned forward, both arms on the desk, and waited a moment until I composed myself. He hadn't really ignored what had gone on with me, but he hadn't acknowledged it either. He continued, now attempting to be more consoling. "She may be one of the 20 percent. She seems like a strong person. I think she has a chance."

This was *not* consoling. I took a deep breath, slid forward in my chair, and stood.

"Thank you for taking the time to meet with me. I'll relay the information to my family. Can I see my sister now?"

CHAPTER 2:

Our Father's Funeral

The days immediately following my father's death were filled with silence. My memory is that no one spoke to me, and I said nothing to anyone. If there were snatches of conversation taking place around me, I never presumed to think of myself as part of them and retreated before I could be expected to participate. My policy was silence and, if I had been able to, I would have made myself invisible.

Our mother's father, Hortaire Ganier, and her two sisters, Léonie Duplessis and Amay Ganier, arrived from New Orleans two days later. Like my mother, they were large people—tall, big-boned, and heavy. At least, that was my impression of them. Our apartment was very small: small living room, small dining room, used as a bedroom all the time we lived there, two tiny bedrooms, a kitchen, and, off the kitchen, a small bathroom with a commode and a tub with white enamel inside and dark green paint covering the outside, including the ornate claw feet. The bathroom was too small for a washbasin, so the kitchen sink served its purpose. How these three additional adults squeezed into that living space, with our mother and four children, is hard to imagine.

On the evening of the third day there was a wake in the apartment. I was sitting alone on the hallway fire-escape windowsill looking down into the street. The day had become quite dark when a long black automobile parked in front of the building, next to the alley on its east side. Two men got out, went to the rear of the vehicle, opened the door, and pulled out a large rectangular box, which I feared was coming to us. I wondered how the men would be able to get it up the narrow staircase to the third floor. Soon I heard the two men grunting below. Then, from the top of the stairs, I saw them struggling to turn the corner up to the third floor. I marveled that they had gotten such a bulky object that far. Leaving the windowsill and standing in the hall, I continued looking down at them. When they reached the third floor landing, I quickly retreated into the apartment, found a place near a living room window, and stayed out of the way while the men arranged the box on a stand with torch lamps nearby.

Grownups, mostly in small groups, streamed through the darkened living room that evening, but my mother continued to spend much of the time in bed crying. In ones and twos visitors entered her bedroom to commiserate and comfort her, but she was inconsolable.

As soon as I could, I retreated again to the fire-escape window and watched the night traffic on 14th Street and Halsted Street—as I often would for many years. I have no memory of seeing my siblings or any other specific person that evening. I felt alone and afraid.

The funeral was held on the fourth day. One of my aunts took charge of me. She found my best clothes; hardly speaking, she pulled me around, told me to put this on and that on, and did what final changes needed to be done to make me presentable.

The funeral Mass was to be held in the chapel of the St. Joseph Mission School. I had first seen the chapel sometime earlier; I don't remember the circumstances. On that first visit, I had been stunned by its beauty. There was a statue of St. Joseph to the left of the small, ornate altar, but my attention was drawn immediately to a life-sized statue of the Virgin Mary, which stood on the right side. Fresh flowers surrounded it, and through a window to its right, bright sunshine streamed in, giving it a bright glow. Although I later attended the school for eight years, I never saw the chapel look as beautiful again.

On the day of the funeral, however, everything was dark—outside and inside. The chapel, which was on the third floor of the school and had many windows, was, like the day itself, covered by an opaque curtain of grayness. The casket stood open on the left side of the sanctuary, just inside the wooden communion railing. Few people were present. Father Cetnar, the Jesuit priest who served as pastor of the mission, gave a brief homily. He used words like "death and life," "earth and heaven," and "pain and joy." But he didn't say anything suggesting he knew my father or intended to speak about him. I didn't understand very much of what was happening.

At the end of the Mass, those attending were invited to file out past the casket, and I had my last look at my father. His pale face looked dry and flat, as if powder had been layered on. It was my father, but there was something very different about his face. I managed to get through this ordeal by letting my Aunt Amay take control and push me along—as if I was to do nothing that would annoy the adults around me. Outside the chapel, the hallway was particularly dark; little light got in from the overcast day and few lights were on. Many of those who had shuffled out of the chapel first lingered along the walls, as if waiting for a parade. I looked back and saw my mother being escorted out of the chapel by two men, each supporting her by an arm. Halfway along the hallway toward the stairs leading out she collapsed in a faint between them. They struggled to hold her, but they couldn't prevent her from slipping away onto the floor. Now on her knees, her body went limp, but the two men kept her from going down completely. After a brief interval in which everything froze, they made a concerted effort and got her back onto her feet. They stood holding her in place, as if evaluating whether to try to go on. Although her eyes were glazed, she finally put one foot forward. They took the signal and moved ahead and past me. I replayed this scene frequently in my memory over the years. Standing motionless, I had accepted that my mother was in pain but I was no longer capable of responding to her.

By the time everyone entered the automobiles parked in front of the school, a slight drizzle had begun. The cars used at the funeral must have been provided by the funeral parlor because, until I was older, no one in our family and no one we knew had one. The long ride to the Lincoln Cemetery was my first time in an automobile.

Whoever the adults were that I shared the back seat with ignored me, and their large bodies squeezed me onto a small space on the right side of the seat. We were all silent. My own thoughts were confused and full of questions. *Was that really my father in that casket? Would I ever see him again? What would happen to us, if we had no father?*

When we arrived at the place in the cemetery where our father was to be buried, the drizzle was more intense. The sky was the color of dirty snow—as if the city winter had been thrown upward out of the streets.

I wasn't allowed out of the back seat, and I saw what I saw through a triangular side window. Although I discovered later that the gravesite is actually in a flat area, I have a clear memory of looking upward as two young black men worked around a mound of dirt and laboriously maneuvered a plain pine box. I wondered what had happened to the rather elegant gray casket that had been at the wake and the funeral. Even then I realized something was not right.

Following the long ride back from the cemetery, a small group of relatives and friends came to our apartment. The adults congregated in the kitchen around the table. Most sat but others stood engaged in animated talk. I looked at them from the distance of the living room two rooms away. A few times they laughed briefly. That was odd to me.

People gradually departed, and when the only people remaining were my mother, my aunts, and my grandfather, the tone of the conversation sounded more serious.

My mother, nicknamed "Loleet" throughout her life in Louisiana, having cleared away dishes used by those who had left, sat across the table from her two sisters.

Léonie placed her cup of coffee into its saucer, braced herself noticeably, and addressed her sister. "Loleet, we have to talk about what you gonna do now Jim's gone. Have you thought about that?"

Loleet looked straight at Léonie and said, "What do you mean 'do now'? I don't exactly know what to do. I'm just tryin' to deal with his being gone. I haven't thought about anything else." She began to whimper and reached for a handkerchief sticking out of the top of her purse.

"Well," Léonie said with a slight edge of insistence, "you need to be thinkin' about it soon." She looked at her father, who took the cue.

"Loleet," he began slowly, "we and the whole family down home in Nawlins and Davant are worried about you and the children. We don't see how you gonna survive up here now Jim's gone. We yo' only family now."

"I know that and I appreciate you coming all this way to see me through it. I really do appreciate it. Your being here has meant a lot to me, and it's made it much easier to manage things."

"You know we love you and yo' children," Amay said. "Of course we had to come to try to help out, and we want you to know you've still got a family. You don't need to carry this load by yo'self."

Loleet dabbed her eyes and reached a hand across the table to Amay, who took it into both of hers. Then she grasped it more firmly, looked at her sister's face intently, and said, "You need to come home, Loleet. We want you and the children to come back, back to Davant, where you belong. Everybody down home misses you, and we all wonder why you want to live in a place like Chicago when you could be raisin' yo' children where you grew up yo'self. We all suffered through the Depression, but y'all up here suffered more than we did down home. We always had food. We never suffered through no winter. Everybody helped each other. That's the kind of place you need to be now, Loleet. Now Jim's gone, there's no good reason to stay here."

Loleet looked back at Amay just as intently, gently pulled her hand free, leaned back into her chair, and said, "I really do appreciate your help and your concern, but I could never go to live permanent back home. I left there because I wanted something more than living in the country. Besides, what would life be like for a widow with four children? How would I support the children and myself alone down there? And in that situation, who would ever want to marry me?"

"First off," began her father, "you don't need to worry 'bout how you gonna manage. You and the young ones can stay with me and the two eldest can go to either Nelson or to one of yo' sisters. Nelson's two boys would be happy to have little Jimmy to help with the farm chores, and Mary June would be a help in any house. Later on, I can give you a piece of land I own near to Nelson, and everyone will pitch in to build you a house of yo' own. You won't have to be separated from the children for too long. We'll work it out, Loleet. Really, it'll be best fo' you and the children."

She hesitated, looked at her father and sisters, each in turn, and envisioned life in the country. She herself had gone to the third grade, and she had little reason to expect more for her children in that little farming and fishing town, where daily survival depended on unpredictable weather and hard physical labor rather than school and education. Without a man to help, farming and trolling in the bayou for a living would be much too difficult. Of course, her family would never let them starve, but she would always be aware that she and her children were dependent on the charity of her family. It was true that the children would be safer off the streets of Chicago and have the security and wholesomeness of a close-knit family. But their lives would be limited in the same way all of her family's lives were limited.

Without waiting for a response, her father went on, "You have to think about the welfare of the children, Loleet. They need to be around their only family, just like you do. They would have their cousins to play with and everybody would pitch in to help you raise 'em up right. It would be fo' the best, believe me."

She continued to think about what it would mean to be back in Davant, back in the country. The people all knew her and would accept her without question, but she didn't like the picture of herself as the pitied widow, who tried to leave but was forced back by a cruel outside world, an object lesson for other women who thought of trying the same. *No*, she thought, *I just can't do that.* Still, she hesitated to say "no" too quickly lest her family think her ungrateful and unreasonable.

"After a while," Léonie said, "if you don't like it in Davant, you could move up to Nawlins or to Gretna, where we are. You have people in the city—people who would give you a hand if need be. You might even find some work in one of the hotels. You did hotel housekeepin' work when you was in New York. Maybe you could do that in Nawlins."

Our mother smiled and responded only to the last argument. "I was treated like dirt in the New York hotels. I can imagine how those crackers would abuse me down there. I don't think I could get use to Jim Crow again. Chicago ain't perfect by no count, but at least I don't have to be reminded every day that I'm second class. I don't have to sit in the back of the streetcar, in the back of the church, in the balcony at the show, or on dirty toilet seats for the 'colored.' I been gone from there for fifteen years. I won't put up with that kind of life again." She knew this was among the least of her objections to their proposal, but it was the first one available that couldn't be seen as a rejection of them or their generosity.

"You'd be surprised how much things have changed since you left," her father said. "Since the war started, things have relaxed some. Creole people pass for white a lot now. They hardly ever be challenged. When I'm alone, I sit in the front of the streetcar, and nobody say nothin' to me."

"When you *alone*, Daddy?" she shot back. "Don't that tell you somethin'? You would be taken for white most any place, but the rest of us can't do that, and neither could my children. But that's not the point. Why should I live in a place where people even have to think about such a thing as passin'. I don't want to be someplace where my children are taught to think of themselves as inferior. No, Daddy, I don't want that for my children."

"It's more than that," her father responded. "Everybody is expectin' things to change after the war—no more Jim Crow laws, no more segregated anything, and no more race prejudice. They say that, 'cause of all the coloreds that's fought and died in the war, it wouldn't be fair to keep us down the way they have for so long. Everything's got to change. Yo' children won't be livin' under the same kinda rules. Believe me. Change is comin'."

"Nowhere near fast enough. Change shoulda come yesterday. Besides, I don't trust that white people will ever do the right thing. They too comftable bein' on top and keepin' everybody else down. No, I'm not gonna count on big changes any time soon, and I just won't put my children through it."

She felt that this objection to the proposal had been taken as far as it could. She went on. "But even if things changed overnight, I wouldn't go back there to live. There just ain't enough there for me to make the kind of life I want to have for myself and the children. I know I can get a job here in Chicago. Down there I would never be sure of havin' more than a kitchen, housework, and growin' vegetables. The children would have to go to terrible schools—even if we were in the city, but much worse in the country. I know. I've been through it."

"Loleet," said Amay, "you just lookin' at all the worse things—what you might have to give up, if you came back. What about the good side? What about bein' near to yo' family? What about bein' sure you and the children will be looked aft'a? What about havin' a peaceful and quiet place to live? The streets here are full of streetcars clangin' along, cars blowin' horns, and people at the bar across the street yellin' and fightin' all night. You want yo' children growin' up 'round all that?"

"There's problems everywhere you go. I know how to take care of myself and the children. I know the people around here, and they know us. We get along just fine. We even look out for each other. It ain't like bein' with family, but we all right here. I even think we use to the noise. After a while, it seems natural—like we would miss it, if it stopped." She smiled. They did not.

"I expected you to be more sensible, Loleet," Léonie said. "Don't you see how unreasonable you bein'? We offerin' you a way out of this place, and you tellin' us you prefer to be here more than with yo' family that loves you and wants to be yo' help in time of need. You been doin' not much more than cryin' in yo' bed all the time we been here. How you gonna be able to be a proper mother fo' fo' children when we gone?"

This last question stung. She sat up straight, turned her body directly toward Léonie and said, "What you sayin', Léonie? I ain't fit to take care of my own children? Is that what you tellin' me? You suppose to be helpin' me out, but instead you judgin' me. I been through hell this week, and I know I'm still hurtin' real bad, but don't you think for a minute I won't do what I have to do to take care of my children." Our mother burst into tears and bent over. She looked up and continued. "How could you say such a thing to me? I love my children more than anything in this world, and you sayin' I can't be a proper mother. That ain't right, Léonie. You know that ain't right." She continued to cry for several minutes, while her sisters and father could only watch.

"Loleet," Léonie finally said, "I didn't mean it that way. I'm sorry, if it sounded like I was judgin' you. We just want to do what's best fo' you and the children, that's all."

"I think we best leave this for later," said their father. "We don't have to decide nothin' right this minute." He rose and, as he left the kitchen, said, "I think I'll take a little walk."

Léonie rose and stood by Loleet. Placing an arm around her shoulder, she bent down and placed her cheek against her sister's. "I'm sorry, Loleet," she said softly. Loleet reached up to the hand on her shoulder and held it. Neither said anything more.

After dinner, when the children were in bed, the four adults again sat at the kitchen table. Loleet knew the ordeal she faced and tried to delay it by offering to make a pot of coffee. They all nodded appreciatively. They were serious coffee drinkers; they had brought their own Louisiana chicory blend unavailable in Chicago.

After she placed the coffee pot onto the stove, Loleet sat and quickly opened by commenting on the need for the children to get back to school as soon as possible. "No point in having them miss more than they have to and fall behind, even though the sisters know all about their daddy's death. I know they'll understand, no matter what we have to do."

"Have they been doin' all right in school?" asked her father.

"Just fine, accordin' to the teachers I talked to a while ago. At least the two oldest should go. Precious and Castie, I think I want to give them more time."

A long silence was broken by Amay. "I hope my family is doin' okay without me. They're probably havin' beans and rice for every meal." Smiles all around.

"I left enough gumbo at my house to last a week," added Léonie.

After pouring the coffee around, Loleet sat, sipped, and turned toward her father. He took this as an invitation to begin. "Loleet, this is Wednesday and we thinkin' about leavin' fo' home on Saturday. I know there's no way you can get yo'self ready for a move back to Davant right away. I understand there's lots to it. Might take weeks or even a month to take care of all you have to do. But you don't have to take everything—certainly not all this here furniture. You can manage for a while with what we have down there, at least till you have yo' own place."

"Daddy, you assumin' we movin'. I told you this afternoon I don't plan to go nowhere. You know I do appreciate your concern and your offer, and I know you love me and the children, but there's nothin' down there for us. I want a different kinda' life for me and my children. I just can't go back."

Her father and sisters sat in silent surprise. Léonie finally responded pointedly, "I suppose that means the life we have down there ain't good enough fo' you. Now you see yo'self as the big-city girl. Well, big-city girl, what has the big city done fo' you? The city done swallowed up yo' husband and left you with next to nothin'. What is it you lookin' fo'? Great opportunities? Glamour? The fast life? Well, so fa', I don't see any proof it's done you much good."

"I didn't mean to say there's somethin' wrong with your life in the country," she answered. "I look back to my life growin' up and there's a lot of good memories. But now, I just don't see it for me and my children."

"What's so special about you and yo' children?" broke in Amay, lifting her body and bobbing her head. "We all happy enough. Why can't you be happy in the life you come from? I just don't understand it."

"I can't expect you to understand. All I'm askin' is for you to trust me to make up my own mind about what my life is gonna be. You all have chosen the life you want, and I surely don't fault you for choosin' it. Jimmy and I wanted something else. I can't say it's better, but it's what we wanted. It ain't glamour or the fast life, for sure. But it *is* opportunities—for education, for good jobs and maybe even professional careers for our children. Is it so wrong to want somethin' more for your children than what you had? I don't think so." She looked at each of them. Silence followed.

She went on. "And I'm not claimin' I'm stayin' here just for the children. I like it here. I like bein' independent. Jimmy and I struggled from the first day we got married, and sometimes we was both near givin' up, not knowin' how we was gonna pay the rent, feed the children, keep warm in the winter. It was hard—real hard—a lot of the time coming through the Depression. But we struggled together, and in the end, I think we were stronger. If the sickness hadn't come on him, I believe we woulda been ready to build a good life here for the children and ourselves. Now he's gone, but I think he woulda wanted me to go on toward what we worked for. I don't expect it to be easy for me and the children, but I have faith that we will survive. I know you must be thinkin' this is all selfishness on my part—not choosin' to take the safe way, maybe even puttin' the children through unnecessary hard times. I don't want it to be hard, but even if it is, I feel like I can do what it takes."

Again, there was an extended silence. Loleet looked at the others briefly, each in turn, and finally at her own hands folded in her lap. She had said her piece and felt good about how it came out.

"You sho' about this?" her father asked and went on without waiting for a response. "We can't make you do nothin' you don't want to, but I wish you would think about it mo'. You might feel different about it afta we leave. You might feel difrent in six months or a year. For my part, the offa' is open. All I can say is good luck and God bless you."

"Thank you, Daddy," she said. "Don't you worry about us too much. If it comes to that, I know I can run home to my people." She flashed a gentle smile at him.

"Just in case," he said, "I'm gonna keep my eyes wide open for a good man wantin' to marry a widow with fo' children. You still young and attractive, Loleet. You ought not to suffa alone the rest of yo' life. There's lotsa good men out there."

"I ain't thinkin in that way right now," she said, "and I doubt any man is out there lookin' for a forty-two-year-old widow with four kids between six and ten. Even if there was, there would be more of them here than in Davant."

They both smiled, but her sisters did not.

"So that's what all this is about," Léonie said. "You think you have mo' of a chance to catch a new husband up here."

"I *said* I ain't thinkin' that way. It was Daddy who brought that up. That's the furthest thing from my mind. For the love of heaven, I just buried my husband today. Please drop this kinda' talk."

"All right, so I guess it's a settled thing now," said Léonie. "You not comin' home to be with yo' people."

"If you want to put it that way."

"OK, then," Léonie continued, as if presenting a new gambit, "I have another suggestion. Now hear me out befo' you start reactin'. First off, you alone. Second, you have next to no money. Third, you have a fifty-cents-an-hour factry job that's none too regula. Half the time you gonna be laid off and on relief. Fourth, you have fo' young children you will be tryin' to raise by yo'self. I say that's too much fo' one person to have to deal with. You may think you able to deal with all that, but I think the children are bound to suffa. You need to have some of it taken off you. Here's what I think. I think the youngest two are the ones that'll need the most attention, and they the ones who gonna suffa most if they don't have enough. I think we should take the two young ones back to Davant with us. I could take Precious, and either Amay or Nelson could take Castie. June and Jimmy are old enough that they don't need as much attention. They can take care of themselves. Amay and I have already talked. What you say to that?"

"You tellin' me I should give up my two babies?" Loleet asked in a tone of incredulity. "You want to take them a thousand miles away from me and have you and Amay raise them? You think that's a better idea? Well, it's not."

"Hold on," Léonie said, holding up her palms as if to ward off the barrage. "This would be temporary—only til you got back on yo' feet and under less pressure. Whenever you was able, you could come down and get'em or somebody could bring'em back to you. Anyway, we do expect to be seein' you—if not this comin' summa, for sure by next summa. Whenever you came, you could decide whether you was able to bring them back to Chicago with you. Who knows? By that time, maybe you'll want to move back to Davant yo'self."

"Now listen to me," she said forcefully, looking back and forth at her two sisters. "That is *not* gonna happen. You think 'cause I been grievin' over the loss of my husband I won't be able to take care of my babies? I said this to you before. Now listen, and hear this clear. There is no relationship between my grievin' the loss of my husband and my bein' able to take care of my children. If you can't stand to see me grievin' so heavy, maybe you should go back sooner than later."

"Loleet, please," their father broke in, "there's no call to be talkin' like that. Yo' sisters are just offerin' you the help they think you need. I said it befo'—there's no way we can force you to take the help we been tryin' to offa you. You have to believe all hearts are in the right place on this. No one wants to separate you from yo' children. We tryin' to see if there's any way we can make it easier fo' you. That's all."

"Well, what I hear," answered Loleet, "is that I won't be able to take care of my children properly. I love my kids, and I would die before I would let any harm come to them. What I hear is that I better pull myself together and stop cryin' all the time. All right, if that's what it takes to keep them with me, I guess I should do that."

Her father shrugged and said, "It was a long day fo' all of us. We shoulda' given you a bit mo' time befo' talkin' 'bout makin' big plans. We can talk 'bout it tomorrow. I'm goin' to bed."

As their father left, Loleet stepped into the bathroom nearby and sat bent over, worn out. She could hear her sisters clearing and washing the dishes and speaking softly. She could tell that they were reassuring each other and expressing disappointment at her response to their proposals. Still, she was determined to resist any plan for a permanent return to Louisiana. When she stepped out of the bathroom, she immediately exited the kitchen without turning toward her sisters but said "goodnight" with a coolness of tone even she found alien.

In the morning, after June and Jimmy had gone to school, Loleet asked her father to accompany her to the Social Security office in order to submit a claim for burial expenses and survivor benefits for the children. He agreed, of course, and Amay and Léonie simultaneously volunteered to stay with Precious and Castie. This simple gesture released them all from the tense distance that had developed between Loleet and her sisters. From then on relationships were amicable, and the exchanges between them grew gradually warmer.

When Loleet and her father returned to the apartment, their mood was somewhat lifted. The visit to the Social Security office had been altogether successful. Loleet had to get a death certificate and birth certificates for the children. Even though she didn't have a marriage certificate, she had been assured that it would suffice for her to submit a sworn affidavit that she had been married to our father.

As they finished a small lunch of the leftover gumbo Léonie had made when they first arrived, Loleet announced that she had an idea. "I was thinkin' last night and this morning that it might work out for the two oldest to spend the summer down in Davant. They wouldn't be too much trouble to anyone, especially if they spent time with different families. I figured that would give them a chance to get to know their family down home—especially all their cousins. It would also give me some more time to spend with the young ones—and also relieve some of the pressure you all were talkin' about yesterday . . . But I would need some help with the tickets."

Her sisters beamed, and their father let out a sigh of relief and said, "Now that sounds to me like a wonderful plan . . . Tell you what: I'll pass the hat 'round the family and send you the money for the tickets right away. When do you think you would want to send them and when would you want them to come back home?"

"I was thinkin' at least for the month of July. If it worked out and they wanted to stay for part of August that would probably be all right too. They would have to start gettin' ready for school around the middle of August."

By the time June and Jimmy arrived home from school, the tension of the day before had completely dissipated. Both children responded positively to the idea of going for a long visit to their mother's hometown and meeting her family. After the painful week they had just gone through, this sounded like a fine adventure. Their only question was why they couldn't all go. Although there was squirming among the adults, Loleet finally said that we couldn't afford to have us all go. We would have to try hard to save for the following summer.

On Saturday morning we all took the short streetcar ride to the Illinois Central Station near Grant Park. Before they entered the final gate, our grandfather and aunts kissed each child and our mother and cried a bit, but our mother cried more than any of them.

June and Jimmy did spend most of July in Louisiana and had a good time wherever they visited. But they came back to Chicago in the first week of August and were home in time to celebrate with the family when the end of the War was announced.

Throughout the remainder of my childhood our mother from time to time packed us all up for trips to visit our father's grave. Those long streetcar and bus rides from 14th Street to 121st Street were usually on warm-weather holidays—Memorial Day, The Fourth of July, and Labor Day—but there were odd Sundays when the weather was dry and warm when she would announce after Sunday Mass that we were going to "visit your daddy's grave." Because I enjoyed standing with Jimmy at the open window, in the front of the streetcar near the motorman, I remember those trips with some fondness, but they were always laced with sadness. For a few years, as soon as we arrived at the gravesite, our mother stared at the small granite marker and cried. After a period of silence, however, she made the sign of the cross, and we did likewise. Then we cleared the weeds, cleaned the gravestone and, if we brought them, planted fresh flowers or a potted plant on the grave and watered them from a spigot nearby. Next, in a clear area close by, we put down a thin blanket and had a lunch of sandwiches and lemonade. Then, while our mother sat in the sun or under a tree, we went about reading gravestones and otherwise exploring. We never stayed very long; we were always home before dark.

CHAPTER 3:

Our Father's Letters

P oor people often fantasize about becoming wealthy. Some scour their memories and let loose their imaginations in constructing plausible avenues for attaining such wealth. In the years after our father died, our mother shared with us, from time to time, two such fantasies, and the four of us in varying measures came to believe in and incorporate them into our own fantasy lives.

The first was based on my mother's having inherited from her father a narrow but long piece of land facing a levee on the Mississippi River and fronting the only road through Davant, Louisiana, where she and her siblings grew up in the circle of a French-Creole extended-family enclave. Soon after the end of World War II the search for oil intensified and oil was discovered throughout that region of south Louisiana. Oil companies promptly leased the drilling rights to all the farmland they could. The leasing fees were modest, but receiving small payments from an oil company always fired my mother's hope that eventually riches would follow.

They never did—not to our family. The only thing we ever received from the land were Christmas boxes of pecans harvested from some particularly productive trees and sent by my mother's brother Nelson, whose own land abutted hers.

The oil companies continued leasing the drilling rights for many years, but never drilled. Oil fields did spring up around the area, but not, alas, on any of our family's sites. Many in our family suspected that they were being cheated; by some device the companies were pumping oil from their land but through other sites. Eventually the oil company stopped paying leasing fees to our family, but my mother never entirely abandoned the hope that oil would be found and we would be rich. Finally, the only thing we received were tax bills for the land, and, after those accumulated unpaid, they stopped as well, and we assumed that the land was taken and sold by the parish or the state. That was just as well, because Hurricane Katrina swallowed up the town, as she did all the small communities along the lower Mississippi, and turned it into swampland for a time.

Our mother got some pleasure from telling us a story related to this oil-riches fantasy. Back in the 1930s, under suspicious circumstances, the parish courthouse burned down along with all its records, including birth and marriage records. Following the 1940 census, the Negro population was found to be twenty percent lower than it had been following the 1930 census. It was an open secret, she told us, that some number of Creole people of the parish who could "pass" for white had simply taken the opportunity to have their race officially changed. Among other things, marriages that would have been illegal according to the state's miscegenation prohibition became a possibility for them.

Then, when oil was discovered in the parish after the war, another demographic shift was found in the next census; this time in the opposite direction. The population of Negroes in the parish was increased by fifteen percent, which indicated to most that the prospect of receiving oil money through family connection was more important to some than hiding their family backgrounds. The old saying, "money talks," became the punch line for many local jokes.

Because there hadn't been a complete reversal in the racial composition of the parish, our mother speculated that some must have decided that going back to being "colored" was too high a price to pay, even for the prospect of oil money. Given the anti-miscegenation law, admitting to having even a drop of Negro blood would have meant the dissolution of marriages and the reclassification of children.

The second fantasy of wealth came to us as a legacy from our father—but through our mother. Eight years after our father died, when I was a freshman at St. Ignatius High School, my mother began urging me to read the documents and letters my father had left in two stiff legal storage boxes—the type resembling huge books and have small doors on the side that can be opened to allow the back to be pulled away and reveal the contents. The only reason she gave for this urging was that, after a few months of studying diligently to succeed at a Jesuit school where kids from my neighborhood had never gone, I was the "bookworm" in the family and, therefore, the only one who would have any interest in what was there.

She also reasoned that, if I could figure out what it all meant, we would all be lifted out of poverty. Our father had told her many times of being mistreated by his stepmother and cheated out of a valuable legacy left to him by our grandfather. I was uncertain what I could find in those papers that my father hadn't known. If I simply discovered what was there and what it meant in the same way he did, how could I hope to do more about it than he had? Still, it was a task my mother had assigned to me and, no matter how reluctant I felt about pursuing it, I knew it was mine.

I had several false starts. The letters and legal documents were initially nothing more to me than a jumble of old papers. There was little to connect them other than my father's name, which appeared on almost all of them—James Julius Turner, James Turner, and in some of the personal letters "Jim" or "Jimmy." Many of the letters had come from Kingston, Jamaica. Most were typed and appeared to be business letters. Others were personal letters written, as if with finely pointed pens, in spidery longhand. Some of the script was strange to me, so reading them was difficult. The letters referred to people I didn't know and situations I didn't understand, and I often stopped in confusion and frustration.

One Saturday, early in the following summer, after intense urging from my mother, I decided to make a serious effort to organize and gain an understanding of what was there. Of all the letters in the collection, approximately a quarter were carbon copies of letters that my father had written. All of those letters were in beautiful and full longhand that always struck me as artistic. I placed all of the letters from Jamaica together; then separated them into those that were personal and those that were typed business letters; finally, I sorted each of the piles into chronological order. Establishing sequential order for the personal letters became very difficult at times because some letters were merely fragments without the first pages; others had no date. In those cases, in order to establish the narrative represented in the letters, I had to read them carefully to figure out the logic of what was being said. After many readings, I realized that the personal letters and the business letters were related.

Next I ordered the correspondence from the United States. An occasional one was in Spanish, and I simply put those into a separate pile. Many years later I learned to read Spanish and found them to be simple letters from my father's friends in the United States, with cordial sentiments and sometimes references to his illness but with no importance in telling the story of his life. The remaining were business letters—some from government agencies, others from lawyers. Integrating these with the Jamaica letters and papers made it clear that most of the letters, both personal and business, both from Jamaica and the United States, were part of the same story. Together they told of my father's lengthy quest to get what he felt he had been cheated of, his legacy from his deceased father. Still, the narrative I pieced together was often broken and incomplete.

Toward the end of one day's inspection, I had nearly completed one of my organizing attempts but didn't understand anything better than I had after previous readings. I felt frustrated and incompetent but didn't want to fail my mother. Among the items remaining to be inspected was a letter-sized envelope labeled "Social Security bills" in my mother's handwriting, which I had been reluctant to open because it was sealed. I hesitated still, but only briefly; I had, after all, been asked to investigate what was there. Inside were five items: a death certificate; a small clipping from a newspaper; a bill from a funeral parlor; a small card indicating the number and location of a gravesite at the Lincoln Cemetery; and a bill for a gravestone.

I gave the gravesite card and the bills only cursory inspections and put each back into the envelope. I stared for a long time at the death certificate. One word was written in large script with no attempt to stay within the bounds of the space allowed for the answer about the circumstances of death: "Suicidal." I was stunned, but then I tried to avoid the meaning.

That's an adjective, I thought. *Why doesn't it simply say suicide? Did the person who wrote that mean the circumstances were suicidal? Or was my father known to be suicidal?* I felt some shame, but quickly became defensive. *Unless there was a witness,* I argued back at the writer, *no one can ever know for certain that a person committed suicide.*

The word "suicidal" rang in my head for a long while. From the beginning, our mother had told us our father had fallen accidentally from a window at work. As we got older and asked how a person accidentally falls out of a window, she added that he had been washing windows. At first, following my discovery, I refused to think our mother had deceived us intentionally all those years. Perhaps her third grade education made it impossible for her to read the certificate and understand what was there—which would also explain why she insisted that I, rather than she, should dig into my father's papers. Perhaps the ambiguity of the word "suicidal" gave her the right—as I had claimed the right—to make an interpretation that was more palatable than the truth. As my mother had attempted to reinterpret the suicide, I had been trying to reinterpret my mother's obvious deception. Suicide had to have been for her not only something to be ashamed of, but also a sin. As much as anything, however, she must have been angry. If our father had committed suicide, it meant that he had left her in a situation so overwhelming that she could barely manage. That the man she loved had done that to her was difficult to accept. Over the years, she let us know frequently how victimized she felt by our father's death—"How could your daddy leave me to raise four children alone?"

Finally, I broke the spell of the death certificate, put it aside, and picked up the newspaper clipping. It had turned rust colored from age, and I felt some concern about whether it could survive much longer, whether even my handling it would destroy it. I assumed that my mother hadn't cut it out herself, because I rarely saw her reading a newspaper, and the possibility that she had been looking carefully through a newspaper within days after my father died was quite remote. Whoever clipped it didn't note the name of the newspaper or the date. The small notice began in boldface "LEAP TO DEATH." The details were brief and emotionless—"fifth floor window . . . down into the alley . . . skull crushed on the concrete . . . died instantly . . . apparent suicide." *This isn't an obituary*, I thought. There was no mention of loving wife and children. No mention of parents and siblings. Only name, address, and employee of some glass company. An anonymous, impersonal, but sensational back-page notice.

I stared at these two pieces of paper for a long time. I wasn't trying to figure anything out about them. The information itself was simply sinking deeply into me.

The feeling of being alone, which I had lived with since my father's death, intensified. I never seriously considered talking with anyone about what I had discovered and what I was feeling. I had no one in those days in whom I confided. My mother? What could I say to her? I had concluded that she already knew about the suicide, and because she hadn't told any of us, it meant there was something terribly wrong about it. It was a secret about which she didn't want to be reminded. The envelope had been sealed for a reason. No, talking with my mother about this wasn't an option.

My sisters and brother? My siblings and I never spoke with each other about anything personal in our early lives together. Mary June, the eldest, was pretty and much involved in being social. Her straight black hair, high cheek bones, and coloring made her look like she had been plucked from a Native American reservation. She was also very much into being "Creole." After going through her early teen years hearing at our kitchen table about whose skin was too dark, whose hair was too nappy, and whose lips were too thick, it made sense that her girlfriends at St. Joseph's had all been the least negroid girls in her class. By the time I learned about our father's suicide she was already a senior at Lucy Flowers Technical High School. Her concerns about friends and getting married weren't of interest to me. If I had had a way to communicate with her about the heavy matters facing me, I would have felt guilty about intruding into her life.

My brother Jimmy (given name: Santiago Julio Turner) was sixteen months younger than June. Jimmy was the only one of the four of us who, because of his light complexion and wavy hair, would easily be taken for white. He and his friends were two to three years older than I, but that age difference didn't matter so much when we were younger. During the summers all the kids played ringolevio in the streets, played softball and tag football in empty lots strewn with broken glass, spun tops, and tried to win marbles. In winters, we had snowball fights and belly-flopped down man-made hills covered with heavy snow. Then, Jim and I separated abruptly when I was around eleven, and by the time I began high school I had only the vaguest sense of what he did outside our apartment.

According to our mother's frequent complaint in those days, Jimmy was always "running the streets." He and our mother sometimes argued about his cutting classes at Crane Technical High School and his spending time in the pool hall near the school. The problems between them intensified following a specific confrontation. Once, after school, although an innocent bystander to a prankish streetcar incident, the police took Jimmy, with all the teenagers present, to the station. When our mother arrived to get him out, she refused to believe his explanation and cried uncontrollably. The burden of guilt she laid on was so heavy that he decided to leave home as soon as possible.

Early in high school he and June began working after school to help the family. They worked at a place downtown that sold sewing patterns by mail order. Nonetheless, he was usually bristling with anger at our mother. If I had confided in him what I had found, I feared he would confront our mother on the spot with hiding the suicide—as if it was somehow her fault. In his worst rages, he blamed her for our frequent periods of being penniless and hungry. I didn't want to stir up more trouble between them.

Precious was fourteen months younger than Jimmy. When we were young, she was best known for her "Shirley Temple" curls, which formed easily in her wavy hair. Throughout elementary school, however, she had been a tomboy. She was a better softball player than most of the boys her age, and she won more marbles than Jimmy and I combined. She and I spent more time together than with our older sibs. We cleaned house together on Saturday mornings, while listening to fairy tales on "Let's Pretend," and learned that good always triumphed over evil. We often took the long walk together to and from St. Joseph's, especially in the early grades, but walking together or being together was never a compulsion. If we happened to show up at the same marble game or the same corner on the way, we walked home together—rarely talking and never really discussing anything important or intimate. We never complained to each other about school or our teachers, about how hard it was being so poor that we were often hungry, about being without a father, or even about our mother, who was beyond reproach to Precious and me.

When Precious graduated from St. Joseph's and joined my sister June at Lucy Flowers Technical High School, she had long since given up being a tomboy, but she had no close friends and little interest in anything. It was as if she was doing her duty and asking little from anyone or from life. I could have found a responsive ear with Precious. At least, my discovery would have interested her. I doubt that it would have changed any feeling she had about our mother or how she saw the world. She was affected by having lost her father in ways too profound for me to understand at the time. She had in my mother, however, both the solace and the burden of a lifetime. She remained safe in the one and carried the other with unwavering dedication.

She also helped the family by taking a job, along with June and Jimmy, after school at the mail-order pattern company. She always looked tired because of the long days of school and the work afterwards. In retrospect, I see a depressed teenager. She was quiet. She made few demands, never got into trouble, and did very well in school. Her life was already set by the time I discovered the truth about our father's death. Did I consider talking with her? Why would I burden her with something more?

After putting the papers away, another year passed before I looked at them again. Whenever I thought about what I had found, I always allowed it to flow into the background. I kept myself safe from it but felt alone with a secret burden. I couldn't make sense of it. I could only carry it.

During the following summer I tried again. I confirmed that the correspondence I had considered business letters fit with those I had thought of as personal. Most of them, beginning in 1930, related to my father's obsession with mistreatment by his stepmother following his father's death.

However, the oldest item in the collection was a hand written letter from my grandfather to my father, addressed as "James Julius Turner, Esquire," dated June 1909, two months after his mother, Daisy Maud Humber Turner, had died. Neither this early letter nor the remainder of the letters described the circumstances of her death. Since my father was only one year old, he was clearly meant to read it when he was older. In the letter, the grieving widower conveyed his deep love for the deceased wife and his son, reassured my father that he would be taken care of financially, and gave him fatherly advice about education, hard work, and prudence. The letter sounded as if he didn't expect to live much longer, but he actually lived another thirteen years.

Eight months after our grandmother Daisy's death, the elder James Turner wed another Jamaican woman, Annie Rebecca Turner, who bore him two daughters, Ivy Merle and Fern, and a son, Roy Collins.

In 1922, when our father was fourteen, his father died. Again, the cause and circumstances of his death weren't described in the letters. A year later, his stepmother sent him to New York City to fend for himself. There was practically no contact between them from 1923 to 1930, but it was clear that she knew how to contact him.

Having placed the letters in chronological sequence, I saw that there had been three periods of intense letter exchanges. The first began in 1930 and ended in 1933 and had to do with the proposed sale of property in Providence, Rhode Island. The second began in 1934, soon after my eldest sister June was born, and ended in 1936. The third began in 1939, ended after our father's death in 1945, and were either about the proposed sale of the last real estate in Jamaica or about his declining health.

In 1930, after many years of being out of touch with our father, his stepmother wrote a letter saying she wanted to sell his late father's last real estate holding in the United States, in Providence. He responded with skepticism and wanted to know how he would benefit from the sale. She wrote back to say that he had no benefit coming to him since she, according to the will, had a life interest in the income from all real estate left by his father. In spite of his expressed concerns, she asked her lawyers in Kingston, Jamaica, to proceed with the sale. They contracted with a Providence law firm to handle the local sale. Having seen James Turner's will, the Providence lawyers insisted upon having a signed agreement for the sale from our father, the only one of the children who had attained majority age of twenty-one.

When they wrote asking him to sign a Power of Attorney authorizing the sale, his adamant response was the beginning of his resistance and struggle:

> . . . I will not sign such a document unless I am assured by you that you will get an authorization from Mrs. Turner who is the executrix of my father's estate, that you pay me personally one-fifth of the net profits of the sale of such property, which is my legal portion according to the will.
>
> I am the eldest child of my father, James Julius Turner, by a former marriage, so Mrs. Turner, with whom you are dealing, is not my mother.

> I have not been treated squarely according to the
> terms of the will up to the present time, and I do not
> propose to sign away any of my rights . . .

There was a copy of the will among my father's papers, and I inspected it more carefully than I had previously. There was no ambiguity about the widow's "life interest" in the real estate; until she died or remarried, she was to receive all income from the property. No mention was made, however, about the disposition of the assets if real estate were sold. My father reasoned that, if the will were to be interpreted by the court to allow the sale, it could be interpreted to allow timely distribution of the assets of the sale.

Having gained an understanding of this issue, I returned to the letter exchange that continued, in February 1931, with a reply from the Providence lawyers. In it they tried to assuage his fears that he would be cheated again. He wasn't reassured and refused to sign without a promise of prompt payment of his share. Soon a more threatening letter arrived from Annie Turner's Jamaican lawyer, who suggested that he would be liable for additional legal costs caused by his intransigence.

At this point, there was something of a standoff. In November of 1931, however, the Providence lawyers attempted to serve my father, living in New York City, with a subpoena to appear at a hearing in Providence to construe the will. Finally, after he had managed to avoid service for some months, the subpoena was advertised three times in a Providence newspaper and a registered letter with a copy of the subpoena enclosed arrived in the mail.

Around this time, and in response to the increasing pressure from the lawyers, my father wrote to the Legal Aid Society of Rhode Island. In his initial letter to that office he addressed the problem of the proposed sale, but he raised another complaint based on his father's will:

> . . . You will see that the Will provides for my
> maintenance, education, and support up to the age of
> 21, but at the age of 15 my stepmother sent me to New
> York to scuffle for a living while she and her children
> live in luxury . . .

This was the first place in the letters revealing the intense resentment he felt, not only toward his stepmother, but also toward his three half-siblings. Again, I went back to the will in order to understand the reference being made. According to the will, the income from the *personal property* (including cash, investments, and debts owed the estate) was to be used for the children's "maintenance, education and support."

In his early letters, my father apparently assumed that the legacy ended when each child reached 21. The will was ambiguous on this point, but it doesn't say anything about an age terminating rights to the legacy regarding "maintenance, education and support."

The Legal Aid Society responded that they had found an attorney in Providence willing to represent him on a contingency basis. They also reported that the Supreme Court of Rhode Island was deciding the meaning of the will.

The Providence attorney who agreed to represent my father wrote to say that he was working to the end of having my father's vested interest decided by the court. After several months the attorney wrote to report that the Supreme Court had found that he had a vested interest in the real property, but that Mrs. Turner's life interest precluded any enjoyment of the property until she died or remarried. In February of 1933, he received a final letter from his attorney, indicating that a buyer was found and, after some negotiating about where the proceeds were to be kept, the Rhode Island court agreed to send the money to the Administrator General of Jamaica. His role would be to give to Mrs. Turner all interest earnings from the funds held. The principal wouldn't grow, and at her death that principal would have to be split four ways.

My father was, no doubt, disappointed by this. Even though he had been judged to have a vested interest in that real estate, he wouldn't receive anything immediately. But, in his first letter to the Legal Aid Society, he referred to other property having been sold after his father's death.

> . . . All other holdings of my late father in Chicago and Providence were sold, and the money kept in her possession in Jamaica. She is the sole executrix and trustee of the will since Mr. Simpson, the co-executor

resigned, so if she succeeds in selling both holdings, she
will be at liberty to go away and I will never hear of her
again . . .

He clearly believed that she had been selling off property ever since
his father's death. He surmised that, in any sales before this contested
one, none of the children, including himself, were of age and therefore
wouldn't have been consulted about such sales. When Mrs. Turner
wanted to sell the Providence property, it was held up only because her
own attorneys in Providence saw that one child mentioned in the will
with an interest was of age and had not agreed to the sale. It was this
scrupulous attention to detail by those lawyers that led to the three-year
struggle over the sale. Based on her experience with previous sales, Mrs.
Turner must have expected that the new sale would proceed as others
had.

The reference to Mr. Simpson's resignation from the role of
executor and trustee is also noteworthy. Other documents indicated
that Aston Simpson had been the elder James Turner's attorney for
many years, possibly as early as his first business transactions in Jamaica.
When our grandmother died in 1909, he was referred to, in the brief
handwritten letter to my father—a one year old—as the person who
would handle my father's affairs until he reached the age of twenty-one.
He also prepared, in 1922, the Last Will and Testament referred to
here. Exactly when the document was written is unclear, but it was
filed in the Jamaica Records Office on August 27, 1922, six months
after James Turner's death on March 10, 1922. In reality, James Turner
had never signed any document such as a Last Will and Testament.
The document lodged in August 1922 had simply been based on the
affidavits of Mrs. Turner and Aston Simpson saying that this was what
the deceased man had, in 1920, told them he wanted. Given the two
year gap between the claimed date of the statements and his death, I
wondered why the will had not been lodged with the Records Office
earlier. One plausible scenario is: In the absence of a will, the widow
convinced Simpson to write a will favorable to her and to him. Her
control of the estate while she remained single was made complete.
They were named co-executors and trustees, for which they collected
generous fees. We will never know whether the will was written entirely
from whole cloth or did represent what our grandfather had intended.

The reason for Simpson's resignation as executor and trustee was that he and Mrs. Turner "had a falling out," which may have had something to do with management of the estate. The resignation was most likely in 1930, because that's when Mrs. Turner hired a different Jamaican law firm to arrange for the sale of the Providence property. Simpson may have realized that there was trustee malfeasance in the earlier transactions: first, some of the principal of the personal property had *not* been lodged in trust; second, the proceeds from any previous real estate sales had likewise not been lodged in trust; and finally, the sale of the Providence property could be contested and lead to a closer inspection of the will.

The second series of correspondence didn't begin until September 1934. It began with a letter from the office of the City Clerk of Newark, New Jersey, which was a response to a request from my father for a copy of our parents' marriage record. In the letter, the clerk noted the marriage date of James Turner and Loretta Carter to have been April 3, 1932. Since our mother's maiden name was Loretta Ganier, this was either a typo in the letter or a mistake in the record itself. It appears from the letters that our parents eloped and took an apartment in Jamaica, Long Island, where they lived until the end of 1932. Early in 1933 they took an apartment in Harlem, where they remained until they relocated to Chicago in 1934.

A second letter, received in September, was a reply from the American Consular Service in Kingston, Jamaica, indicating that no evidence of his United States citizenship had been found in its records. There were several letters in the collection suggesting that my father was trying to establish his eligibility for United States citizenship. Yet another letter from the American Consulate was a reply to my father's letter seeking help, because he was "being discriminated against with regard to provisions of his father's last will and testament, by which certain moneys were stipulated to be paid for your support, maintenance, and education." The Consulate declined to get involved in what was clearly a civil matter, but suggested he write to the Administrator General of Jamaica and sent him a list of Jamaican lawyers.

Why start up the campaign again at that time? The only coincident event that I could see was that a month earlier, August 15, my sister, Mary June, was born in Cook County Hospital. Moreover, by this time the Great Depression had a firm grip on the country. It's likely that the answers to the above question were: first, dire poverty; and second, a new dependent. Our father would have felt the pressure of responsibility even as his prospects for making a living worsened.

Although he must have been disappointed, yet another time, by these responses from the Consulate, he did follow through on both suggestions at the end of the letter. First, he sent an appeal to the Administrator General of Jamaica asking for his intercession in the matter. This was the same Administrator General who had in trust the proceeds of the sale of the Providence property and had been giving the annual interest earnings to Mrs. Turner. He also declined to get involved and suggested that he try to negotiate with his stepmother.

My father then wrote to his stepmother, putting forth his complaints. This icy and distancing response revealed her anger:

Mr. Jas. J. Turner

Chicago, Ill.

Dear Sir,

In answer to your letter of Oct.'s date I beg to state that you have a misconception of the value of your late father's estate.

If you will go over the "will" you will find that all Real Estate was left to his wife for life.

The personal property consisted of loans made without any security whatever and most of which I have been unable to collect up to the present . . .

My father wrote a response, dated November 16, in which he asked for a full accounting of the estate's real and personal property. In her response of December 20, Mrs. Turner first reviewed what had happened in connection with the Providence sale, including his resistance leading to greater legal expenses, the court decision that she had a life interest in the real estate, and the depositing of the proceeds into a trust, from which she received interest income for life.

The stipulation in the will concerning personal property, including cash and various debts owed to the estate, was a different matter. The Jamaican court ruled that all such were to be put in trust and invested, the income of which was to be distributed as follows: first, Mrs. Turner would receive 6% for her fee as trustee; second, one quarter of the remaining income would go to Mrs. Turner; and third, the remaining was to be used for the "support, maintenance, and education" of the four children. The actual amount collected wasn't known, because the debts were repaid to the estate over a long period and in varying amounts. In her letter, Mrs. Turner admits that some of the collected debts were *not* put in trust and invested for income, but instead " . . . used for living expenses." The further phrasing of the letter suggests that *none* of the collected debts were put in trust, which would have been a breach of the trust.

The Administrator General's second suggestion was that he pursue his claim in the courts. In February of 1935, he sent a lengthy letter to the Supreme Court Office of Jamaica. Again, he described the history of the case and his claim that he had been treated unfairly. He also implored the court to do a number of things to secure his full rights in the estate: obtain an accounting of the income from personal property; compel Mrs. Turner to pay him what he was owed for the years he had not receive any support; obtain a full accounting of the administration of the estate; and finally, remove Mrs. Turner as executrix of the estate, because of neglect of duties concerning him.

The registrar of the Supreme Court's Office sent a brief reply suggesting he consult a solicitor. On the list of solicitors in Kingston, he found the name of Colin Orrett, a friend from his days at Jamaica College Prep School. My father sent him a similar letter, asking that he take up my father's cause. Orrett did pursue the case to the point where he was able to get a full accounting of the estate. When my father wished to pursue a claim of fraud, Orrett reluctantly agreed, but he needed a substantial amount of expense funds to do so. My father pleaded with him to take the case on contingency, but Orrett responded that it would be unethical for him to take a case on such a basis.

The following March our father located another close childhood friend, Charles Blanchett, who was living in Morant Bay, Jamaica. He wrote essentially the same letter describing his situation and asking whether he could do anything to help. An Air Mail response from Harold Norton, a lawyer, indicated a willingness to take the case. Soon, however, he was told that Mrs. Turner had relocated to England and that pursuit of a case would be very expensive. Three years passed before the third series of letters began.

CHAPTER 4:

Final Struggle And Illness

Although it's unclear why our father became particularly desperate in September of 1939, he sent two letters to Jamaica early in that month. One was to Harold Norton, the attorney in Morant Bay, asking him to reopen the case, because he had learned that Mrs. Turner had returned to Jamaica. Norton responded that he would proceed only if he was sent a certain amount of money. My father wrote back to say that he was without funds and would have to delay pursuit of the case.

The second letter was a remarkable—and pathetic—plea for help to his stepmother:

Dear Mrs. Turner—

Due to the great economic depression and unemployment, I find myself without any funds whatsoever. I am about to be put out of my rooms. I have not eaten a bite for 7 days. I have not a suit of clothes that is fit to be worn. My creditors are hounding me from all sides. This situation has got me in a terrible state of nervousness, sickness, and absolute desperation.

Therefore, I am appealing to you as a last resort and in the name of humanity to come to my aid and send me all the funds possible at this time. Send $25.00 or $30.00 or more by Air Mail or the fastest way possible to help to relieve my misery and suffering at this time . . .

Mrs. Turner replied in about a week. There was no copy of her letter in the records, but based on a letter he wrote to her six months later, she responded that she was sorry he was having such a hard time but she had no funds to send him. His response, apparently written six months later, two days after his thirty-second birthday, was full of bitter sarcasm:

3/23/40

Dear Mrs. Turner,

I received your very kind and sympathetic letter of last Sept. 14th. I wish to extend to you herein my sincere thanks and appreciation for *such extraordinary courtesy.*

I greatly regret to hear that you were stone broke . . . It touches me very deeply that no one will even give you a job. It seems as if some employer would realize your executive ability and employ you. You would really be an asset to some good business house for you have brains to make money. If I were a big employer, I would give you a job as I know that you are undoubtedly outstandingly clever and have the talent necessary to be of great benefit to any business. I wish to keep up correspondence with you in order that I may become just half as smart and clever as you are. In fact, you are a shining example of what the youth of the nation should aspire to be. Please give me all the ideas that you have in mind . . .

Soon after sending this letter, he opened another path to getting help in his quest for the legacy he believed he deserved. He located and wrote to his half-sister Fae, in Jamaica. At first, I didn't understand who she was, but I soon saw that she was yet another child of the elder

James Turner, my grandfather, but not a child of Annie R. Turner. The contents of her letters suggested that Fae was a child out of wedlock with her own grievances against Annie Turner. Her mother had been their father's assistant in his money-lending business and kept the books recording the debts owed him. After the elder James Turner died, Annie Turner, who knew about Fae and her mother, obtained a court order to take the books as part of the estate. In his first letter to Fae my father had introduced the problem he was having with getting a fair hearing on the status of his legacy. In her response, which was mostly about her family and updating on her life since he had left Jamaica in 1923, there is the following sentence:

> . . . Mrs. Turner forged Dad's handwriting and came for all the books that had the names of the people that owed us monies, so you see, Jimmy, I shared the same fate as you did . . .

In September of 1942, he also sent a letter to Merle, Mrs. Turner's eldest and his half-sibling, which led to a brief correspondence. Her response was primarily an updating on her own marriage and three children. In her letter she makes no reference to any rift between him and her mother.

When Mrs. Turner heard from Merle that she had received a letter from her stepson James, she sent her own letter, which began the final confrontation in their lengthy struggle. In it she asked him to sign off on the sale of "Everton," the family home in which he grew up and the only remaining property from the elder James Turner's estate.

In his reply, he asked that Merle and Roy write directly to him to give their opinions of the proposed sale. Both sent letters saying they saw no other way than to sell the property as soon as possible, and they understood that they would receive nothing from the proceeds. Still, he was wary and didn't reply. After ten months, Mrs. Turner wrote again, this time more insistent. After explaining the benefits of an early sale and reminding him of his past costly recalcitrance, she threatened to side-step his objection " . . . and put it through the Supreme Court of Jamaica."

There is no record of a response to that letter, but my father wrote to his sister Fae, asking that she help him find a lawyer in Jamaica who would represent him in this matter. Fae sent his letter and a request for help to Gilbert Knowles, a friend in Mandeville,. His response was that he felt, because the case was complicated and long-standing, it would require considerable expense, and asked to be sent at least ten pounds. Again, my father was faced with the restriction against contingent legal representation, and, of course, he couldn't send anything.

Instead he received a December 17th letter from Mrs. Turner's lawyer, in which he reviewed the history of the will, the control of the estate by Mrs. Turner, and the rationale for the sale of the Eureka Road house. He ended his letter by proposing £100 in payment for his agreement to the sale.

The response from my father was business-like and brief, but his writing also showed some signs of declining clarity.

> Gentlemen:
>
> I have your kind letter of last Christmas concerning the matter of the sale of the property known as 6 Eureka Road, in St. Andrew. I have very carefully noted its contents.
>
> I feel, of course, that my share in the property is worth twice the amount that has been offered in your letter. Two hundred pounds will be more justified taking in consideration the fact that Mrs. Turner is not my mother as you have stated, but my step-mother, and I suppose that you are her lawyers. Then again, property values have recently inflated in the island to a great extent . . .

The response from the lawyer, in February 1943, included a new proposal. "Will you take £200 and convey any interest you might have in the place? If you will, we will confer with your step mother and let you know definitely." Whatever came of conferring with Mrs. Turner was left unclear because no further letters from the lawyer were in the files, but five months later my father wrote his final letter in this fight over the estate:

Gentlemen:

I received your inquiry last winter asking whether I would accept £200 and convey any interest I may have in the place. The matter has been given careful consideration and it has been found that this sum would be far from satisfactory and also that it might be best to have proceedings to wait, at least, until the war is over.

Needless to say I am rather skeptical about the matter indeed . . .

Since £200 had been his own proposal, it's difficult to understand why he didn't promptly agree. That amount of money would have been substantial, given the plight of our family. The availability of jobs during the war, however, probably led to improvement in the family's financial situation. He certainly sounds less desperate than he did in 1939. On the other hand, based on several of the personal letters, he was already quite ill. By that time he may have been experiencing signs of what was to come.

After hearing nothing back from the lawyer about the proposal, my father must have concluded that Mrs. Turner had balked at the £200 price for him to withdraw his objection. Nothing more was communicated. After his death, there would have been no further barriers to the sale of the property.

The struggle between our father and his stepmother was played out in the letter exchanges between 1930 and 1943, but the roots of the conflictual relationship undoubtedly lay in their history. Based on the records available, it would be pointless trying to arrive at a final judgment about the legal merits of their claims. We must conclude, however, that Annie Turner won the struggle; she was finally able to sell both houses under dispute, and our father received nothing from either sale; nor did he or his heirs ever receive anything for his "maintenance, education, and support." Still, there were many questions left unanswered.

Throughout this period there were signs in the letters of his failing health. In his September 1939 letter to his stepmother, he referred to ". . . a terrible state of nervousness, sickness, and absolute desperation . . ." In his March 1940 letter, he referred to himself as sickly. In her December 1942 letter, Fae refers to how sick he had been. In January 1943, Merle began her letter with the following:

> . . . It deeply grieves me to learn how sick you are, and having a wife and children dependents makes it more difficult. Although it could be hard, could you not get into some hospital or institution, or arrange at some clinic where the proper tests could be made and some treatment undergone? Every sickness has some control these days. That country is up to date. Please do something. Sickness is no respecter of persons, and there is nothing to be ashamed of. Will yourself and try anything. I am sorry you are suffering. May God guide and help you . . .

When I first read this as a teenager, I didn't understand the nature of his illness, but I did wonder why she thought he might be "ashamed."

After more than a year of being out of touch with her, he wrote to his sister Fae. She began her response of March 13, 1944:

> Dear darling brother, I received your letter and was glad to hear from you, for I was very worried about you. I could not imagine what had happened. We were all so very sorry to hear that you are sick, but trust in the good Lord that you will soon be ok again . . .

It is impossible to know how he had described his illness to her. I realized later, however, that the date of the letter meant that he was in Elgin State Hospital at the time.

The following letter was sent, from the hospital, to our mother and clarifies the nature of his illness:

3-15-44

My dear wife:

> It was more than fine of you to be so sincere and punctual in your visits on Sundays. And most of all

what you have to be admired for is your virtuous tolerance, patience and understanding in regard to my peculiar spells of anxiety, hiccups, shakes and what not. Of course, funny as it seems—it is all uncontrollable at this time. But it will sooner or later come to an end; so that you may be helped in your life's struggles of difficulties. It is to be regretted that anyone as kind, considerate, and fine as you are should have had the great misfortune of having a neurotic husband. Your nobility and your courage cannot be overestimated. But remember what I spoke to you about—these things are deep rooted causes and not just mere accidents that happen. So, they must be forgiven and overlooked. If there ever was a wife and mother that deserved consideration, it is you. And I cannot express too highly my deep appreciation for all the kindness and consolation that you have shown . . .

. . . With love and kindest regards to you and your angel children. Do not beat them under any circumstances. It may affect their nerves in the future . . .

Very affectionately yours,

Jimmy

This is the first place in the letters where there is an explicit description of the symptoms of his illness. I didn't understand the meaning of mental illness or how such an illness caused those particular symptoms.

In a letter to Jimmy, the postscript gives more of a hint about the type of hospital he was in:

Dear Jimmy (Mary June received a similar letter),

My son, I am so glad to see you write me such a nice letter. It was so thoughtful of you.

I also appreciated your nice card.

Daddy will be glad when he is well so that he may be able to see his lovely children again.

Remember, in Daddy and Mamma's absence that you are the little Daddy and June is the little mother.

With love and kisses to you all.

> Very lovingly yours
> Daddy

Show this to Mamma.

Bring suspenders, rubbers for snow, 2 good ties (not red).

I received grounds parole card before I mailed this letter. So I can walk out and get fresh air whenever I care to.

Reading these letters as a teenager, I didn't remember his period of absence when I was five years old. But I began to understand more about my older siblings. A heavy load of responsibility was placed on them; after our father's death, that burden must have felt still heavier.

He received only two more personal letters: one, while still in the hospital, was in Spanish; the other, from his friend Charlie Blanchett, whose name I found scattered throughout the personal letters. Both letters referred to his illness and hoped for his recovery. Charlie's included this poignant passage:

> . . . I am very sorry to hear how ill you have been, and I think if you got a change of climate for a few weeks it would perhaps cure you . . . I really feel for you, and if I could afford it, I would offer you some assistance, so that you could come out and spend a few weeks with me here. I feel that returning home and seeing the land of your boyhood would have a great effect on you and this would take off the strain that you are shouldering, by relaxing you would recover from it. What has brought this on you? Have you ever neglected yourself in any way? I candidly think that you worry too much . . .

The last letter he received was from the United States Department of State, dated November 11, 1944. He had sent a letter to the department asking for a statement of his citizenship. Nothing in the papers indicated why he had wanted this certification, but the response must have been devastating:

> Sir:
>
> With reference to your letter of June 23, 1944, you are informed that while it appears from the records that your name was included in the application upon which your step-mother, Mrs. Annie Rebecca Turner, was registered as an American citizen on September 24, 1923 showing that you were born at Kingston, Jamaica, British West Indies on March 21, 1908, it further appears from the records pertaining to members of your family that the birthplace of your father, James Julius Turner, was variously stated as Cincinnati, Ohio, Chicago, Illinois, Peru, Indiana, and the British West Indies. Moreover no conclusive evidence of your father's birth in this country has been received by the Department. Accordingly, the Department cannot undertake to furnish you with a statement as to your citizenship status until it has received satisfactory evidence of your father's birth in this county of the nature set forth in the indicated paragraph of the enclosed circular. It is further requested that you furnish the Department with a statement explaining, insofar as you may be able, the aforementioned discrepancies, relating to your father's place of birth . . .

The irony implied by this letter must have struck deep. He had no way to prove his right to citizenship; his stepmother, who was born in Jamaica, had, in 1923 obtained United States citizenship on the strength of her marriage to his father, who had died a year earlier; finally, the person who had sent him away from his home at fifteen and whom he blamed for much of his difficulties in life, could claim such citizenship, whereas he could not.

There were no more letters addressed to my father in the correspondence files. There were, however, two hand-written letters addressed to my mother following his death. One was from Annie R. Turner; the other from Isabella Phillpotts, Daisy Humber Turner's mother and our great grandmother. I didn't feel, as a teenager, the cynicism I later felt about the motivation for Annie Turner's letter.

April 15, 1945

Dear Lolita,

. . . I can quite imagine how upset you are from the loss of your dear husband and then to have people questioning and annoying you as to the way he died. When Jim was very sick and suffering terribly he didn't do away with himself, then why should he do that when he was feeling so much better as to be able to go to work. He must have tried to get a little fresh air at the window and one of those dizzy spells took him.

. . . Since 1929 I've never seen him. During his boyhood days he was normal, strong, and healthy. I think it is very unfortunate that he should have left us that way . . .

. . . I asked if you owed for the funeral, and how much, so if you could ask the undertaker for a transcript of death from the Board of Health, and a duplicate bill from him of funeral expenses and send to me, I would send it to Jamaica and see if the gov. would release me a few dollars to help you. I know how hard it is when one's heart is broken with sorrow to be burdened with debt and expenses of living going on every day . . .

According to the terms of the elder James Julius Turner's will, our father's death meant no further barriers existed to the sale of the Eureka Road property and that, given that he died before Annie Turner, his heirs were cut off from the estate. I never knew whether my mother replied to the letter and sent the death certificate and funeral bill, or whether Annie Turner sent any money. I did know that, by the time I began reading these letters, eight years had passed, and we had heard nothing further from our father's Jamaican family, and I didn't understand why.

The following letter was from his grandmother and struck me as a genuine expression of grief and compassion:

Mrs. I. Phillpotts
12 May/46

My dearest Lolita,

    I received a letter from Emmy Reid with the sad news of Jim's death. I could not write before as I have been ill in bed with rheumatism. I have just been able to sit and use the pen. I can imagine it must have been a great shock to you, with 4 children around. I hope you are trying to cheer up as much as you can. I am trying to cheer up. He is my first grandson. The Lord has relieved him of the great suffering. Kiss the kids for me. It was a good thing some time ago he sent me the whole family picture, including yours and his. I shall be pleased to always get a letter from you.
    Take care of yourself and accept love and kisses.

Grand Mother

Again, we had no further contact with our great grandmother or her family.

Although I had put in a serious effort and felt I had a better grasp of the narrative of our father's life, there was much I didn't understand. What I could say definitively: first, his mother died when he was an infant; second, when he was 15, a year after the death of his father, his stepmother sent him to New York City to fend for himself; third, when his stepmother asked him to agree to the sale of property in Providence in 1930, he refused, leading to litigation and the eventual sale without his approval; fourth, although he never succeeded, from that point on he frequently made the case to various parties and agencies that his stepmother had been guilty of trustee malfeasance and that he should have been receiving funds for his "support, maintenance, and education" ever since leaving Jamaica; fifth, he married our mother and relocated to Chicago, where there were business associates of his deceased father; sixth, he had a mental disorder of some kind and was hospitalized for some unknown period in Elgin, Illinois; and seventh, he had committed suicide at the age of 36, leaving his wife and four children.

The questions remaining were many. How had his mother died? What were the reasons that his stepmother sent him to New York at age 15? What was the nature and frequency of his contact with his family in Jamaica before 1930? Was there truth to the claims of wrongdoing by his stepmother? What was the specific nature of his illness? What were all the factors leading to the suicide? Why had we never heard more from Jamaica for eight years following his death? Again, I packed up all the papers and put them away. It would be twenty years later, 1974, when I began a long course of psychotherapy and was the age my father was when he died, before I read those papers again.

CHAPTER 5:

"Why, Ma?"

O ur father's suicide in 1945 profoundly impacted me and my siblings, but I can describe with intimate knowledge only its effects on my life. The major legacy from our father: Ma told us frequently that our father had wanted us to "get all the education you can." Our family's economic situation was precarious before he died; afterward, we were very poor. But the psychological and behavioral change that occurred in me following my father's death made possible another extraordinary turning point—admission to the all-white St. Ignatius Preparatory School in 1952. This could open the door to educational opportunity, and a chance to fulfill our father's wish.

After my father died, I changed from outgoing and aggressive to quiet and passive; adults, including my mother, adult relatives, the parish priest, even the nuns at St. Joseph's Mission School referred to me as a "good boy" and sometimes as "quiet." My newfound politeness and accommodation felt natural and were rewarded. But I did all the things my male classmates and neighborhood friends did, including various pranks.

One memorable instance of misbehavior did *not* go unnoticed. Raul Murillo, whose family lived on the second floor, was my best friend through most of my childhood. One hot summer night, when we were nine or ten, he and I sat on the outside ledge of the third-floor hall fire escape window. Looking down past our shoes through the metal grating and saying very little, we were bored. "I need to pee," I said without moving.

"So do I."

"I don't want to go in yet," I said. "I'll have to stay in, if I go in now."

The fire escape hung directly above the entry door to the building. Looking down from the third floor we saw no one. Nor was anyone in sight on either side of the street. It was late. We looked at each other, as if sharing a lark, pulled out our penises and sent a shower down to the sidewalk. When I saw a palm come out of the entryway, as if to check for rain, I was first stunned, then appalled to see the man who lived in the basement apartment step out and look up—just in time to get the full brunt of the shower of urine. Raul and I quickly drew back into the hallway, zipped up, and dashed into our apartments.

Sitting quietly in the living room, I hoped that somehow there would be no consequences for this prank. Ten minutes later, however, there came a knock on the door. When my mother answered, I could see from the dining room, where I was now skulking, the neighbor's face and my mother's back. They spoke quietly, but when the door closed my mother confronted me with folded arms and a stern, piercing stare. She asked, "Did you really do that?"

"We were just playin'," I said with my head down. "We didn't know somebody was standin' in the doorway."

My mother scowled, gave my left thigh a stinging slap, pointed an index finger at my face, and said, "Don't you ever do that again . . . That's nasty . . . I thought you were a good boy . . . Promise me you won't do nothin' like that again."

"I'm sorry . . . I promise," I said tearfully.

She gave a declarative "humph" and returned to the kitchen. I went to bed on the living room couch feeling glad the scolding and punishment were behind me, but I also worried that I would later see the neighbor and be unable to face him. I don't remember ever seeing him again.

In spite of the rare occasion of such lapses, my image as a "good boy" held. I was a dedicated altar boy, became a crossing guard as soon as I could, and ran errands and did odd jobs for the nuns. In addition to being a "good boy," I began to get the top grades in my class from fifth grade onward, and eventually received the American Legion Award, the highest award given at our graduation. All this explains why I was chosen to be "the experiment."

When I was growing up in Chicago, the neighborhoods and suburbs, like most American urban areas, were even more racially segregated than they are today. Blacks and whites lived apart, and that reality was the basis upon which school segregation was maintained in the north. Occupational discrimination may have been severe, but keeping the races totally separate in the world of work would have been impractical. Even black professionals, however, found that success *didn't* include access to white communities and suburbs—neither working class, like Cicero, nor middle-to-upper-middle class, like Oak Park. Segregated neighborhood elementary schools were the general rule—even for Catholic schools. The Catholic and public high schools were as racially segregated as the elementary schools.

The city had two broadly defined areas where blacks lived during most of the twentieth century; the boundaries were firmed up by the Race Riot of 1919. Between 1934, when our parents arrived from New York City, and 1940, our family lived in the larger of the two, on the South Side. This was an area of predominantly black communities, strung together and stretching south out of the "Loop" from 21st to 72nd Streets, which came to be known later as the Black Belt and Bronzeville—comparable to Harlem in New York City. During those six years, my family lived in four different apartments—on Michigan Avenue, Wabash Avenue, South Park Boulevard (later renamed Martin Luther King Boulevard), and Prairie Avenue, all between 29th and 36th Street. This was a working class community, but most people were unemployed during those years. My family's several evictions were based on failure to pay rent, and each move was to greater dilapidation. When we were finally evicted from 2922 Prairie Avenue, where the rent was $20 dollars per month, my parents had to find cheaper housing.

The only recourse was the other black area, the Near West Side. This area stretched narrowly westward from the railroad yards at Canal Street to Western Avenue, between 12th Street—after the war renamed Roosevelt Road—and 16th Street. The black communities of the South Side were affluent compared to this area. It was here, toward the middle of the Great Migration (1910-1940), that blacks from the South found low-cost housing. The particular neighborhood where we lived, located at the eastern end of the Near West Side, was called the Maxwell

Street Area. It had been a largely Jewish enclave from the middle of the nineteenth century, but it gradually changed. Only elderly Jews stayed on long after the young and middle-aged families had moved to white neighborhoods and suburbs. By the time we arrived, almost all of the residential housing was taken up by blacks and Latinos, while most of the commercial property and businesses were owned by Jews who had moved out but returned, on a daily basis, to make a living. Maxwell Street was, like the Lower East Side of Manhattan in the early twentieth century, a Mecca for bargains. On Saturdays, Sundays, and holidays, when the weather was favorable, and sometimes when it was not, Maxwell Street and the streets that crossed it were teeming with small shops, pushcarts, open-air stalls, tables and blankets displaying new and used merchandise, crowds of bargain hunters, blues singers, and tourists gawking at the spectacle.

Until the 1950s, Roosevelt Road, a wide boulevard running west from Lake Michigan, was the unofficial boundary between the Maxwell Street Area (and all the adjacent black neighborhoods) and the strictly white neighborhoods to the north. On the "white" side of Roosevelt Road, about five blocks west of where we lived, stood Holy Family Church. Attached to it was an elementary school and St. Ignatius High School. As far as I could see, only whites attended these schools. St. Francis Assisi church and school, on the south side of Roosevelt Road at Newberry Street, served the Latino community; both the masses and instruction were in Spanish. Although we lived closer to St. Francis and Holy Family schools, my siblings and I attended St. Joseph's Mission School, an all-black school.

Following graduation from St. Joseph's, most of the boys attended Crane Technical High School, which my brother Jim attended, and most of the girls attended Lucy Flowers Technical High School, from which my sisters graduated. When I graduated, I expected to follow my brother to Crane Tech. However, the parish priest had a meeting with my mother. Although no graduate of St. Joseph's had ever attended St. Ignatius, he had convinced the administration of the school to take a chance on me. I was to be a social experiment. They understood that my mother couldn't afford the tuition, so she paid a nominal fee—when she could.

Although I barely understood the implications, I didn't hesitate to accept the challenge. During the summer I had to take an entrance test by special arrangement. When the principal graded my exam, he looked at me soberly and said, "Not very good. We will have to see."

When I finished my first year at St. Ignatius, I received Class Honors—I had the best grades in my particular class of 30 students. The parish priest proudly announced this in St. Joseph's parish bulletin. In my second year I did the same each semester. Academically, I was succeeding beyond the expectations of those who had decided to see whether a kid from the ghetto mission school could succeed in a competitive—i.e. white and middle class—school. At the end of that school year, I was assigned to the Classical Honors track (two years of Homeric Greek and two additional years of Latin) for my final two years.

During the summer I made another attempt to understand my father's letters, but soon gave up in frustration. I was also feeling what sociologists call "the stress of upward mobility." Although I never felt I fit in at St. Ignatius—I had lunch alone every day—I also began to feel estranged from the black community. My response was to become the membership registrar at the local Chicago Boys' Club, which offered little pay but allowed me to work with younger boys and interact with the staff. I also hung out with AJ, a friend from St. Joseph's, much of the summer and we joined a West Side social club called the Torches. Aside from an occasional house party, where we charged a quarter to come in and dance, we were really a street gang getting into turf battles with other gangs. When school started again in September, I held onto the commitments I had made during the summer—including the Torches and my job at the Boys' Club—but now I studied Greek, Latin, and Advanced Algebra deep into the night as well.

By the middle of October I burned out, got strep throat, and within a week had joint pain and swelling in both knees so severe I had to use my arms to crawl up the stairs to get to our apartment. During a feverish night, I was reeling in pain. My mother took me to the Mandel Clinic the next morning, and I was admitted into Michael Reese Hospital with a diagnosis of rheumatic fever. After a month of bed rest, and because I also had two damaged heart valves, I was transferred to a convalescence home called Herrick House, in Bartlett, Illinois, for children with rheumatic fever and associated cardiac problems. Within a week I had a flare-up of the fever, but this time the pain and swelling were in my shoulders, upper arms, and eventually both hands. I spent a month in the infirmary. I remained at Herrick House for the remainder of the school year, so when I returned to St. Ignatius, I had to repeat my junior year.

This time I was placed in the highest tier class of the Classical Honors track with the brightest students. My grades were even better than they had been, so I achieved First Honors—but *not* Class Honors. The parish priest surprised me when he confronted me with this lapse.

The big event of that academic year for me was winning a third-place gold medal in a school-wide short story contest. Our English teacher knew he could make extraordinary demands on us, so submitting a short story for the contest was a class assignment. I didn't hesitate or think long about what to write about; I simply sat and began writing, as if it were already there in my mind. At the time, it didn't occur to me that the story, published in the 1955 Christmas issue of the school's semi-annual magazine, was about my father's death, but, when I cried while reading it to my therapist twenty years later, I knew the tears I shed were for my father, my mother, and myself.

The story, entitled *Why, Ma?*, told of a six year old boy living with his parents and four older siblings in a racially mixed neighborhood. He was going through that stage of development when knowledge of the world is soaked up by asking questions—especially "Why?" The little boy of the story had only his mother to provide the bridges between observations of events and their causes, and he relentlessly pursued her for them. Much of the story tells of the love between the two. For the mother's part, witnessing and participating in her child's development made her feel both pride and gratitude. However, she sometimes felt annoyed by the repetitiveness of the questions—especially when she had no good answer or when a series of logical questions led to a contradiction: " . . . but why . . . ? but why . . . ?" When he asked her questions like why some white people hated black people, she had to say "I don't know" or "that's the way some people are," and she found it painful to see the bafflement in her child's face. But her annoyance was mostly with herself and what she felt were her inadequacies. For the little boy, the impasses that sometimes arose were inconsequential compared to the experience of his mother as the fount of all knowledge and love. At the climax of the story, the boy is struck by a car and killed near the house. A white boy of his age had pushed him into speeding traffic as a prank; he had meant to simply frighten him but failed to hold him back at the last second. The mother is, of course, devastated by this loss and asks, "Why, God?" Hearing no answer from God, she chooses to see the loss as a test of her faith. She finally reaffirms her faith in a loving and all-knowing God, but she is left with the question "Why?"

The father never appears, not even to comfort the mother after the death of the child. There is no explanation for his absence. Likewise, none of the boy's siblings ever makes an appearance. Only a loving mother or an omniscient God could possibly have the answer. If this story was my attempt to resolve the mystery of my father's death, these distortions of the real-life story may well have been a disguise for answers I couldn't handle. The story is framed around and ends with the question "Why?" When I had put aside the letters in the previous summer, I felt frustrated by not knowing why various things had happened. Why had our grandmother died at the age of twenty-one? Why had our father killed himself? Could his illness be the reason? Could someone, especially his stepmother, be blamed?

Not perceiving the connections between the short story and the unanswered questions of my family history, I had simply seen the award as a sign that I could write well. But, in spite of the pleasure I had in writing and encouragement from English teachers in high school and college, something kept me away from writing another story—until now.

Only much later did I realize the psycho-historical context for the question the boy asked his mother about whites' hatred of blacks. I wrote the story in late 1955. Emmett Till, a 14 year-old black Chicagoan, had been brutally murdered in Mississippi that August. The story and the pictures were talked about everywhere in the black community for many months. I remember seeing gruesome pictures of Till's remains in *Ebony*, *Jet*, and *The Chicago Defender*. I was the only black student in my year and only one of three in the school at the time. I felt isolated, fearful, and mystified. I had taken the writing of the story as an opportunity for a muted protest.

The following summer, I wanted to work to help out. For several weeks, I worked as a day laborer for a "temp" company; one day in a steel mill, another delivering telephone books, each day having to pull out my birth certificate. After a long search, I got a job as a page at Michael Reese Hospital, where I had been a patient two years earlier. The work was full time and hard, pushing patients from place to place, delivering records around the hospital, and by the end of every day I was too tired to do anything. I felt uneasy and didn't look forward to my senior year.

Around the middle of the summer, I came upon pamphlets and other material from the Society of the Divine Word (SVD) inviting application to study for the priesthood. They were starting a special program for students who had not gone the usual seminary route from the beginning of high school but later wanted to enter religious studies. The major appeal was that the order had two substantial missions in Africa, in Ghana and The Congo. Did I have a calling? Was this a way to reestablish my roots? I applied, was accepted, and talked with our parish priest, the principal at St. Ignatius, and a few other priests I trusted. No one tried to dissuade me, although the principal informed me that some at the school had hoped I would want to be a Jesuit. When I told him that the major appeal of the SVD was its focus on missionary work, he pointed out that the Jesuits were largely a missionary order.

The seminary was St. Paul's in Epworth, Iowa. There were only a dozen students; some were a bit older, some had been in the army, others had simply worked for a time following high school graduation. One of the things these "late-comers" lacked was knowledge of languages—Latin, Greek, but also German—the order originated and had its Mother House in Germany. When the education director realized I had already had three years of Latin and a year of Greek, I was sent to the seminary, Holy Ghost Seminary in East Troy, Wisconsin, where students studied Latin from the first year. Because the seniors I was joining were in their first year of Greek and had already three years of German, I was allowed to skip the Greek classes and studied German on my own.

I was happy there. The bells that signaled the beginning and ending of everything, including prayers, chapel, classes, work, meals, recreation, and bedtime induced serenity.

In the spring the seniors entered a period called postulancy, preparation for going into the major seminary as novices the following fall. As part of the process, each postulant had several individual meetings with the Principal of the seminary. I thought these were counseling sessions in which we would be invited to work through any doubts before making our initial vows. Although I didn't realize it until later, they were really screening interviews to identify any problem candidates. Having been invited to express my concerns about anything troubling me, I launched into a criticism of the Church and the Order for its abetting of racism. I knew, I told him, that the order had a mission in Louisiana where blacks still had to sit in the back during mass. I asked, "Why would the order tolerate such a thing?" The principal gave an unsatisfactory answer, but I dropped the subject. I don't remember why it came up, but I also spoke about my father—what I had found out about his illness, hospitalization, and suicide.

My mother arrived to pick me up on graduation day. Before we left, a priest I didn't know invited her into a private but visible area of the administration building. Though out of earshot, I could see them having a rather intense conversation. I never inquired, nor did my mother tell me, what the conversation was about. When I left for the summer, I looked forward to rejoining my peers as a novice at the major seminary in the fall of 1957.

That summer I took a job as a summer camp counselor at the convalescence home, Herrick House, where I had been a patient three years earlier. On one of my first weekend visits from Bartlett to Chicago, my mother handed me a letter she had received from the Director at the major seminary. The letter was sent to her because the order thought it best that *she* break the news to me: I was *not* to show up at the seminary in the fall. The history of my father's mental illness was said to be the major factor in the decision. As soon as I realized the meaning of the brief letter, my hands came together and crushed the paper into a ball. I straightened the letter and read it again, I asked, "How can this be happening?" My mother, clearly despondent, sat at the kitchen table. I handed her the un-crumpled letter and asked, "What does this mean?"

"I know how disappointed you must be," she answered, and through her tears she said, "I'm so sorry."

I immediately turned around and returned to my room. For years I assumed that my mother, who had made it clear that she didn't approve of my going into the priesthood, had said something in the conversation with the priest to sabotage my chance to be a priest. When, several years later, I worked up sufficient courage to share my assumption with her, she told me that she had been confronted with the information I had given to the seminary director. She said that she had never understood why I would tell them about my father. Then I realized that I had considered my conference with the seminary Principal to be confidential—comparable to the sanctity of the confessional. It turned out not to be. I apologized to my mother for all the years I had blamed *her* for my not becoming a priest.

After recovering from the initial shock of the rejection from the seminary, I explored avenues of appeal. I had conferred with my parish priest, with a well-known director of a Catholic retreat house where I had sometimes volunteered as an acolyte, and with a black priest I knew at a parish on the South Side of Chicago. When I shared my problem with the director of Herrick House, she suggested I try obtaining my father's records from Elgin State Hospital, which happened to be in a small city close to Bartlett. I received a response that included the following:

August 8, 1957

Dear Mr. Turner:

Our records indicate that your father was committed to this hospital by Cook Country Court on 1/21/44. He remained until 4/29/44 when he was given a conditional discharge. An absolute discharge was issued on 4/29/45. This was as Without Psychosis (Not Insane), and we have no further record of a recurrence of Mr. Turner's illness.

Perhaps you would like to show this letter to the persons interested, since it should indicate to them that, legally, your father would not be considered mentally ill and that the illness he experienced at the time of his hospitalization was brief in nature. We know no manner in which his illness should affect you, or any other member of his family, and we feel that it is regrettable that this has become a factor in your plans for the future . . .

When I showed this to the director of Herrick House, she agreed to ask the medical director of the convalescence home to write a letter to see whether the hospital would send him more details or release the records to him. He received a similar, though briefer, response from the Hospital Director, who gave some additional information orally. The most significant description was that my father had a head tic and brief episodes of shaking.

In spite of the designation of "Without Psychosis," it was clear to my supporters who read these letters that words like "commitment," "illness," "diagnosis," and "Psychoneurosis" would be unlikely to persuade the Order to waive its policy against accepting candidates with a family history of mental illness. Given that they had the death certificate indicating "suicidal" and noting that the "final discharge" was granted more than a month after my father's death, they expected that the Order would question any assurances that he was "Without Psychosis."

Because I had been told that it was likely that all missionary orders would have similar restrictions, I finally gave up hope. Several supporters suggested that there wouldn't be such restrictions in various dioceses around the country. I was given several suggestions, and I wrote letters to them all—mostly in the Midwest. Some didn't reply; others were mildly encouraging. Then I received a response from a diocese in Indiana. It was brief and simply indicated that the diocese had "no need for colored priests." I was still reeling from my disappointment from being rejected by the SVDs, and this response threw me into a tailspin of emotions—first disbelief, then anger, despondency, and finally bitter resentment at the hypocrisy of the Catholic Church. Still, I was also given to self-blame and wondered how and why I had indicated that I was black in my letter. Perhaps, as in the case of my revelations about my father to the SVD, I had unconsciously sabotaged my stated desire to become a priest; perhaps I had managed to find a face-saving method of withdrawing. In the end, I had to acknowledge that both my disappointment in and resentment of the Church were just, but I also concluded that I had been ambivalent about pursuing the priesthood. I ceased to do anything more in that direction and, although I continued to be a practicing Catholic for several years, my smoldering resentment remained.

Because the end of my attempts came late in the summer, I had made no other plans—not for going to college or for making a living. I asked to continue as a counselor at Herrick House while, for two semesters, while I attended Elgin Community College. In the following Spring, Barbara, a co-op student from Antioch College, arrived to work as a counselor and stayed for four months. During that time we began a relationship that culminated in our marriage three years later, when we were both finishing our college degrees—she from Antioch College and I from DePaul University. We both worked fulltime for a while but were eager to attend graduate school. We earned master's degrees in Clinical Psychology from DePaul, did year-long internships at Chicago State Hospital, and went on to earn Ph.D.s from the University of Chicago—she from the Committee on Human Development and I from the Psychology Department. After I received my degree in 1966, I was obliged to work for the Illinois Department of Mental Health because I had been supported by the state throughout my graduate training. By spring of 1968 Barbara was close to finishing, so we decided to apply for academic jobs around the country. Given the difficulty at the time for married couples to get academic positions in the same institutions, we felt fortunate to have both obtained Assistant Professor positions at the University of Massachusetts in Amherst—she in Human Development and I in Psychology.

Because of the Catholic Church's stance on the use of birth control and our desire to delay starting a family, we had stopped attending Mass within a year after getting married. The hypocrisy implied by going simply led us to stop. I was also still harboring unresolved resentments against the Church because of its rejection of me and because of my assessment of its own hypocrisy. But when our first child, Adam Justin, was born, we arranged for his baptism at St. Brigid's Church in Amherst. Our daughter, Shomari Megan, was baptized at the same church in 1974, the year we both received tenure. That was the extent of our children's religious training. We were "lapsed" Catholics.

Possibly because of the strain of working toward tenure, the strains in our marriage (based, in part, on being an interracial couple during the Black Power Movement), and the strains of having a young family, but also because I was approaching the age my father was when he died, I became depressed. When I began psychotherapy that year, I didn't immediately identify the unanswered questions about my father as the underlying source of my problem. However, as I probed deeper, my question became whether I was fated to follow him. As I read *Why, Ma?* to my therapist I cried. He asked what my tears signified, but I couldn't articulate anything more clearly than to say it was "so sad." As the therapy work progressed, I was able to unravel some of the complex feelings and role attributions I had given to the three main characters—the missing father, the grieving mother, and the child. As in the story, the reasons for my real father's absence had always been a mystery—even after my discovery of the death certificate. What did it mean to say someone was suicidal? What were the reasons for taking his own life? What had our father meant to say by doing something so drastic?

Although our mother was always loving and caring, she made it clear to us that she felt aggrieved about our father's leaving her to raise four young children alone. In the story, the mother has only the little boy as an object of love, but her mood is somber and she doubts her ability to care for and protect him. This may have been an accurate picture of my mother immediately after our father died, but these weren't characteristics through most of her life. In the therapy I concluded that they were projections of my own feelings.

Finally, the interpretations had to make sense of the little boy and his death. As alluded to earlier, in one of my earliest memories, from before my father's death, I see myself as an outgoing—even aggressive—child. After my father's death, I was "a good boy." If this strategic shift had become a way of coping, perhaps the little boy's eagerness to know was a way of reasserting a more forceful, although hidden, self. Why did he have to die? Rather, why did I have to arrange his death? What would be accomplished by doing so? We explored several possibilities. The therapist was most attentive to the psychodynamic possibilities: first, when my father died, I was six, a ripe age for the fantasy that I had wished for, and thereby accomplished, my father's (my rival's) permanent disappearance; second, the death of the little boy was just retribution for what I had done and headed off fears of Oedipal incest. I preferred a somewhat less Freudian, but still deterministic, interpretation: having witnessed the intensity of my mother's grieving following the loss of our father, and the deep love it implied, I wanted my mother to grieve for me and love me in the same way.

The therapist and I spent many sessions spinning out complex interpretations for even minor details. The story began with a description of the street where, following a rainstorm, cars that had been parked pulled away revealing the rivulets of water flowing from the center of the street down toward the sidewalk and into the gutter. Those "tears" foretold the sadness that would come later. And another: it could be no mystery why my three siblings (and, for that matter, the many people flowing through our real apartment throughout my childhood) were left out of the story. I wanted my mother to myself. Finally, we also realized that there was an off-stage character in the story: the unresponsive, and therefore disappointing, God.

Like the mother of the story, religious faith was a major part of who my mother was. Not even the death of her husband or her child would have led her to reject that faith. The seventeen-year-old author of the story, however, may have expressed my father's doubts about the existence of God, which were present in the letters left behind. It was remarkable that within months of writing the story, I decided to become a priest and entered the seminary. When I made a verbal slip in psychotherapy and said " . . . I decided to go into the cemetery . . ." we speculated that in the seminary I had found yet another way to punish the guilty child.

While in therapy I felt that I was gaining useful insights into my complex set of emotions and motivations. But I still hadn't answered the questions about our grandmother's death, our father's suicide, and our family in Jamaica. A full year into the therapy, I realized that there was only one way to get answers to these questions: I had to go to Jamaica, find our family, and ask the questions. The therapist supported this idea, and much of the remaining months of therapy were spent preparing myself for what lay ahead.

CHAPTER 6:

Return to Jamaica

W hen I began to talk about my father in therapy and think seriously about travelling to Jamaica, I hadn't seen his letters and papers in many years. In 1974, my mother assured me that she still had them, though some might have been lost when she and Precious moved from Chicago to Los Angeles in 1961. Precious agreed to make a copy of the remaining files for me. When I received them, the letters and papers struck me as being in the same jumble as when I had first read them at thirteen. I dug in, organized them as I had earlier, made lists of all the people who could still be alive, noted the relationship to our father and their last known addresses, and again familiarized myself with the story. Both my eagerness to go to Jamaica and my anxiety about doing so grew.

In fall 1974, when Barbara and I were due for our first sabbatical leaves, they had to be delayed for administrative reasons. This gave me another year to think about and plan what I knew would be a critical journey.

Although Barbara worried about the implications of my strong identification with my father, she saw the importance of this endeavor for me and agreed that we should use our delayed leave to spend the following year in Jamaica. We had no trouble writing proposals to justify a year of research in Jamaica because she and I had worked together since 1969 on a longitudinal questionnaire/interview study: "The Family Origins of Achievement Motivation." For decades research on blacks in America had reported on the exceptional achievements of Jamaican-born immigrants; we wondered whether this was a reflection of differences in the cultures or based on selective migration. We wrote our sabbatical proposals to gather questionnaires and interviews in Jamaica to match what we had from the United States, received small research grants, and began making preparations.

I took on the major responsibility for arranging the Jamaica sabbatical. We knew that we would need the cooperation of an academic institution in Jamaica. Jamaican colleagues at the University of Massachusetts provided me with the names of professors at the University of the West Indies at Mona, a suburb of Kingston. After exchanging several letters, the Social Science Division and the Registrar of Appointments informed us that we could only be granted unpaid appointments and various University privileges once we arrived. We were pleased with this outcome, because it left us free of any formal obligations but provided a base from which we could carry out the research projects.

The academic preparations, however, weren't the only ones I needed to make. How was I going to find the lost Jamaican family with whom we had had no contact for almost thirty years? After searching libraries for telephone directories of Jamaica, I discovered that I could purchase one through the local telephone company. It's difficult to say what I expected to find there, but I thought knowing retail establishments and service providers could help in our adjustment. I also had some hope of finding family this way. When I received the book, I immediately looked for the Turners in the white pages. The only real hope I had was for either Roy Collins Turner or Fern Turner, two of my father's half-siblings, but there were no Turners with given names that matched. From his letters, I had discovered the married names of two of my aunts—Merle Steele, *nee* Turner, and Fae Wehby, the child of our grandfather with his assistant. There were multiple listings for these two surnames—Merle Steele and Fae Wehby were among them. I was taken aback by the notion that, after almost thirty years, all I needed to do to find my family was open a phone book. I decided to wait until we were in Jamaica before trying to contact any of them.

Preparing for the yearlong sabbatical was arduous. The documents needed seemed endless. United States passports were the easiest to get—birth certificates and notarized affidavits that we were who we said we were. Obtaining Jamaican visas, on the other hand, was fraught with snags and delays. We had to get proof of financial solvency—a letter from the University of Massachusetts treasurer's office indicating our tenured professor status and the amounts of our sabbatical half-salaries. The Amherst police department gave us letters to the effect that they could find no criminal records or outstanding warrants for us. Our physicians wrote reports indicating we were all in excellent health and were up-to-date on all required immunizations. We began the application and interview process in early February but didn't receive the visas until the middle of August, two weeks before we were to leave. Because we were uncertain about the transportation system on the island, we decided to ship our automobile. We shipped the car and most of the personal belongings we took to Jamaica out of New York City by boat.

We left Amherst on August 28, 1975. We missed our afternoon flight in New York City by minutes and had to wait in a motel for a morning flight on the 29th. This turned out to be fortunate, because we would have arrived in Kingston at night with sleepy children, luggage in tow, and no prearranged transportation to the hotel. We discovered later how much more of a hassle that would have been, especially since Adam's ears bled in reaction to the airplane cabin pressure.

We arrived in Kingston in the late morning. When we first stepped from the airplane and walked along an extended canopy to the main building of the airport, tears welled up and I had to fight off an unanticipated impulse to kneel and kiss the ground. I think I aborted it because I feared such a gesture would be too strange for the children to understand. After all these years, I had come to my father's country of birth which, after being sent away at age fifteen, he never saw again. I had no feelings of anger or recrimination, but only the sense that I had completed a circle he had promised himself but had never been able to fulfill.

We were able to get through customs, rent a car, and be on our way by early afternoon. On that first ride through Kingston, we were surprised by the mixture and proximity of opulence in the hills and tin shacks and other signs of utter poverty at lower elevations. Goats, pigs, and cows wandered freely through the streets, and there were few signs of traffic control. Overstuffed buses and jitneys slowly skirted and wobbled through potholes deep enough to damage axels. The hotel was pleasant, with colorful murals on all the walls in an atrium, with rooms facing a flower-filled courtyard. But our room was small; the children slept in the one bed and Barbara and I slept on cots brought in.

We had to endure this tight arrangement for about a week, after which the university's housing bureau granted us an apartment near the campus. We were pleased to have a two-bedroom two-bath apartment with a kitchen and spacious living/dining room. The one surprising amenity, which pleased the children most, was the well-maintained swimming pool. Within a few days I retrieved the car so we could collect our belongings from the dock and set up our household. We enrolled Adam, age 4, in St. Margaret's elementary school, a private school near our apartment. We hired a "helper" for three days a week to clean, cook some meals, and baby sit.

Within two weeks of settling and getting our bearings, Barbara and I were ready to visit the University of the West Indies (UWI) and meet the faculty. The chair of the Social Science Division, with whom I had exchanged letters in setting up our visit, was a friendly and talkative man of about fifty. We spoke with him for several hours about our projects and what we thought we needed from him and UWI. He escorted us to a prearranged interview with the Registrar of Appointments, an attractive middle-aged woman with a severe demeanor. I found it impossible to draw a smile from her on any topic, and her questions implied a level of wariness we didn't understand. We learned later that some suspected us of being C.I.A. agents, while other faculty possibly feared we might take their jobs. Half of the faculty in Social Science lacked doctorates and few were doing any research. Nonetheless, we eventually got our formal appointments as Visiting Research Associates, positions providing us with library privileges, access to lunch and the bar at the Senior Commons, and our modestly priced university housing.

Later that first day at UWI, the chair introduced us to as many faculty members as he could find in the building and to some who happened to be passing through. They were cordial enough, but we never found anyone who had any interest in the research we were to do there. The closest we came to becoming socially accepted on the campus was being bought drinks at the Senior Commons.

Within weeks of the beginning of the fall term, and before we were able to launch our research, the faculty and staff at UWI went on an extended strike. The entry gates to the campus were blocked by picketing strikers; and then, two days later, tanks and armored vehicles patrolled the campus and the surrounding streets. The campus was closed to everyone. That was our first hint of how volatile the political situation on the island and campus was. Since we were unable to go to campus, our research plans went on indefinite hold. By the end of the sabbatical year, we had scaled back the project to just a questionnaire study. With the requisite approvals of faculty and student groups, we asked instructors of large lecture courses to permit us to collect data in their classes, thus sufficiently (though minimally) fulfilling the research mission of the sabbatical.

Of course, for me, the research project on family socialization was less important than the personal search for my own family. Although I had found the names of my two aunts in the Kingston telephone book, I decided that it wouldn't be prudent to initiate contact by telephone. In mid-September I wrote letters to Merle Steele and Fae Wehby. In these letters I introduced myself as a son of their brother, James Turner, who had died thirty years earlier in the United States. I told them I was in Jamaica with my family and doing research at UWI. I referenced their letters to my father and provided enough information to assure them that I was their nephew. Finally, I expressed my wish to meet them and any others on the island to whom I was related.

It turned out that neither of my aunts was on the island at the time. I received a call from Donald, one of Fae's sons, who informed me that his mother was living with one of her daughters in Ontario. He had reached her by phone to tell her about my letter, and she had asked him to read it to her. He reported that she was overjoyed by the letter and the prospect of meeting us when she would be returning to Jamaica in late October.

In the meantime, Donald said he had spoken with his two sisters about organizing a gathering to introduce us to the family. The party was held at the home of his sister and brother-in-law, Beverly and Orville Higgins. We found them all to be delightful, welcoming, and generous people, but none of them could provide me with any information about my father. None had ever met him nor could anyone remember seeing a picture of him. The little they might have been told about him by my aunt Fae when they were young was long forgotten.

We enjoyed working out the name to describe our familial relationship—half first cousins. We had a good time whenever we were invited to their homes for the occasional dinner or social gathering. It was from these families that we received the most information about island social structure. They were all regarded as middle-class. Donald worked for the local telephone company; his wife taught Spanish in a public high school; Beverly's husband, Orville, was a manager of a large department store in downtown Kingston. When we told them our research was, in part, about perceptions of racial discrimination, they claimed race discrimination didn't exist in Jamaica; what mattered and distinguished people was social class, which correlated highly with wealth. They did acknowledge that there was a "shade system" of race in Jamaica—black and white at the extremes, but brown, yellow, and red as distinct categories broadly recognized and accepted. This was explained, in part, by the waves of imported labor during British rule that brought in immigrants from various parts of Asia and the Middle East. They and their friends would be thought of as politically conservative in the United States. They saw Jamaican government policies under Michael Manley as leaning too far toward socialism, and some were wary about the new friendship between the leaders of Jamaica and Cuba. Still, they were my closest relatives in Jamaica, and I was pleased to have found them.

When my aunt Fae arrived in late October, she first stayed with Beverly and her family. Our first encounter with Fae was cordial but lacked the warmth I had expected. Unlike her letters to my father, she was quite reserved. When I showed her a copy of one of her letters expressing concern about his health, she inspected it but made no comment. More surprising was that she asked me nothing about my father or his death, about our family in the United States, or even about me. Looking back, I regret how little I pressed her for information about my father. I could have spent time extracting details about my grandfather, her mother, my father, and their relationships. I never asked her for even basic information or details. Each time I was alone with her, I came away feeling as if I had been with a stranger who was withholding something. Was she afraid I would reveal something her children didn't know? Did I fear what I might learn if I interrogated her? I didn't want to stir up something that would make her uncomfortable. I was also afraid some underlying resentments I was harboring would emerge and alienate her. Reading her letters to my father always gave me the impression that, while he wrote about our suffering in poverty, her letters suggested that she and her family were succeeding as small business entrepreneurs. Still, she never offered any assistance to my father and his family, and after he died, she never attempted to contact our mother.

This experience of Fae was reinforced when my mother and Precious visited. I told each of my cousins I was eager to have my mother and Fae meet; the responses from Fae and the cousins were noncommittal. Since Fae routinely moved around from one to another of her three children on the island, it was left unclear how and where the meeting would take place.

Fae was staying at her daughter Carol's home when my mother and Precious arrived, so a meeting was arranged to take place there. The home was in a cluster of modest, but modern, townhouses in Kingston. The first-floor apartment had its own small deck leading to the front door. When I introduced my mother and Precious to Fae and Carol, no one on either side smiled. I didn't expect the women to embrace, but the stiffness, even coldness, I observed disappointed me. After the introductions, I expected that we would be ushered into the apartment. Instead, we were invited to sit on the crowded deck outside. Barbara was busy with our two small children throughout the visit. Whenever I looked at the faces of my mother and my aunt, I saw only the slightest of smiles, and neither woman spoke more than a few sentences. My mother didn't question Fae about my father and his early life in Jamaica. Fae didn't ask about her half-brother's life in the United States or his death, nor did she ask how my mother and her children survived after my father died. Neither woman seemed interested in having a conversation.

Carol offered us cold drinks, and we sat hardly speaking. At one point both Fae and Carol went inside the apartment and didn't reemerge for ten minutes. I wondered whether they were inside conferring about what to do with us all on the deck. After they had been absent for a while, my mother leaned toward me and asked in a tone of mild scorn, "Is this something like the projects?"

Donavan, Carol's teenage son, was sitting silently nearby and let out a muffled snort, which we all chose to ignore. I was too stunned and embarrassed by my mother's insensitivity and condescension to say anything. Precious, too, looked away and said nothing. After Donavan went inside, we were left there alone. I felt very uneasy and soon suggested to my mother and Precious that we should leave. No one objected, and when Fae and Carol came back to the deck, I rose and announced that we had enjoyed the visit but were obliged to leave. Fae and Carol expressed regret at the brevity of the visit, but both smiled for the first time.

I never spoke to my mother, Precious, or Fae about this encounter. I felt mortified but never understood whether this feeling was more for my mother, Fae, or me. I was left with questions I hardly allowed myself to ask. What had I wished would happen when the two women met? What was it that really happened? Why had the two women been so cold toward one another?

My mother had given me, in my early teens, the assignment to study my father's letters. I expected my mother to be pleased that I had managed to use his papers to reconnect with the Jamaican family. She never expressed any such pleasure. I never raised the topic with her again, but I was disappointed. I concluded that my mother was, by her silence, communicating her own disappointment in what I had done—reconnecting with the family but without getting anything from it that could be regarded as the long-lost legacy our father had pursued. Had she come to Jamaica hoping that I had found the wealth she had dreamed was there? If so, she never said.

Fae had expressed, in her letters to my father, such warm and loving sentiments that I had expected the same in person. She had been inexplicably distant in our first encounter, and this picture of Fae had now been supported by the way she responded to my mother. Was this simply a reflection of her personality? Was she simply shy or lacking in personal warmth? Was this the way she was seen among her own children? I never knew because I was afraid to ask.

My disappointment in the outcome of my mother's visit led to a very rare episode of open anger and resentment between us. Close to the end of their weeklong visit, we went on a driving tour of the Blue Mountains. The roads there were unpaved, narrow, and full of large stones. On the way down, we met a car coming from the other direction, and in order to give plenty of room to pass, I moved slightly off the road. Unfortunately, there were large rocks lurking in the tall weeds. *Blam*! *Blam*! The two left tires blew out. We had only one spare. Precious and I were fortunate to get a ride from a plainclothes policeman to the first town at the base of the mountain. He helped us arrange the purchase of a new tire and a ride back up the mountain to pick up my mother, Barbara, and the children. By the time we all got back to our apartment, we were all stressed and exhausted.

When I went into my mother's bedroom to ask how she was, she began to scold me. "Castie, why were you driving so fast? How could you be so reckless? How could you let your sister be exposed to such danger by letting her go into that man's car with you? I was so worried about what might happen to her. That's what happens when you drive fast."

I was taken aback and immediately exploded, "Ma, it was an *accident*! I was *not* going fast and I *wasn't* driving recklessly. The road was narrow and I had no way of seeing what was under the weeds at the side of the road. I will *not* accept blame for such an accident."

"How could you put your sister in such a dangerous situation? Anything could have happened to her!"

"What could have happened to her?" I asked angrily. "She wanted to go down with me, and I was with her every minute."

We continued this bitter exchange for less than a minute, but by the end of it my mother was crying and I was fuming as I walked from the room.

I knew there was something very unusual about this episode even as it was happening. Rarely had I done anything that made my mother cry. I had long witnessed and withstood without defensiveness our mother's attempts to make her children feel guilty. I had accepted it without either verbal counterattacks or taking on any heavy guilt feelings. I had always been the "good boy" who would never add to my mother's hardships or pain.

My mother's reaction to the automobile crisis was predictable, but my response to her this time was not. So, what could explain my behavior? Clearly, I was still reacting to the failure of the visit with Fae. Without having allowed myself to work through my frustration at that failure, at the next situation of stress, I had an uncharacteristic emotional outburst.

In the middle of our confrontation, I had felt justified in defending myself against my mother's accusations. The next day, however, when Precious told me that our mother was in their bedroom upset and crying, I regretted having responded so harshly. I went in to her and apologized but didn't try to explain away my reaction to her scolding. She said nothing but did allow me to embrace her; she blew her nose and flashed a smile of satisfaction. The crisis was over, but, since they were leaving the following day, there was little remaining time for either reflection or repairing. My mother and I never spoke further about the incident, but the next few times I visited California, others in the family told me they had heard all about my mother's complaints and hurt feelings.

The letter to the second aunt, Merle Steele, was still unanswered when my mother and Precious left Jamaica, and when Barbara's mother, Irene, visited for a few days around Thanksgiving. The letter was never answered; I met my aunt nearly by accident. In response to an ad in the major Kingston newspaper, I entered a weekend tennis tournament in Port Antonio, a resort area on the north coast. Noting that my aunt's address as listed in the phone directory was on a major route to the north coast, I decided to drive past for a look. The house turned out to be at the top of Stony Hill Road, a winding, narrow but well-maintained street populated by increasingly large and impressive mansions the higher I climbed. As I drove up the long driveway to the house, I noted that the grounds were overgrown. Still, I thought the abundance of trees of many varieties, neatly arranged hedges, and the many flowerbeds suggested past grandeur. Because I hadn't received a reply to my letter, I didn't expect to find anyone there, so I was surprised to find a car parked close to the far side of the house—almost completely hidden from the view of the main road. I was immediately struck by a large cage-like structure jutting out of the back of the house. The bars of this forbidding structure were made of heavy wrought iron. In its design there had been no attempt at ornament, or even attractiveness. Although I looked carefully, I didn't see a gate or door. I could see two French doors into the first level of the house and realized that access was only from the inside of the house.

After parking in the shade of a large tree facing this enclosure, I approached warily. When I got close to the cage, a tall, thin man stepped into the enclosure from the nearest French doors and looked at me suspiciously. His light olive coloring, full head of iron-gray straight hair, and handsome face reminded me of the pictures I had seen of my father. *Is this possibly a relative?* I thought.

"May I help you?" asked the man. His deep-set dark eyes kept their focus on me.

"Hello," I said, with a tentativeness I failed to hide. "I'm looking for Mrs. Merle Steele."

His inspection of my face became even tighter, and he said, "I'm sorry, but she's not available at the moment. May I tell her who was inquiring after her?"

"I sent her a letter at this address some time ago," I said, "but received no answer. I was on my way to Port Antonio for the weekend. Since the address was on the way, I thought I would pass by. Actually, I hadn't expected to find anyone here."

"Yes," the man said, "she's been off the island for some time. She now lives in New York City. May I ask what business you have with Mrs. Steele?"

"Well, it's a bit complicated. I believe I'm related to her. My name is Turner. My father was James Turner. I gather from some letters I have that Mrs. Steele was my late father's sister. I'm here in Jamaica with my family on sabbatical leave from the University of Massachusetts. My wife and I are associated with the University of the West Indies at Mona. I was hoping to take the opportunity to find anybody from my father's family still living here. I found Mrs. Steele listed in the Kingston phone book. As I said, I sent a letter of introduction but received no reply, so I didn't know whether the letter ever reached her."

The man kept his focus on me throughout this brief speech. He finally asked, "You're Jimmy Turner's son?"

"You knew my father?" I asked quickly.

"No, no," he responded, "but I do know *of* him from Mrs. Steele."

"May I ask who you are?" I inquired, wondering whether he was another relative.

"Oh, I'm just a friend of Mrs. Steele's," he said. "She asked me to accompany her and her daughters to Jamaica to take care of some business."

"Well, may I leave my address and telephone number?"

"Of course." He stepped into the house and reemerged with a half-pad of paper and a pencil, which he passed through the bars. "Write down the best way she can reach you."

As I wrote on the pad, I said, "I won't be reachable until I return to Kingston Sunday afternoon."

"I'll tell her that," he said, taking the pad and pencil. "I'm sure she'll want to talk with you."

I left elated by this unexpected prospect of meeting yet another aunt. When I returned to our apartment on Sunday, Barbara reported that Merle Steele had telephoned. I called the number she had left. After a brief set of cordial greetings, she invited us to visit soon, and we arranged to be there the following evening.

We were met at the front door, which was on the opposite side of the house from the caged area, by two smiling young women, who introduced themselves as Jeanette and Jackie Steele. Both were pretty and dressed in American clothes with no influence of Jamaican culture. They spoke like New York City natives—again, with no hint of a Caribbean accent. Behind them stood Merle who, when the two sisters moved to the side, stepped forward with a broad smile and outstretched hand. She was a small, attractive woman with straight black hair, a round face, and surprisingly light complexion. Introductions were animated and pleasant all around. The three women were particularly taken with Adam and Shomari, who stayed close to Barbara and me but responded with polite smiles. The male companion I had earlier met was the only one not smiling, but he finally stepped forward and introduced himself as Woody McKinsey.

As we were ushered from the foyer, I realized that the inside of the house was even grander than could have been imagined from the outside. A broad spiral staircase led up and past a large chandelier hanging from a two-story high ceiling. The stair-railing, floor, and side panels were of a dark polished wood. The furniture in the foyer and the large living room, the only rooms we were invited to see, was of fine quality, though dated and faded. The two young women brought cold drinks, fruit and cookies, placing them on the coffee table encircled by the sofas and easy chairs we occupied. We established that Merle and my father were half-siblings, making me her half-nephew, and Jeanette and Jackie my half-first cousins.

We established that Woody was not family; he was long-time friend of the Steele family, who had grown up in Jamaica but lived much of his life in the United States. Although he looked a bit too young to be a companion to Merle, he seemed too old to be romantically attached to either of my cousins. I never discovered the exact nature of his relationship with any of them. He stayed mostly in the background of our conversations, but he followed what transpired with a skeptical eye.

After we had talked generally about my family in the United States, Merle began to direct all of her attention toward me. I responded by moving closer and leaned in her direction. After a few exchanges, it was as if we were in a private conversation. Barbara and my cousins talked about the various food shortages on the island and the experiences they'd had with surly store clerks, then went to pick lemons from trees on the side of the house.

"Aunt Merle," I said softly and hesitated, " . . . I hope it's all right for me to address you that way." She responded with a slight and noncommittal nod, and I went on. "A big part of the reason I came to Jamaica was in order to find my father's family here. I was only six when he died, so I barely knew him, and he had little opportunity to tell his children about his family and early life in Jamaica. But he was careful to keep important letters and other documents, and my mother stored them after he died. When I was in high school, she asked me to look at them. Among these letters were several from you, but he didn't keep copies of the personal letters he sent. So I don't know what he said in his letters to you."

"Oh dear. I never kept letters for very long. I'm sure I threw out most when we moved to New York. We exchanged a few letters over five years, and I do remember some of what he said in those letters, though. In the last of them, he began saying he was ill. He said it was a problem with his nerves—spells of some kind."

I reached into a folder and pulled out the letter. Handing it to her, I said, "This is a copy of a letter from you where you refer to his illness."

She read it slowly. She looked at me somberly and said, "I heard later that he had died. I was so upset. So sad. I never knew the circumstances. First, I heard it was an accident, then that he killed himself. I was so upset. We all were. I couldn't believe it."

"The death certificate reads 'suicidal' under circumstances," I said. "Our mother told us, he fell accidentally while washing windows. I didn't know the truth until I was in high school and looked through his papers and letters. Considering all he was going through, it's very likely that it was suicide."

"He had some nervous or mental problem?" she asked.

"He did have a brief stay in a psychiatric hospital," I said, hesitating to tell her everything. "He must have been depressed."

"So sad," she repeated. "He was so intelligent . . . and such a handsome man he grew up to be. He sent me a picture of himself and the family once. I don't think I still have it, but I remember he was so handsome and he looked happy at the time. I don't know when it was taken . . . probably sometime during the war. I remember the little army and navy suits you and your brother wore. I remember remarking on how pretty your mother was too. Your mother is Spanish, right?"

"No," I said stumbling in surprise at the question, "my mother is from the Louisiana bayou country. Her people are French . . . French Creole."

"That's odd," she said with a puzzled look. "I was sure he told me once that she was Spanish. Her name is Lolita, right?"

"Her family from Louisiana called her Lolita," I said, uncertain where this was going. "That *is* a Spanish name, but I never understood why they called her that. As far as I knew, in Chicago, she went by the name Loretta Turner. All the documents I ever saw named her "Loretta.""

"That's strange," Merle said bemused. "I always thought she was Spanish . . . well, it doesn't matter . . ." Looking at the letter again, she went on, "Is this a copy I can keep?"

"If you wish," I responded. "My mother has the original. I could always get another copy made . . . And, speaking of pictures, I have a picture I believe is of you." Detaching the black-and-white photograph from the paper clip that held it inside the folder, I said, "This is one of the few pictures my father had."

Merle looked at the picture of herself as a young woman. She neither said anything nor changed her expression. I could see the same woman sitting before me as in the picture. The features were the same; the straight black hair; the serious and penetrating stare; this was Merle. She struck me as much lighter than I would have expected from the photograph. Whenever I had looked at this picture in our family album over the years, I had thought of the portrait as quite daring—her shoulders bare, she held with one hand a dark patterned and frilled shawl lightly at the cleavage of her breasts in a way suggesting that there was nothing beneath; and those dark eyes.

I finally said, "I don't have a copy of the picture, but I could have one made and send it to you."

She handed the picture back with a lighthearted dismissal. "I was so young. No, thank you. I believe I have a copy somewhere in my albums back in New York. Odd that this is the only picture of his family you had."

"There were a few others," I said, "but you mentioned sending pictures in one of your letters. I guessed that this would be one from you. When we first arrived tonight and I saw you, I knew I had been right. You do look much the same."

"Not to me," she said with a broad smile. "That picture must have been taken before I got married . . . maybe forty-some years ago."

I returned the picture to the folder and said, "You were quite young when your father died, I believe."

"Yes, I must have been around twelve. Jimmy was two years older. We all adored our father. He was a wonderful man . . . handsome as they come. You did know he was an American Indian, didn't you?"

"Our mother told us we were part Indian, but I never quite understood what she meant. Sometimes she would say "West Indian," so I didn't know whether that referred to our father being from Jamaica or what. Also, most of the addresses on the letters ended in 'West Indies' or 'British West Indies.' It was his being from Jamaica was what I thought she meant."

"I'm sure your father knew about being American Indian," she said. "One year our father took Jimmy along on one of his trips to America. I was so jealous! And hurt too. When they came back, Jimmy showed off a beautiful Indian headdress he received on the reservation where our father was born. He claimed it made him a member of the tribe, like our father. He made it worse by teasing us, saying that he was the only one—that the tribal membership didn't extend to us. I really got angry and hated Jimmy for a while."

"Did he say anything more about the reservation?" I asked. "Where it was? What state?"

"I think it must have been Ohio. What I remember is that the tribe was called Miamis and all I could learn later was that there had been reservations all around the Midwest—Ohio, Indiana . . . in that general area . . . and one of the tribes was called the Miamis. He was careful to say that it was pronounced like Meeyamee, unlike how people pronounce the city name Miami. On a driving trip many years ago, I went through that area looking for the reservation. We never did find anything like a reservation, and we could never be sure where he was born because the government didn't keep records of Indian reservation births when he was born—I guess about 1863."

"Are you saying my grandfather was a full-blood American Indian?" I asked.

Merle looked surprised and said firmly, "Yes he was. Anybody who saw him knew he was very different from people here in Jamaica. He had straight black hair; his body was dark but it had a reddish tinge to it; his skin was as smooth as a baby's; and he had very little body hair. Yes, I'm sure he was."

"Did he tell you this himself or did your mother tell you?" I asked.

"I remember him talking about it," she said, "and my mother also told us this after he died. One particular thing I remember was his reservation name, which translated as 'Lonesnake.'" Merle lifted her body a bit and looked at me with some intensity. "He told us, when he left the reservation, he had to have a regular English surname, so he gave himself the name James Julius Turner. I never asked him how he chose that name, but he made it up." She stopped, narrowed her gaze, and asked, "You believe me, don't you?"

I was taken aback by this question, but responded immediately, "I have no basis for doubting anything you tell me about my grandfather and father. I didn't know any of what you just told me. Of course I believe you."

"Well, I'm glad," she said. "It's all true . . . Of course he never told us much about his life on the reservation, but he did talk about how he became well off later. He said he was on the road for a while doing all kinds of work. Then he got a job transporting and trading in corn and other commodities in Chicago and travelled all over. He saved enough to start doing some buying and selling on his own. He did pretty well in the commodities business and then started buying real estate. Most of the real estate was for rental income and as investments. When he moved to Jamaica, he started making a living lending money. Again, he did quite well, and decided to settle down here. That's about all I know . . . When he died, my mother had a lot of trouble collecting what was owed him."

"Do you know anything about my father's mother?" I asked. "I mean his biological mother."

"All I know is that she died when your father was a baby. Then our father married my mother and they had three children, including me."

"Do you know how she died?" I asked.

"No," she replied. "I never did know anything about that."

"He never talked about her at all?" I asked, with a slight hint of skepticism.

"Not that I can recall," she replied with a tone that suggested she understood the emphasis at the end of my question. "I was pretty young when our father died. I don't remember my mother saying anything about her. I don't think my mother knew her or any of her people. Anyway, I don't remember meeting any of them."

"What about my grandfather—your father?" I pursued. "Do you know what he died of?"

"The only thing I remember was that he had a heart condition and suffered a great deal with the heat. As I recall, he died at home in bed . . . He's buried in the cemetery outside the St. Andrews Parish Church in Half Way Tree. We used to go there sometimes, when we lived nearby. If you want to go there, the grave is close to the front of the cemetery."

"I *would* like to visit it," I said. "How do I get there?"

"Just a minute—I'll draw a map," she said and left the room.

Woody, who was the only one remaining at the coffee table and had been following the conversation in silence, asked, "Now that you've found family here, what plans do you have?"

"Just finding my father's family means a lot to me," I said. "My father died so young, and I had very little sense of his history. I guess it's partly the "roots" thing people talk about. Maybe I needed to feel like I had more of a history. Actually, I have been wondering lately about Jamaican citizenship based on my father's birth here. I don't know anything about what the rules are about such things, but I thought I would find out."

Woody responded with mild alarm. "I wouldn't jump into something like that, if I were you. What do you have to gain? Do you know whether you could also keep your United States citizenship, if you took on Jamaican citizenship? No, I would be very careful about doing something like that. I would be very careful indeed."

I was surprised at this response and said, "Frankly, I'm not sure why it occurs to me to do that. I imagine it would meet some type of emotional need—somehow connect to my father in a way I have never been. Maybe it's just sentimentality. But I'll consider what you're saying. Of course, I should understand a little better what it would mean to me and what the implications would be for me as an American citizen."

"I would be very careful," he said. "There could be more disadvantages than you can foresee. There are many problems right now in Jamaica—political violence, more and more restrictions—just be careful."

Jackie, Barbara, and the children rejoined us. Merle reentered holding a half sheet of paper, which she handed me, and said, "This will get you there. I wish I had time to go myself, but we're here for just a few more days."

"You may be wondering what happened to Jeanette," Jackie said with an embarrassed smile. "We have to always keep a lookout with flashlights in the back of the house to make sure no one is coming up the hill after dark. The house has been robbed and vandalized several times, and whenever we're here we're afraid."

Merle nodded and added, "Things haven't been the same in Jamaica since Independence. We never felt safe after that. For days crowds of people would parade by yelling at us from the road saying we had to give up our big house and leave because the revolution had come and we were no longer going to live in luxury. It was awful. I'll never forget how afraid we were. It was a good thing my husband knew people in the government and the police. We had police guards for a while."

"That does sound frightening," I said. "When did you leave for New York?"

"We bought our apartment in Manhattan and have lived there most of the year since around 1966. We would like to sell out here, but if we sell, the government won't allow us to take the money out. So, we're stuck."

The children were getting restless and it was past their bedtime, so we rose to leave. I was, however, eager to have another conversation with Merle, so I said. "What you have told me already I find fascinating and useful. Is it possible we might get together again before you leave? I'm sure to think of more questions. When are you free to come to dinner?"

"May I call you about that tomorrow?" Merle responded. "I have your telephone number."

Woody took up the guard duty in the rear as we readied to leave. Merle said goodbye at the door and my cousins walked us out to the car. After the children and Barbara were seated, I turned back and said impulsively to Jeanette and Jackie, "It's been very important for me to meet you all. I do hope we'll keep in touch."

They both beamed and said excitedly, "Oh, this is important for us as well. We're sure to see you again."

As we drove back down Stony Hill Road to Mona, I felt pleased about the visit and thought this was the beginning of new family ties. I never saw either Jeanette or Jackie again—on or off the island.

CHAPTER 7:

"But am I at the place?"

The afternoon following my meeting with Merle, I went in search of our grandfather's gravesite. Merle's map was perfectly clear. When I arrived at the central square of Half Way Tree, a busy intersection, I could see the large church looming up from one of the side streets. As I drove past the entrance of the church proper, the lawn sign announced that I had found St. Andrews Parish Anglican Church. I could see a three-foot-high wall and gate ahead. I soon saw headstones and knew that I had found the object of my search.

As I walked through the large opened iron gate, I was struck by how small the cemetery was. *This is,* I thought, *the resting place of relatively few.*

The headstones varied in size and ornament, and were, with few exceptions, lined up in rows. On each side near the entry were two small mausoleums of white marble, darkened by age and exposure. The road quickly narrowed to make several paths through the cemetery. Since Merle had indicated that my grandfather's gravesite was near the front, I began immediately walking through the rows and reading headstones. The earliest interments had been in the middle of the nineteenth century. Since my grandfather had died in 1922, I concluded that placement of graves couldn't have been chronological. After completing my walk through three rows, I became tense, fearing both finding and not finding the grave. I stopped abruptly when I spied a large flat marble slab that seemed out of place. It was parallel to the ground but rose above it by approximately six inches, and the inscription was partially obscured by dirt and leaves. Unlike the other gravesites, this one had no headstone, but in a space somewhat wider and longer than a large casket was this flat slab of marble. I knelt on the edge of the marble and brushed its face and found the name *James Julius Turner 1863-1922*. I took a deep breath and stared at the name for several minutes.

Why am I here? I thought. *What is this all about?*

I hadn't anticipated these questions. The body beneath the slab was my grandfather's, a man I never met, a man whose life was largely a mystery to me. What could finding his burial place tell me? My own father had been an infant when his mother died. His father's death thirteen years later had made him an orphan.

At that moment I felt my father's loss. He must have felt alone. When my father died, I had felt that same aloneness. The difference was that I had felt bonded to my mother; he hadn't had such solace.

Our mother had also served as our father's surrogate, giving us directives beginning with " . . . your father always said . . ." and ended with his aspirations for his children: " . . . nothing more important . . . good education . . . college graduates . . . professional careers . . . good life . . ." He had completed only two years at the Kingston College Preparatory High School. Where had he developed such aspirations? He was fourteen when his father died. Had there been time for high aspirations to have come from his father, whose remains I stood above?

As I looked down at the slab, I wondered whether our grandfather had picked or designed it himself. This monument was so different from those around it—simple but elegant. Did the style have some meaning, possibly related to his being Native American? Did he choose the site—close to the front of the cemetery? He was chronically ill, with sufficient opportunity to make his own burial arrangements.

Although I was in the cemetery for about an hour, no one else appeared. I didn't regret the lack of company but thought it sad that the graves were probably neglected. I wondered how long it had been since anyone had visited our grandfather's grave. Picturing our father's gravesite in Lincoln Cemetery on the outskirts of Chicago, I saw our mother and my siblings, as children, standing near the small, roughly hewn head stone—"James Julius Turner, Beloved Husband,

1908-1945." I wondered if anyone had visited *that* grave, since we had all left Chicago.

When Merle called that evening, we invited her and Woody for dinner on the day before they were all leaving for New York City. I don't recall whether we had invited my cousins and they were otherwise engaged or whether we didn't invite them, but they were not part of the dinner party.

I didn't think much about what I wanted to talk about with my aunt. I may have simply thought that this was yet another way to firm up the new family ties. I had learned a great deal from the first visit, but I didn't know what to expect from this meeting.

The children were already in bed by the time Merle and Woody arrived. Merle smiled as she entered and handed Barbara a box of candy. I was surprised but pleased by this small gesture. Woody came behind her with the same non-committal, unanimated countenance I remembered from our first two meetings. Over cold drinks we talked about the children, our work, and about the differences we found living in Jamaica. Merle talked about having taken care of some family business and regretted that they were no closer to being able to sell the house.

"It's such a wonderful house," I said. "It's too bad it has to be left unoccupied so much of the time. Can't you find someone to rent it, at least?"

"You really think the house attractive?" she asked. "You should have seen it when it was our main residence. Then it *was* wonderful. My late husband had it built for us not long after the war. Now it's a shell of what it once was. So much has been stolen or damaged. It needs so much to be really livable. We can stand the inconvenience for a week or two at a time, but it's hard to stay longer. We feel tense and out of place in Jamaica now. So much has changed."

"You mean the political situation?" I asked.

"That's a large part of it, but it's the way people act here now. There are beggars everywhere. The store clerks act as if they resent having to provide service. You can't feel safe anywhere you go. It's so sad."

"So far, we haven't had any big problems," I said. "We've gotten used to the children begging outside every store. We find the banks slow and hard to deal with. But we took my mother and sister to Montego Bay, and we all had a good time. We took a train tour into the interior of the island. They enjoyed it. We were thinking about going to the beach with some friends."

Jonathan shook his head slightly and looked incredulous. "The beaches were once nice to go to. I guess they are still beautiful, but now you won't be able to stand the people you have to go by to get there. Now they let just anybody go to the beaches here, so they fill up with people you wouldn't want to be around."

"Like what people?"

"Riff-raff," he said. "People smoking ganja and drinking. People changing into their swimsuits right on the beach—like nobody else is there. Pretty disgusting."

Barbara called us to dinner. Given the warm weather, she had prepared a modest cold bean dish with salad, pita bread, and iced tea. After everyone was served, we ate for a while chatting about nothing in particular. The brief silences between this chat made me slightly uncomfortable.

"I went to my grandfather's grave on Thursday," I said. "The church and the cemetery were quite impressive. I'm really happy you told me about it."

Merle looked at me with a broad smile and said, "Oh, I'm so glad you found it. I thought you wouldn't have much trouble. How did it look?"

"I was very moved by being there," I answered. "It gave me the feeling of going back in time. Some of the headstones were from a hundred years ago. I found my grandfather's near the front, as you had told me it would be. It looked like he was buried where most of the others had been buried at least fifty years earlier. I couldn't figure that out."

"I think what happened," Merle said, "was once they filled up to the back of the yard, they started squeezing more all over, where they could find space. Of course, that could go just so far."

"My grandfather's gravestone did look different from those around it—more modern."

"I never noticed that," Merle said. "My mother and I went over there a few times when I was living on Constant Springs Road. As I recall, my father actually picked out the grave marker himself."

"I wondered about that. I gather he had been ill for a while before he died, so he had time to make his own arrangements."

"Merle," I began again, "I think I would like a copy of my grandfather's death certificate. How would I go about getting one?"

"That's no problem. Just go down to the Island Records Office in Spanish Town. They keep records back more than two hundred years. You have to know basic information like full name and approximate date of death. I think I saw a copy many years ago, but I wouldn't know where to look, if I had one."

"For that matter, I would like to get a copy of my grandmother's death certificate. The only thing I know about her is her name and the year she died. I do know her maiden name too: Daisy Humber."

"Doesn't sound familiar," Merle said. Looking at Woody, she asked, "Ring any bells for you?"

"I can't say it does," answered Woody. "You may have to go through a few ledgers to find it, but with the married name and the year, you should be able to find it."

"Spanish Town," I said as I wrote it on a pad nearby. "Do you happen to know the address of the Records Office?"

Woody responded, "If you can get yourself on the main road to Spanish Town, when you get there, just ask anybody. The Records Office is right in the center of town. It's not such a big place."

There was something I wanted to raise, but the thought of doing so made me tense. I steeled myself and addressed Merle directly. "You mentioned visiting my grandfather's gravesite with your mother, when you lived in Half Way Tree years ago. I guess she must have lived with you for a time."

"She lived with me sometimes, with Roy sometimes," she said. "But she also travelled quite a bit after she started working as a nurse-companion."

"I gather from my father's letters that there had been considerable conflict between him and your mother." My throat tightened and my voice cracked as I forced myself to go on. "Something about his father's legacy . . . He thought he had been treated unfairly by his stepmother."

She pursed her lips, looked away, and said, "I never did understand it myself. I know their relationship was very shaky for years. I tried not to get involved. I felt like your father and I had started to have a warm and friendly correspondence. Then I heard he died."

"Did your mother ever tell you what his complaint was? Did he say anything in his letters about it?"

"All I knew was that my mother, when she needed money, wanted to sell off property left by our father in the states and the house we all grew up in here in Jamaica, and he refused to sign a release for the sales unless he was given a share of the proceeds. She was able to go ahead with one of the sales by petitioning the court in America, and he received nothing. I think she sold the house here after Jimmy died. I never asked her anything more about it. I had my own children and my own concerns."

For the first time I felt in control of myself and of the direction of the conversation. "One of the things never made clear in the letters my father left was your mother's reason for sending him away to New York after your father died . . . I believe he died in 1922 and my father was sent away in 1923 . . . he was fifteen."

"My mother didn't speak with any of us about it before it happened," she said. "We never talked about it . . . until much later. The only thing my mother told us was that she thought it was the best thing at the time for everybody, including Jimmy. She thought he would be able to make a good living in the United States . . . where his father had grown up and lived most of his life."

"Well, it was more difficult than expected, I guess," I said. "Apparently there wasn't much contact of any kind between your mother and my father between the time he left in 1923 and 1930, when your mother wanted to sell property in Rhode Island. Whenever my father referred to that period, he says 'I had to scuffle on my own.' Then your mother wrote to him to get his agreement for the sale. I think he must have felt much misused."

"Unlike your father, the other two children and I were still underage when that happened, so we didn't have to be consulted," she said. "I only found out about it a few years later. My mother told me she thought Jimmy was just being willful, because the will was clear that the living from the real estate was hers until she died."

"But he claimed that the bulk of the *personal* property was intended for the support and education of the children. After leaving Jamaica he got nothing."

"I really can't say anything about that. We didn't have much ourselves. We got by, but my mother was always fretting about money—complaining about our school fees, saying how trades people were trying to cheat her."

Merle pulled at her napkin, looked toward Barbara and Woody, and reduced her eye contact with me. I felt I needed to back off a bit but wanted to continue probing.

"And when my father died, how did you find out?"

"At that time I kept up a correspondence with Jennie Hanson in New York City. They were old friends of my mother."

"How did she find out?"

"That I don't recall," she replied. "All I remember is how upset I was. It was weeks before I felt like talking to anybody about it. I know I couldn't write to anybody about it for a long while." She took out a small white embroidered handkerchief, dabbed her eyes, looked at me, and said, "So sad."

I retreated somewhat and allowed the intensity of the moment to recede. "Yes, it *is* a sad story. I think things are clearer to me now than they were. It has been very helpful and important—talking with you like this. I feel fortunate to have found you and that you were able to share so much with me."

"I'm glad it's been helpful," she replied. "Talking about these things brings back some sad memories, but I'm so happy to have met you and your family. Perhaps someday I'll meet your mother. I'm sorry I missed her on this trip."

"I plan to write to my mother and my sisters and brother. I know they'll all be excited to hear what you've told me about my father—especially about our grandfather being Native American. I think *that* will be something of a surprise."

"I would like to stay in touch when you get back," she said. "When will you be going back home to Massachusetts?"

"At the moment we're thinking sometime in mid August, so we'll have time to get resettled, prepare for our classes, and make arrangements for the children. We could go down to see you when we're all settled. Or you could come up to see us during fall foliage. September and October are beautiful in western Massachusetts."

Having exchanged addresses, Barbara and I escorted Merle and Jonathan to the front door. The farewells were cordial but not warm.

When they had left, I looked at Barbara, held her in silence, then, without warning, I burst into tears. I became immediately self-conscious, fearing that our visitors could hear me, because the windows were open and there hadn't been sufficient time for them to reach the ground floor landing and the parking lot. I continued to cry while holding Barbara, but I made no more audible sounds.

The tears continued, as if they might wash away the pain of that encounter. I neither expected nor fully understood the meaning of my tears at the time. Barbara didn't ask for an explanation, and I didn't offer one. I couldn't have explained. And it has remained a mystery, since after that evening, Merle and I never met or spoke again. I wrote her one lengthy letter several months later, while still in Jamaica, but she never responded.

One morning of the following week I drove to Spanish Town. A policeman escorted me to the ornate double doors of the Island Records Office within ten minutes of my arrival. The large room to which I was directed was similar to the reading room of a public library. Approximately ten four-by-twenty dark-wood tables were lined up and filled about a quarter of the long narrow room. From the high ceiling hung two large fans moving so slowly I wondered about their utility, but the room was pleasantly cool. Behind the counter that cut the room in half one could see tall shelves filled with books of uniform size. At the counter a young woman greeted me with a broad smile and asked if she could be of service.

"I'm looking for birth and death records," I said.

She gestured toward a small box with a stack of paper cut to about the size of three-by-five cards and said, "Please write down each name and approximate date of birth or death on a separate piece of paper. Also include the parish."

"The parish?" I asked, puzzled. "What if I don't know the parish."

"Do you know the city?" she asked.

"I'm pretty sure Kingston."

"Well, you should probably look at the ledgers for two parishes, St. Andrew and Kingston," she said. "When people think of Kingston, sometimes they don't realize it covers two parishes."

"Should I write out a separate sheet for each parish for each person?" I asked.

"No, not necessary," she said, "but write down both parishes for each person requested."

Sitting down with several sheets, I first made out birth certificate requests for James Julius Turner and Daisy Humber. I had seen several documents among my father's papers indicating his date of birth. Based on my father's letters, I knew Humber was my grandmother's maiden name, but I had to guess the likely years for her birth. When I searched the Kingston parish ledger of 1908, I promptly found the reference number for James Julius Turner and obtained a certified copy. Using that number, with the following information:

Date and Place of birth: 21 March, 1908; "Happy Retreat," Windward Road, Kingston.

> Name: James Julius
>
> Sex: male
>
> Name and Dwelling of Father: James Julius Turner; "Happy Retreat," Windward Road.
>
> Name and maiden name of Mother: Daisy Maud Turner, formerly Humber.
>
> Rank or Profession of Father: Real Estate Agent.

After trying unsuccessfully to find a birth record for Daisy Humber in both Kingston and St. Andrew parishes, I moved on to finding the death records. Again, my father's letters had given me the approximate date of his father's death, and I soon held a copy:

> Date and Place of Death: March 10,1922; "Everton", Eureka Road, Saint Andrew.
>
> Name and Surname: James Julius Turner.
>
> Sex: Male.
>
> Condition: Married.

Age last Birthday: 59 years.

Rank, Profession, or occupation: A Usurer.

Cause of Death: (a) Chronic Endocarditis; (b) Acute
   Bronchitis.

Certified by: Oswald D.F. Robertson, M.D.

Signature, Qualification and residence of informant:
   James J. Turner, son, present at the Death.
   "Everton", Eureka Road, Saint Andrew.

I was surprised by several pieces of information provided by the
certificate; first, 59 struck me as an advanced age for a man with young
children; second, the occupation, usurer, which I associated only with
Shakespeare's *Merchant of Venice*; and third, my father, at the age of
fourteen, was the only one present at the death of his father—at least
the only one able to give information.

From what Merle had described of his early life in the United
States, I could have surmised that our grandfather was older than either
of his Jamaican wives. I calculated that, since my father was fourteen
at the time, our grandfather was 45 when my father was born. Since I
hadn't found a birth record for Daisy Humber, I didn't yet know the
difference in our grandparents' ages.

I became defensive. *My grandfather? Usurer? Banks lend money
and that's not referred to as usury*. In my father's letters there had been
references to unsecured loans counted as part of his father's estate.
Perhaps the term and the independent business of lending money at
unregulated interest rates were neither unusual nor unsavory for the
time and place. My father's birth certificate had listed his father as a
real estate agent. Had he become a moneylender only after being in
Jamaica for a while?

The final document I wanted was my grandmother's death
certificate. Based on references made in my father's letters, I knew only
that her death had taken place in the spring of 1909. How old was she
when she died? How had she died? I had no idea. Childbirth? Some

tropical disease? When I received the copy of our grandmother's death certificate, I held my breath and read:

> Date and Place of Death: 21st May, 1909, Kingston Harbour.

> Name and Surname: Daisy Maud Turner.

> Sex: Female.

> Condition: Married.

> Age last Birthday: 21 years.

> Rank, Profession or Occupation: Gentlewoman.

> Certified cause of Death and Duration of Illness: That the said Daisy Maud Turner committed suicide by drowning herself.

> Signature, Qualifications and Residence of Informant: Certificate received from Leonard Gray, Deputy Coroner, Inquest held 16 June, 1909.

> When Registered: Seventeenth June, 1909.

As I stared at the word "suicide," my face became hot; the back of my neck tightened. Emotional confusion held me suspended. When I looked up, the clerk at the front counter was looking at me, and I wondered whether I had unconsciously made some sound that drew her attention. I wasn't crying, but the feeling of tears hovering led me to rub both eyes. Taking a deep breath, I turned away from the clerk and the documents.

Nowhere in my father's letters and documents was there any indication that his mother had taken her own life. If my aunts Fae and Merle had been aware of the suicide, what reason could either have had for withholding the information from me? If I assumed that they didn't know, then perhaps my father didn't know either. I was transported to the moment when I discovered my father's death certificate declaring him "suicidal." Overwhelmed by the discovery was how I felt then—and at that moment. I gathered up my materials but could not stand up for several minutes. Images of my father and my grandmother near death washed over me like sudden rainstorms. No shelter available; simply wait for them to pass. When they did, I was temporarily unsure where I was, but tears were coming down both cheeks. The clerk looked in my direction. I wiped my face and left.

On the way back to Kingston, I thought about the implications of what I had just discovered. Both my grandmother and my father had taken their own lives. Why? My father's letters provided some motives for *his* suicide—years of frustrated attempts to get what he considered his legacy, his illness, and his severe depression. But what would lead a twenty-one year old mother of an infant to do such a drastic thing?

When I told my cousin Donald Wehby about my discovery, he said that a suicide on the island would have been a major event—especially the suicide of a "gentlewoman." He suggested that I check the *Kingston Daily Gleaner*, the island's major newspaper of that period, to see whether it was reported. Within days I was perusing the microfilm files in the newspaper archives, where I found the initial report of the death of Daisy Maud Turner, on the front page:

Daily Gleaner

Kingston, Jamaica

Thursday May 25, 1909

"Tragedy at Rockport"

Drowning of Mrs. D. Turner on Friday Night

Sad Circumstances.

Left Half-way Tree for Mandeville; Stopped

On the way

Body Found on Saturday

Mrs. Daisy Turner, the wife of J.J. Turner, a coloured American, was drowned at Rockport on Friday night last and the circumstances surrounding the affair are extremely suspicious . . .

A second, much longer, article appeared in the middle of June, reporting on the inquest, which took place on June 16. The front-page headline and introduction were as follows

Daily Gleaner

Kingston, Jamaica, Thursday, June 17, 1909

"Suicide at Rockport"

Enquiry into the death of Mrs. D. Turner

Evidence is Presented

Drove in a Late Car to the

Rockport Gardens

The letters read in court.

A coroner's enquiry touching the death of Mrs. Daisy Maud Turner, the wife of J.J. Turner, whose body was found in the sea at Rockport on the 22nd of May last, was held at the Parade Court House yesterday before Leonard Gray, District Medical Officer for Kingston . . .

By the time I finished reading and obtaining copies of the two articles, I was sweating profusely and felt simultaneously elated and sad. On the one hand, I had a fresh and important detail in the history

I was seeking. On the other hand, I was heavy with sadness, imagining how our grandmother must have suffered.

The next day I drove through Rockport but found no way to get access to Kingston Harbour from there. Months later, sitting at a window in the university's library rereading the *Gleaner* articles I had found, I fell into melancholy. Then, looking south toward the harbor and east toward the Blue Mountains, I felt impelled to address our grandmother:

Kingston Harbour,
Jamaica
1976

ELEGY FOR AN UNKNOWN GRANDMOTHER

Dear loved gentlewoman, grandmother—
Never known but by your ending and leavings,
Staring sightless to the bottom of the bay.
At the age of thirty-six I have come at last
To see your death at twenty-one and know
That you could be my own lost child
And comfort you as the fish never could—
And comfort myself in life.
I am your flesh and I feel I know you
As I imagine, through time,
Your tears were scarcely different
From your laughter—even on that day.

But am I at the place?
On the beach? By the boats?
I would see the spot, but I will not,
Just as the years and lives cannot come again.
I see only the azure sky of May
Holding off the few tearful clouds
That creep out of the Blue Mountains
To form your final shroud.
The tempests rage only in the hearts
You left behind, the babes and unborn.

105

We are your children, your legacy of life,
All here late to weep against your passing.
And, knowing nothing of why you left,
We understand.

CHAPTER 8:

The Long Day

On the morning of May 21, 1909, in Half-Way Tree, an affluent suburb of Kingston, Jamaica, Daisy Humber Turner began packing a small trunk in preparation for an extended visit, with her mother, to her mother's family in Mandeville, a three-hour bus ride away. Her mother, Isabella Phillpotts, stood nearby holding one-year old James and pleading with Daisy to get some rest before the next day's trip.

"Don't worry about the baby," her mother said. "We'll do just fine. I stocked up on everything he needs and I have nothing to do but watch over him until we leave."

"I know he's in good hands with you, Mama. I know everything will be all right." She said this with a pointed look, which she saw her mother hesitate to question.

Daisy's head, bent over the trunk, felt heavy. She could hardly get herself to move. The few items in the trunk seemed distant and unfamiliar. She turned away and sat by a nearby window overlooking the courtyard and driveway below, stared blankly at a large billowy cloud, and sighed. Daisy thought, *Mama, if you only knew the pain I feel. I wish I could tell you. You would understand if anyone could.*

"Dear, I wish you would tell me what's making you so unhappy," the older woman said, still gently swaying with the baby in her arms. "The doctor said the melancholy would pass. Still, it troubles me to see you so sad. You've been dragging yourself around for a month, barely eating, waking up, and walking around in the middle of the night. I noticed you went to bed with your clothes on last night. You even had your boots on. This isn't like you, Daisy. Is there something you're not telling me? Whatever it is, we can work it out somehow. Please, Daisy, let me know what's the matter. Let me help you, dear."

Daisy continued sitting motionless, her eyes unfocused on the space beyond, wrapped in her own cloud of grayness, hearing her mother's voice as if from a distance. No, she couldn't tell even her mother. What could she tell her? She didn't completely understand it herself.

The weeks and days before and right after the baby was born had been the happiest of her life. Now that seemed such a long time ago. Why had that happiness left her? The baby was healthy and beautiful. James, she knew, loved her. He said he adored her, but she felt his doting affection was as if for a child. It was true that he was twenty-five years older than she. Still, Daisy felt that having a baby made her a woman, grown up and worthy of being treated as such.

She sat there, remembering when she first met him.

He strode confidently through the lobby of Kingston's Myrtle Bank Hotel where she was helping in her mother's curio shop. His appearance was striking—tall, lean, reddish brown complexion, straight black hair brushed back flat, a well-tailored suit with a watch chain dangling from his vest. His suit was dark brown, and he held a black bowler hat close to his side. She was particularly struck by his skin. Jamaica, she knew, was full of people from different parts of the world, different races, and all kinds of mixtures. The British had imported labor from all over the Empire, and all the combinations evolved into the Jamaican "shade system" of race; social status was largely based on where one fell on that scale. The two extremes of this scheme were clearly understood by all: whites the most privileged, blacks the least; everyone else somewhere in the middle. The mixing process had led to Browns, Yellows, and Reds, to complete the system. But, for Daisy, this man was hard to categorize. He had the coloring of a brown person but, unlike any she had seen before, his sleek skin was more of a ruddy hue. He had no beard nor any sign of one, as if he had never shaved.

The man perused the shop's offerings but repeatedly looked her way. After several glances, she smiled shyly. He smiled in response, picked out some postcards, walked to her, and extended his hand graciously toward her.

"How do you do," he said. "My name is James Turner. I'm staying in the hotel for a few weeks. I think I've seen you here before."

Daisy was embarrassed and, at first, she could only smile and look down at their clasped hands. Finally she asked, "Will that be all?"

"I was hoping you would tell me your name after I gave you mine," he said with a teasing smile. "I don't know many people in Jamaica. I hoped you would be one of my first acquaintances."

"I'm Daisy Humber," she said finally. "My mother owns this shop and sometimes I come to help her out. I usually come on Friday and Saturday and sometimes other days, when my mother can't come herself—like today."

She turned to the desk and tallied the charges on a quarter sheet of lined paper, presented the bill to him, and looked up, again with an embarrassed smile.

He returned the smile, handed her a five shilling note, and said, "You may keep the change—just for being so beautiful and pleasant."

The money was many times more than the price of the cards, and Daisy said, "That's good of you, but I can't accept. My mother would be very upset, if I took such a gift from a stranger." She opened a small drawer in the desk at the front of the shop, made change, and handed him the coins.

"I understand," he said, accepting the coins. "Well, I hope to see you here again. Perhaps I'll find another way to show appreciation for such a pretty face and charming manner."

James made a slight bow, smiled, and walked out of the shop and toward the main hotel exit.

Watching him walk away, Daisy was breathing rapidly and could feel her heart pounding hard against her chest. What, she thought, is happening to me? She was mesmerized for a few moments, wondering who he was and where he came from.

She woke from her reverie when her mother asked, "Daisy, are you all right, dear?" and approached her at the window. "I'm worried about you. You've been sitting there like a statue for an hour. Are you all right? Should I take you back to see the doctor?"

"Sorry, Mama," Daisy answered. "I guess I was just thinking about the trip tomorrow. Maybe the change will do me good. I really haven't felt like myself. I don't feel like the Daisy I used to be. Something's changed, Mama. I don't know why, but I feel changed."

"I don't understand it either, dear," said her mother. "You have everything to make anybody happy. Does it have anything to do with James being away from you and the baby so long?"

"I don't know, Mama," Daisy said. "I feel so empty, so alone. It's difficult to bear. I don't know how I can stand feeling like this much longer. I just wish it would end."

Isabella moved closer to her, lightly placed a hand on each shoulder from behind, bent over, placed her right cheek against her daughter's left cheek, and said, "Mother's here for you dearest. Mother's always here for you."

Daisy crossed her arms in front of her, reached for her mother's hands and held them. Tears formed and began to roll down both cheeks. She bent her head and began to sob. Her mother held her shoulders more firmly and joined her daughter in tears. There they remained for ten minutes—the mother wanting to comfort her child, the child inconsolable.

Then Isabella became aware of the baby stirring in his crib in the adjoining room. Gradually she loosened her hands from Daisy's, straightened up, wiped her face with a small handkerchief from her dress pocket, and walked toward the child's sounds.

Daisy felt as if her body were falling into itself, and she had to hold on. With her arms still crossed she held herself tightly, then tighter still, and finally with all her strength. Gradually relaxing her hold, she took a deep breath, then another, focused her eyes, and looked around the room. She took another deep breath and felt more composed—even at peace. She stood up, approached the partially filled trunk, inspected what was there, and resumed her packing. She could hear her mother with the baby in the adjoining room and was grateful that she didn't have to attend to him. Weary and detached, she couldn't face being the child's mother.

When she finished packing, she went to the small desk near the window, found a pencil on top, opened a drawer from which she took a half sheet of white paper, and began to write. She felt increasingly calm now. She now knew clearly what she had to say and what she had to do.

Having written the brief message, she opened the trunk, placed the sheet of paper on top of its contents, and closed it. She secured the trunk's two latches but didn't lock it. She pictured her mother reading the message later. The image of her mother's response saddened her, but she suppressed it quickly. Again sitting by the window, she stared at the distant clouds. One of the largest hung over the ridges of the Blue Mountains and was set against a blue sky. It made her think of a funeral shroud slowly falling onto a supine body. The thought was comforting.

Isabella quietly reentered the room and saw her daughter still sitting by the window. Concerned and eager to interrupt what she imagined were her daughter's sad ruminations, she asked, "Have you finished your packing?"

Daisy didn't respond, but when her mother repeated her question she turned and said, "Yes, all done."

"I need to go to my house for some things to take for the trip tomorrow," Isabella said. "Would you like to go with me? Getting out of the house might do you some good."

"I think I will. Bertha will take care of Little Jim this morning. I'll send for Nathaniel to bring around the carriage."

It was close to noon by the time they reached their destination on East Street in Kingston. Isabella walked through the rooms of her modest but neat and tastefully furnished home, as if she were expecting changes over the weeks since she had last been there. She stopped at the kitchen in the rear of the house, gathered some jars of spices, and placed them in a cloth sack taken from a hook on the back door. When she entered her bedroom on the second floor, she took a small suitcase from the closet and filled it with several items of clothing—stockings, undergarments, two long skirts, and her best Sunday dress. From the top of her dresser she took two small framed pictures; one of Daisy in a graduation gown, and the other of Daisy sitting, her infant in arms and James Turner standing at her side. Placing them atop the packed clothes, she sighed at the thought of all that had changed.

As the buggy stopped at her daughter's Half-Way-Tree residence, Isabella Phillpotts said, "I was thinking of asking Bertha to fix some lunch for us. How would that be?"

"Fine, Mama," Daisy replied, without turning toward her mother.

When they sat down for lunch, Daisy stared at the food—akee, fish, salad and tea. She asked, "Do you suppose it's true that akee is sometimes poisonous, Mama?"

The older woman hesitated. "They say so, but only when you eat it before it's ripe." She continued, "Are you worried about the food? Believe me, dear, this akee is fine."

Daisy took a portion of fish, some salad, and a small amount of the akee, which she didn't eat. After they finished, Daisy said, "I would like to see a priest."

Her mother looked startled. "Why? What made you think of that? What do you want to see a priest about?"

"I feel the need to speak to a priest."

"But you haven't been to church since you came back to Jamaica. Why would you want to see a priest now?"

"I can't say why, but I do. Please, Mama, don't ask me to explain." Daisy looked away. "There's a Catholic Church near here, on Half-way Tree Road. I think it's St. Michael's. Will you come with me? Bertha can watch Little Jim."

"Of course I'll go with you."

Daisy asked Bertha to tell Nathaniel, her carriage driver, to prepare to meet them in front of the house in half an hour. She had a good idea how long it would take Bertha to find Nathaniel and how long it would take him to appear with the buggy.

In the meanwhile Daisy freshened up, found her favorite daytime hat, and filled her cloth purse with various small items, some coins, and two letters she had recently received from her absent husband. She sat erect at her dressing mirror and looked into her own eyes. Again she fell into a trance-like reverie.

There she was that April day in 1906 on a ship heading to New York City. Standing on the upper forward deck, she could feel in her body the excitement at the prospect of an adventure she never dreamed of.

It is real, she thought.

The man who was to be her husband was standing at her side.

"I'm so excited! When will we get to America, James?" she asked looking up to him with a bright smile and adoring eyes.

"About noon tomorrow," he said, smiling back. "Are you pleased you came now?" he asked. "I know it was difficult leaving Jamaica—your mother, your brothers, your family and friends."

"I just hope I don't miss them too much," she said. "But even more, I hope they don't hate me for leaving with so little notice. I can't help thinking it was wrong to run away with you this way. But I love you so much, James, I just couldn't let you leave without me. Will it be all right, James? Tell me everything will turn out for the best."

"Of course it will," he said. "I will make sure it does. Don't worry. I'll take care of everything."

"Will we get married when we get to America, James?" she asked, looking squarely into his face, as if to read a response before he began one.

"We'll have to see about it when we get there," he answered, looking away. "It may turn out to be more complicated than I thought. Getting a divorce in the United States can take time. I'll have to go to court in Rhode Island. I just don't know what may happen."

"But we will get married, won't we?" she pressed. "Please tell me we'll get married in America."

"Please, Daisy, don't worry about it," he said. "Everything will be all right. I'll keep my promise as soon as it can be managed. I just can't say for sure when that'll be."

"Oh, James," she said holding his left arm with both of hers and looking into his face. "I can't wait. I'll be Mrs. Turner—Mrs. James Turner of America and Jamaica."

She looked excitedly at him again. "Will I be an American when we get married, James?"

"Yes, you can be," he answered with a gratified smile. "That's the law. The spouse of an American citizen is automatically eligible to become an American."

She held his arm to her face and sighed. They both looked out into the Atlantic's dark waters. She relaxed, but felt his arm tense under his great coat. No matter, she thought. All will be fine . . .

Daisy was roused by a quiet tap. Bertha stood with the door ajar and said in a timid voice, "Mrs. Turner, Nathaniel has brought the buggy 'round. Should I tell 'im you're comin', ma'am?"

"Tell him I'll soon come."

She stood up, smoothed her hair and dress, placed her hat on her head and secured it with a pearl hat pin that James had given her when they were in New York City the first time.

It was nearly two o'clock when Nathaniel pulled up at the rectory of St. Michael's church. He got down from the driver's seat, opened the right side door, and stood waiting for the passengers to step down. The two women spoke quietly and, after a brief discussion, agreed that Daisy would go in alone.

While Daisy was in the rectory, her mother waited in the buggy and tried to imagine what her daughter was saying to the priest, who had greeted her cordially at the entry. When, after forty minutes, the rectory door opened and her daughter stepped across the threshold, Isabella was inexplicably relieved. Daisy turned back, however, and appeared to be thanking the priest. She bent her head, and the priest made a sign of the cross and ended by placing a hand on her head. Then he said a few more words as he handed her what turned out to be devotional reading materials for her stay in Mandeville.

On the journey home both women were silent. Isabella glanced repeatedly at her daughter, whose gaze was fixed but indifferent to the passing avenues and landscape.

When they arrived at the house, Daisy announced that she wished to take the buggy and visit a lady-friend at some distance.

"It will be a long time before I'll see Winifred again," Daisy explained. "After all, I haven't seen her in quite a while."

When her mother expressed surprise but offered to accompany her on the visit, Daisy insisted that she only wanted to have a brief visit and would be back soon. "No need to bother yourself. You must be tired from going back and forth today."

Nathaniel had stepped down and waited impassively as the two women spoke quietly. Still, he understood well what was expected of him. He assisted the older woman from the buggy, walked a few paces at her side, and returned to the driver's seat. Once there, he turned to look at Daisy, who had both hands over her mouth, as if to stifle sobs. He turned and waited for some signal from his employer. After several minutes he turned in her direction again. She was wiping tears from her eyes and cheeks. Again he turned away and waited.

Finally she said, "Nathaniel, do you remember where Mrs. Stephens lives? We went there some while ago."

Nathaniel replied, "Yes Ma'am. I believe so. Laws Street in Kingston? That's a good distance."

"Yes it is," she said, "but I won't be visiting for very long. We should return by six o'clock."

"Yes, Ma'am," said Nathaniel and took up the reins to begin the journey.

After they had traveled about five minutes Daisy asked, "Nathaniel, did you remember that my mother and I will be taking the bus to Mandeville tomorrow?"

"Yes, ma'am. Your mother reminded me about it while we waited for you at the church," he replied. "Will you be needing the carriage in the morning to meet the bus?"

"No. My mother has arranged to have my brother Laurence take us and help us with our luggage."

"Yes, ma'am."

"We'll be away for a good while, Nathaniel," she said. "When we're ready to return, we'll let you know by post or telegram. You'll be in charge of the horse and carriage while I'm away. I know you'll take good care of them."

She continued in something of a distracted manner. "Mr. Turner won't be back from America until the end of the summer. He's so bothered by the summer heat in Jamaica, has to run back to New York or Chicago or Rhode Island—or wherever he goes. He has delicate health, so the summers take too much out of him. He also has business there he has to attend to. Money business. Personal business also." After a moment she continued. "I was planning to go to America myself. Just for a visit. America is nice, but I couldn't be away from my family for long. Now I don't think I'll be able to manage it at all."

Looking in his direction now for the first time, she asked, "I don't suppose you've been to America, have you, Nathaniel?"

"No ma'am. Never have been. No need. Hear it's cold. Don't need dat," he answered.

When they arrived at Winifred Stephens's home just after 3 o'clock, Nathaniel stopped the buggy in a small circular driveway in the front of a large but modestly appointed structure. Before Nathaniel could get down to assist her, Daisy stepped quickly out on her own and assured him that she expected the visit to be brief. As she approached the front door, it was opened. A young woman of about Daisy's age greeted her with a warm embrace.

An hour and a half passed, and Nathaniel wondered whether his employer still intended to return home by six o'clock. Just after five o'clock the door of the house opened and Daisy appeared, followed closely by her friend. They spoke a few moments, embraced, and gave each other cheek kisses. Mrs. Turner approached the carriage with a somber expression but said nothing as she entered and sat.

After several minutes, Nathaniel looked back at his employer, who sat with closed eyes. He took the silence to indicate that Mrs. Turner wanted to go home. He drove off calculating that they could be there by six thirty. After half an hour, as they approached Crossroads, Daisy asked him to stop at the bus stop on Hope Road. He was surprised but complied without a word.

"Nathaniel, it appears that I have forgotten to give Mrs. Stephens something very important. I have to turn back, but you need not take me. I'll return to Kingston on the Hope Garden streetcar. I'll take the next car, and you may take the buggy home. Please tell my mother I'll return this evening on the last car."

She could see that Nathaniel was concerned at this request but he only asked, "Are you sure it wouldn't be better for me to take you back, Ma'am? It's no trouble you know."

"Thank you, Nathaniel. I'll be perfectly fine. Besides, I wouldn't want you to keep your family waiting dinner."

"Yes Ma'am."

Silent and composed, Daisy sat in the buggy until almost six o'clock, when the streetcar arrived from Hope Gardens going toward Kingston.

"Remember, Nathaniel," she said as she stepped down, "tell my mother I'll be taking the last car. She shouldn't wait up for me."

Nathaniel nodded and said as she walked away, "I'll surely do that, Ma'am." He then added, "Be well, Ma'am."

He watched her cross the road, signal the car with the wave of her right hand, and board. She recognized the car driver, greeted him, paid her fare, and moved to the middle of the half-filled car.

Her plan, she thought, was working. She knew that the Hope Gardens car crossed the Rockport Gardens line in Kingston's central square. She would wait there for the Rockport Gardens line, which she knew turned around at Brighton Beach on Kingston Harbor. As always, she sat erect with her bag on her lap and stared blankly ahead. She pictured her destination; at first she shook at the image but then grew calmer. *This is the only way*, she thought. Once her body relaxed, and knowing that the trip would be a long one, she allowed herself to slip back into her reverie.

Daisy pictured the first time she saw "Happy Retreat" on Windward Road in Kingston. It was a modest but sprawling Victorian whose front faced the bay from a considerable height and whose setting was in every way delightful. The grounds and the walks were a pleasure to experience—poinsettias of various hues in full bloom and fruit, evergreen, and palm trees in abundance. She was taken with the place when first she saw it and liked the idea of having her first child there. When they had found "Happy Retreat" two months before her due date, she was pleased that she would have the time to become accustomed to the place and to prepare properly for the baby. She waited patiently a full month, but now the baby had come.

There she lay facing her nursing newborn. She was exhausted, but she felt a peace and joy that she had never before experienced. A boy, she thought. James will be so pleased. We'll have to name him after his father, but we'll call him Little Jim.

It was well after 10 o'clock in the morning before the midwife allowed the child's father into the room where he found Daisy seated on a sofa near the crib.

When their eyes met, they both smiled broadly. The embrace and the kisses were prolonged. Pure joy for both.

James turned and took the few steps to where the sleeping baby lay and looked at him for several minutes. "Daisy, the baby is beautiful," he finally said. "So big and healthy looking. Thank you for giving us such a wonderful child."

"Oh, James," she replied, "he is beautiful, isn't he. He'll be as handsome as his father, so we will name him James and call him Little Jim. I can't wait to show him to my mother and the family."

James looked again at the newborn. This time his gaze lingered, with a question in his face. Still, he echoed Daisy's joyful pronouncement. "We will call him Little Jim."

Daisy noticed the change in his expression and asked, "What is it, James? Is there something wrong?"

He turned back to face his wife, smiled, and said, "Wrong? What could possibly be wrong? You've survived as healthy as ever. Little Jim is as healthy and beautiful as we could possibly have hoped. No, my darling Daisy, nothing is wrong. You've made me the happiest man alive. And I promise you, we'll be the happiest family ever."

Daisy smiled, stepped over and looked at the baby, then again at her husband. She felt uneasy. She didn't understand her husband's brief hesitation. Her heart skipped a beat at the thought that something could spoil their happiness.

The streetcar conductor called out, "Kingston Square. Rockport connection—Rockport Gardens and Brighton Beach!"

As she started up, Daisy realized that during the long ride the twilight had darkened into night. When she reached the front and began to step down, although she had her own wristwatch, she inquired as to the time from the car man. He pulled out a pocket watch from his uniform vest and reported, "Ten minutes after eight, Ma'am."

"Thank you," she said, then asked, "Do you know when the next car to Rockport Gardens will come by?"

"I'm afraid you have a good wait, Ma'am," he answered. "There's only one car on dat route and I believe you just missed it going in that direction. It'll take him thirty minutes before he turns at the gardens. Then thirty minutes to come here again and another twenty to the end of the line. Then another twenty minutes back to Kingston square. I guess that puts it at about one hour and forty minutes, Ma'am. As I said, a good long wait this time of night."

"Thank you. I'll simply have to wait," she said. "The square is well lit and I see benches by the streetcar stop. Good evening to you."

"Good evening, Ma'am," he said with a nod and drove on.

Daisy sat on the bench but soon decided that when the streetcar came from Brighton Beach she would take it to the end and make the return trip rather than wait in the square the entire period. She stared into the distance.

The days at "Happy Retreat" were peaceful in spite of the newborn's spirited demands for nourishment and attention. For a week Daisy felt that she was going to burst with happiness. She stared often at the baby even while he slept and yearned for him to awaken so she could feed him or simply enjoy looking into his eyes.

Still, she had the feeling that something was wrong. Her husband was already talking about traveling back to America, and she felt as though he was gone already. "How could he leave when I have just had our baby," she thought. Whenever she even hinted at questioning his plans, he promptly made light of the brief period he would be away or spoke to her as if he were speaking to a child of limited understanding. He explained, with a smile, that he had important business affairs to take care of in America. He had to make a living for his family. She forgave this condescension because, after all, he was so much older and wiser. In comparison to him she was not only young but also had very little worldly experience. She had never left the island before he took her to America three years earlier.

Even among Jamaica's middle class, girls were not expected to stay in school past the age of sixteen—the age she left Holy Cross Convent School. After that the expense of sending a female to school was wasted, since they were likely to spend their adult lives as homemakers, bearing and rearing children, supporting and pleasing a husband, and providing the connections between the older generation and the new. These responsibilities didn't require formal education. She knew her numbers well enough to deal with tradesmen and banks, and she could write a legible and coherent letter. What more would she need? What more could she reasonably expect?

She was usually content, but before she met James, she was rarely happy. Most of her life had been spent concerned with what others wanted of her, sometimes even certain she couldn't live up to the expectations of her family. She had spent most of her time feeling empty and useless. Her elopement with James was her first real rebellion—both her freedom from others' expectations and her assertion of her status as an adult.

When she looked up, she realized that the Rockport Brighton Beach car was passing her on its way to the end of the line. She would have to wait another forty minutes before its return. The windows of some of the shops in the square were lit, so she wandered past them. Leaving the central square, she walked at a good pace through some of the familiar and well-lit residential streets leading into the square. She avoided eye contact with the occasional person she passed—including two patrolling constables. When she found herself across the street from the entrance to the Jamaica Asylum for the Insane, she stopped and stared at it. She had intended her walk to pass the time waiting for the streetcar. How had she happened upon that spot? She had never been there, but she had heard horrible stories about the people inside and how they were mistreated. But what did that have to do with her? She imagined herself inside, surrounded by mayhem. She cringed.

The streetcar heading to Rockport passed her on its way to the square, and she realized that she had to hurry back to catch it.

On the final leg of her journey she cycled between moments of panic and strong resolve that calmed her. Then images of her mother, her child, and her husband brought on quiet tears and gentle dabbing.

Opening her husband's last two letters from America, she reread them slowly, lingering on each word. *He'll take care of everything,* she thought. *Everything will be fine.* Then, *Too late,* and returned them to her purse.

When the streetcar jerked to a stop, Daisy's startle straightened her spine. The motorman, looking back at her, the only passenger, called out, "Rockport Gardens." Her eyes focused, she gathered herself, rose, and moved to the exit.

When the motorman tipped his cap, Daisy saw the question in his face. She also knew that he would not presume to comment on the late hour or tell her the gardens and beach would be closed. As she left him and headed up the road toward the park and the harbor, she wore a gentle smile.

As she walked, Daisy felt calm and clear-headed. She was determined now to do what she had come to do. Her step was steady and measured. Before her was the garden, with its several walking paths, one of which led to the harbor and the pier. *By now it must be past ten o'clock,* she thought, but didn't bother to look at her watch. The lighting was dim on the path, but it was bright enough not to impede her.

As she approached the pier, she noted the stillness of the air, the water, and the trees. The gate leading onto the pier was closed and a lock and chain secured it. But the prohibition was merely symbolic, since Daisy had no difficulty simply bypassing the gate by stepping down to the sand, walking twenty paces down the beach and around the fence, and back again to the pier.

The full moon and the clear, still air made walking the long pier dreamlike. *Perhaps it's all a dream*, she thought. *Perhaps I'll soon wake up and all will be well.*

As she approached the end of the pier, she instinctively slowed and shortened her steps. She had never learned to swim, but she felt no particular fear of water. The thought of being surrounded by water felt more like a comforting return to a familiar place. The water would receive her and gently hold her, and she would fall asleep floating and warm. The suffering would be over.

She carefully leaned over the edge at the end of the pier. The water, ten feet below her, was dark and she could barely see the small ripples of waves gently kissing the pilings holding the pier. She looked across the bay and down the beach where, at a distance, lights flickered and swayed slightly, as if attached to boats or buoys. The evening was turning cooler, the breeze ever so mild.

Daisy placed her purse on the pier, opened it, and touched the letters she had earlier placed there. She then carefully removed the pearl pin from her hat, removed the hat, stuck the pin back through its side, and placed it beside the purse. She stood erect on the edge of the pier and stared into the distance. Her heart began to race, and her limbs felt weak. She said, "God help me." Then, "God, protect my baby." She stepped forward and closed her eyes.

CHAPTER 9:

"Every Heart Knows Its Own Burden"
Proverbs 14:10

On June 16, 1909, at the Parade Court House in Kingston, Isabella Phillpotts, in her early forties, petite, with olive skin and simple dress, quietly entered a small, windowless but well-lit hearing room. The wood-paneled walls and sconce lights reminded her of a funeral parlor. She was tense and wished she could be invisible. Although the room was less than half-full, she promptly sat in the aisle seat of the last of six well-worn wooden benches on the left. The heavy air seeping in from the midsummer heat, the size of the room, and the tight arrangement of the tables and chairs felt claustrophobic. Overhead the single ceiling fan's slow, creaky whirring only added to her discomfort.

At the end of the room furthest from the entry door, a four-by-eight rectangular table with an armchair faced the benches. On the left side of the table was another armchair, also facing the benches. To the left of that chair and against the far wall was an armless chair at a tiny table where a young man holding a notebook sat staring blankly into the distance. Isabella guessed he was the recorder. To the right of the long table were two rows of five armchairs perpendicular to the far wall. Two tall heavy-set black men dressed in simple uniforms of dark blue pants and grey shirts with official-looking arm patches stood by the doors in the far corners.

From the back of the room Isabella couldn't see all the faces of the dozen or so people seated in the benches. In the front row on the right side, however, she recognized James Turner by his slick dark hair and ruddy skin. When he turned to look about the room, he noticed her and gave a slight nod, which she returned. Leaning toward the man to his left, he whispered, and the two men had a brief exchange. She thought she knew the man, but he didn't turn to look back.

At exactly 10 A.M. the door on the right side of the far wall opened, and the bailiff ushered a line of men to the ten empty seats. Within a moment the door on the far left opened, and the second bailiff announced the arrival of the presiding coroner. A tall white man in a dark suit strode heavily into the room carrying a thick folder with sheets sticking out at odd angles. Standing at the chair behind the rectangular table, he indicated with a hand gesture that those present should be seated. In a distinctly British accent, he described the purpose of the hearing.

"I'm Leonard Gray, Assistant District Medical Officer. We're here to inquire into the death of Daisy Maud Humber Turner, who deceased on May 21 of this year. The coroner's office, with the help of the Jamaica and Kingston Constabularies, has identified and summoned parties who can provide evidence in this matter. As the presiding officer, I'll take the lead in questioning, while the jury will have an opportunity to ask clarifying questions. After these inquiries, the jury will recess in order to deliberate and render a majority decision as to the cause and circumstances of this death. All others present are requested to remain silent throughout the proceedings unless acknowledged by me."

With a slight gesture, he looked to his left. "The empanelled jury consists of ten citizens representing a cross section of Kingston parish, and the foreman is John Bolton Reid. Please stand, Mr. Reid . . . Yes . . . Thank you."

Isabella saw a light-skinned colored man about fifty, of medium height and rotund body, whose gray and brown moustache hung down so far over his upper lip that his teeth would not have been visible even if he smiled—which he did not. He wore a dark brown suit, a stiffly starched white shirt and a tie nearly as dark as the suit. Throughout the inquiry he remained erect in his bearing and attentive to every detail of the process. He projected a business-like and conscientious attitude. In the nomenclature of Jamaica, the other nine included three who would generally be taken as white, five others as varying shades of brown, and one as black. They all wore suits, some well worn, some of good quality, all dark.

A heavyset white man seated in the front bench on the left side stood and requested permission to speak.

"I'm Inspector McCrae of the Kingston Constabulary," the man said. "I wish the court to be aware that the police had great difficulty getting information from Mr. Turner. He refused to give a statement, and it was with great difficulty that we managed to get him here."

At this point the man sitting next to James Turner likewise stood. When acknowledged, he said, "My name is Aston Simpson. I am an attorney present to observe the proceedings on behalf of Mr. Turner. Mr. Turner is in delicate health and when he arrived here from the United States, he was repeatedly harassed by the police to give a statement. Having recently lost his wife, he was understandably distraught and felt unable to respond to such a request. He is present today, however, and will give whatever evidence he can." With this last, the speaker rotated to his right and extended his arm as if introducing his client to the coroner.

The coroner looked briefly at Mr. Simpson, then at James Turner, who was now standing, again at inspector McCrae, and finally back to Mr. Simpson. He said, with a tone of finality, "Very well. We accept the explanation . . . and we appreciate the presence of the deceased's husband—under these difficult circumstances. Now, may we proceed?" No response.

"Let us begin. The list of those summoned to give evidence isn't long, but I believe that my office has been thorough in identifying the appropriate parties. That is, it appears to include those who saw the deceased on the day of her death and those who were present at the recovery of her body the following day. Others who might have given evidence are off the island or otherwise unavailable. Their testimony would not have added materially to the outcome of this hearing. As I indicated earlier, the coroner's office has come to no final conclusion, at this point, as to the cause or circumstances of Mrs. Turner's death. The jury must attend to the evidence carefully and come to a majority decision based on that evidence."

He turned to the court and said, in a somewhat louder voice, "Nathaniel Gal please come forward."

Isabella relaxed. She had feared that she would be called to testify first. However, as Nathaniel, Daisy's coachman, moved toward the front, she felt sorry for him. She knew him to be a shy, gentle man, and could only guess that he felt as intimidated and anxious as she did.

Nathaniel, a short, stout black man of about forty, faced the coroner stiffly. The latter handed him a bible and asked, "Do you swear to speak the truth as you know it, so help you God?"

"I do."

As Nathaniel gave his testimony, Isabella felt that he was comporting himself well and described the day of Daisy's death simply and clearly. He drove Daisy three times that day and had spent more time with her than anyone else had. Still, nothing he reported could explain how the day had ended.

Some of the information was new to Isabella. She was unaware of Daisy's several visits to Brighton Beach with Winifred Stephens. Nathaniel reported that, on one occasion, Daisy had inquired about the depth of the water at the end of the pier. Isabella wondered whether, if she had known this, she would have been sufficiently alarmed to take more drastic steps to protect her daughter. She cringed as she acknowledged that she had seen many warnings, and yet felt unable to do anything. How could she have forbade her to go out? She couldn't watch her every minute. Still . . . the guilt feelings, mixed with constant anguish, had welled up frequently since that day.

As Nathaniel reported, the errand to pick up things from her own home had gone without incident. On the trip back she had even allowed herself to hope that there had been a genuine improvement in her daughter; she was preoccupied, but her mood was less depressed. Then she remembered that, at lunch, Daisy had surprised her with a question about the akee and later a request to see a Catholic priest. Looking back, Isabella realized that these were warning signs, but Daisy hadn't allowed her to question her about them. *In any case,* she thought, *what could I have done?*

Isabella's arms tightened around her purse when Nathaniel described his return to report that her daughter would return on the last streetcar. *I knew something was wrong. Why didn't I insist on going with her? If only I had called the doctor that morning.*

Finally, the foreman asked whether Daisy had appeared depressed. Nathaniel's answer surprised her. "No, she went about as usual." Isabella remembered that Daisy was crying when she left her in the carriage. *How could he not see that something was wrong? And the idea that she would travel on the late car alone! He must believe he is protecting the family. Or maybe he thinks he could have done something more. If that's what it is, I'll make it clear to him that there was nothing he could have done.*

The next witness, Thomas Arboin, was sworn and identified as a streetcar driver on the Rockport line. He described his encounter with Daisy the evening of May 21 as unusual only in the late hour of her ride. He had first seen her that evening near the Asylum on Rae Street. Later he picked her up in front of the New St. Michael's Cathedral. He had seen her several times and recognized her. When asked by the foreman whether she behaved in any way strange, the motorman replied, "She had on her same sweet countenance."

Isabella was touched by this description. Indeed, Daisy had always been a sweet child, easy to raise and dutiful. Both at home and at school, she was well behaved. She asked herself, *What happened?*

Charles Henry Bernard, a black man in his early twenties, came forward stiffly when called. In his grey and dark blue uniform, he was impeccably neat. He stood as if in a military parade while he held the bible for the swearing in. He was clearly tense but was trying to manage the situation by putting on a serious face.

"Be seated," instructed the coroner without looking up.

Isabella expected that this young man would be treated with less respect than others had been. Nonetheless, she was offended when the coroner's first question came out gruffly. "What are you?"

"Constable, sir," responded the witness, looking quickly at the coroner as if surprised to be asked such a question. Isabella noted a barely perceptible smile and imagined the young man was reassuring himself that this process would be easier than he had feared.

"Of what force?" asked the coroner off-handedly, as he inspected some sheets in front of him on the table.

"Sir?" asked the policeman, clearly mystified. Now his anxiety showed again.

"Of what force?" repeated the coroner, now looking straight at the young officer.

"Britisher, sir," answered the officer. He stared at the coroner as if hoping this was the response sought.

"We well know you are a Britisher," snapped the coroner. "What we want for the record is the particular force you are a member of."

The policeman now showed signs of agitation, looking straight ahead, frozen. Nothing came out. Everyone stared but he couldn't focus his eyes even on the coroner.

After a few seconds, the coroner was clearly annoyed and pressed him sarcastically, "Of British Guiana? Honduras? West Africa? Trinidad? Royal Irish? Or what?"

At first the policeman appeared puzzled and increasingly anxious. Some of the jurors smiled, others snorted their amusement.

"Jamaica Constabulary, sir?" the policeman finally blurted out, but with a hesitating question mark in the final breath.

The coroner assured the officer that he was correct. "Now would you tell us everything you know in the case of the death of Mrs. Daisy Turner."

The policeman relaxed somewhat, pulled out a small notebook from the buttoned breast pocket of his shirt, and read. "On the morning of May 22nd of this year I went to Brighton Beach where I found a lady's trimmed hat, a hat pin, shawl, and hand bag on the wharf. I took charge of the things and examined the contents of the handbag. It contained some blue car tickets, two prize drawing tickets, two letters, and coins totaling 2 pounds, 6 shillings, and 4 pence."

"What did you do next?"

"I returned to the Rae Town Police station, handed over the things I found, and informed the officer in charge where I found them."

The coroner held up the items the policeman had described. "Are these the items?"

"Yes sir."

"For the record, I'll read the two letters found in the purse," announced the coroner.

He held the two sheets of lined paper before him and read the first.

"May 12, 1909

My dear darling little wife:

Just a line to let you know I am still on board the ship but will land about 7 o'clock.

127

Poor Jim. I see him day and night.

I feel better since I got out of that heat.

I will pray for you to get well soon, so you can come over here. I think you will be ready the last part of June. So, you be sure and let the doctor fix you up. I will come over to New York as soon as I get through with Howland.

I wish you and Jim were with me. I would feel much better. I love you with all my heart because you are my only friend I have on earth. I will surely keep my promise to you as soon as you get to New York.

Remember me to your mother and all the folks. Spend as little money as you can now.

James Julius Turner"

He looked up but immediately read the second letter.

"May 14, 1909

My dear little wife and baby:

I just finished talking to my friend Mr. Lee, so he said you can come any time, so let the Doctor fix you up soon as he can and come over if you want to for the change. Let your mother look after the things. The change will put you all right. I won't have my case come up in court for a month, so don't worry about me.

It is nice weather in New York. I only wish you were here to enjoy some of it. Remember me kindly and I will keep my word if I live. I love you with all my heart. Kisses for you and some for Jim.

J. J. Turner

Isabella, who hadn't seen the letters, was startled by some of what they alluded to. She wondered what was meant by the promise mentioned in the letters. James had always been generous to Daisy and her family. *What could he have promised to give her?* The reference to a "case in court" made her wonder what legal problems were involved. She thought, *I don't really know this man. For all I know, he could be a criminal.* The phrase "if I live" made her wonder whether James's health was much worse than she had been told.

The next witness, another uniformed, trim young man of medium height and olive complexion, spoke confidently. "My name is Peter Francis and I'm the Acting Corporal of the Water Police, Jamaica Constabulary. We patrol Kingston Harbor and other waterways near Kingston." He pulled out a breast pocket notebook. "On May 22nd of this year I received a call from police headquarters instructing me to proceed to the wharf on Brighton Beach at Rockport. When I and four other officers arrived at the pier, Detective Sergeant Cunningham called my attention to something white lying at the bottom of the sea in about three fathoms of water. We pulled up the dead body of a woman fully dressed. The body was conveyed on the boat to the Water Police Station, and from there it was taken to the mortuary."

As the constable ended his report, the tears Isabella had been holding back gushed forth. With her hands over her nose and mouth she was able to cry silently. *My dear child,* she thought.

Detective Sergeant Edmund Cunningham was the next witness. He was a tall, broad-shouldered man of about forty, wearing a loosely fitting dark suit. His complexion was light brown. His auburn hair was wavy but brushed back tightly. He approached the coroner's table unhurriedly, stood at ease while being sworn, and sat down heavily into the chair. His eyes wandered about the room while the coroner searched through his papers. When the latter asked what he knew of the matter, the witness pulled himself up slightly, relaxed his back into the chair, inhaled deeply and began. "On the morning of May 22nd a call came into the station reporting a missing person. The caller said that Mrs. Daisy Turner, his sister, had gone out the previous evening but hadn't returned and that her mother was concerned. I invited the caller, a Mr. Laurence Humber, to come to the station to make a missing persons report. This is standard procedure. He agreed to meet me at the station as soon as he could. Meanwhile, within the hour another call came in from the police station at Rae Town. It was reported that a constable had found a hat and purse at the end of the wharf at Brighton Beach near Rockport. By the time the deceased's brother arrived at headquarters,

I had begun to wonder about a possible connection between the two reports. I spoke briefly in my office with Mr. Humber, informing him about the reported find at Brighton Beach wharf. He agreed to accompany me to the Rae Town Police Station. I asked the duty officer to call the Water Police Station and ask that a boat meet us at the wharf on Brighton Beach. When we arrived at the Rae Town Police Station, Mr. Humber didn't hesitate in identifying the hat and purse as belonging to his sister. We soon reached Brighton Beach. Humber remained at the police car and I proceeded out onto the wharf. At the end of the pier I looked down into the water. I could see something white, but the water was too deep for me to make out what it was. At that point a boat from the Water Police arrived. I gestured to the officer on deck to move the boat in closer to the wharf because I could see something white in the water near the end of the wharf, where I stood. Using a grappling iron they soon pulled up the dead body of a young woman fully dressed. The body was placed in the boat and taken down to the Water Police Station. I arranged for the body to be transported to the mortuary and I was present when Dr. Gifford did the post mortem examination."

The detective pulled a memo pad from the inside pocket of his jacket, and read. "The doctor removed a lady's gold watch, five gold rings, a gold pin, two brooches and a fine silver chain with a heart attached. I took charge of the items and later turned them over to the coroner's office. I was the investigating officer since that time."

"And what has your investigation revealed?"

"We were able to ascertain a general idea of the deceased's movements on the day she died. It appears that she traveled to the wharf alone and was alone when she drowned."

He looked back and forth between the coroner and the jury and waited.

"Thank you for such a detailed description," said the coroner. Then to the jury: "Are there further questions for this witness?"

The foreman turned and scanned the faces of the other jurors. Finding no reaction, he turned to the detective and asked, "Were you able to estimate the time of death, detective?"

"When I inspected the recovered wristwatch I noted that it had stopped at approximately ten minutes past eleven."

The foreman asked, "How would Mrs. Turner have gotten onto the wharf at that late hour?"

"The gate leading to the wharf was indeed locked, but she wouldn't have had any difficulty getting onto the wharf by simply bypassing the gate and entering from the beach area."

"Are there any residences in that area of Brighton Beach?"

"There is one private home within sight of the wharf, but no one there had any knowledge of what happened on the night of the drowning. "

"Are there no police patrols in that area in the evening?" the foreman asked quickly and with a tone of mild irritation.

The detective made pointed eye contact with the questioner and said, "I do *not* have knowledge of the patrol schedule of that area."

The coroner, looking impatient, said, "If there are no further questions, the witness is dismissed with our thanks."

Dr. Howard Gifford, a medical examiner for Kingston, was called next. His post mortem examination was described as routine, and he filed a written report concluding that death was caused by drowning.

The doctor looked at the coroner, who simply nodded somberly over hands folded under his chin. Realizing, after a few seconds, that the witness had come to the end of his statement, he simply asked, "Do you have anything further to report in this matter?"

"I do not."

"Does the jury have any questions for the witness?" asked the coroner, looking directly at the foreman.

"Did you examine the brain, doctor?" asked the foreman.

"I did not."

"Given the circumstances, you didn't consider it necessary to examine the brain?" the foreman asked with a hint of incredulity.

"A detailed examination of the brain would not have added anything useful in making a determination of the cause of death, which was the only purpose of the post mortem examination."

The coroner, after shooting a look of irritation at the foreman, asked the doctor, "The cause of death was easily ascertained I suppose, doctor?"

"Yes, easily."

Finally, Isabella's name was called. She felt her body tense but knew that she would be able to get through this process. Holding her purse with both hands close to her stomach as she walked forward, her eyes darted between the coroner and the jury. During the swearing in she stared at the coroner. When she sat and looked back toward the seats in the gallery, her eyes fell upon James Turner. There was no discernible expression in his face, and that blankness, she felt, mirrored her own fragile control.

"First, I want to say how sorry I—and no doubt all present—feel for your loss," the coroner said, looking directly at Isabella, who covered her mouth with her right hand and looked down into her lap. She sighed, looked up at the coroner, and said, "Thank you."

The coroner stretched both arms in front of himself, reached for a pencil and began, "What was your daughter's age?"

"She made 21 her last birthday."

"And where did she reside?"

"She lived with me all her life until she went to America for six months in 1906."

"Please describe what you know concerning her living arrangements and movements after that."

"About twelve or thirteen years prior to the earthquake I opened a curio shop in the Myrtle Bank Hotel, in Kingston. I remember seeing James Turner in the hotel for the first time in 1906, but I wasn't introduced to him. Sometimes I would see him buying cards at the stall in front of the store, when Daisy was there helping me. I noticed them talking a few times, but I didn't make anything of it. Then, one day in March of 1906, Daisy told me she would be leaving for America the next day. I was surprised and upset, and I tried to persuade her not to go, but it was no use. She even refused to tell me anything about how or why she was going. We argued all that evening. When I got up in the morning she had gone. Two weeks later I received a letter from her in America, saying she was with James Turner and they were engaged. She sent me a few more letters after that and she sounded happy. In October, she returned to Jamaica with Turner, introduced him as her husband, and said she married him in America. They lived at the Constant Spring Hotel for some time and then took a furnished house on the South Camp Road. I often went to see her there."

The coroner broke in. "And she seemed happy to you at that time?"

"She seemed quite happy—then."

"Please go on."

"After the earthquake she went with her husband to Mandeville and then to Dr. McCarty's in Montego Bay, because Mr. Turner was ill and needed the cooler climate. They were there two or three months. When they came back, they stayed with me a few days until they left for America—March or April, I believe. They came back to Jamaica in August, and they stayed with me a few days again. Then they went to live at Phoenix Park on the Hope Road and later to Hagley Park on the Rockport Road. Daisy was in a delicate condition through this period and gave birth to her son in March 1908. In June they moved to a house at the corner of East and Laws Street in Kingston. That same month Mr. Turner left for America and didn't return until October, when they all moved from Laws Street to Arnold Road. Then, toward the end of January this year, they moved to Hagley Park, and I moved in with them on March 22."

The coroner again interrupted. "Was there a particular reason for your moving in with them at that time?"

"Daisy wasn't feeling well and she began to worry me and Mr. Turner. It seemed like her mind was changed. She often sat with her head leaning on her hands and wouldn't talk. She sometimes cried hysterically and complained about pain across her forehead. Once she blamed herself for the earthquake. Nothing I said could persuade her otherwise, but she never mentioned it after that. And her baby she loved so much? She often took no notice of him. She would sometimes quarrel with me and say she was being watched. Sometimes she would go to bed fully dressed with her stockings and boots on. She became careless in keeping her house and took no notice of her servants. One day she told me she felt she wasn't the same Daisy. She said she had everything to make her happy, yet she didn't feel the same."

The jury foreman raised a hand and, when acknowledged by the coroner, asked, "Did your daughter receive any medical attention?"

"In April, her doctor, a Dr. McCriedel, examined her. Afterward he advised that she should be kept quiet and anything dangerous should be removed from the house. He also suggested that we take her to a Dr. O. D. Robertson, a specialist, and we did so . . . in May."

The coroner interjected, "I believe that Dr. Robertson has been summoned to appear here today and will give testimony later." He went on. "Mrs. Phillpotts, you indicated that you were living with your daughter at the time of her death. Please describe what you know of her movements around that time."

"After Dr. Robertson examined Daisy he advised me to take her away for a rest and a change of air and scene. After Mr. Turner left for America at the beginning of May, I suggested that we go for a visit to my family in Mandeville. Daisy agreed and I made plans for us to go by bus on May 22. On Friday morning, May 21st, we traveled in my daughter's carriage to my home on East Street in Kingston, so that I could pack some things for our trip on Saturday. When we returned, we had lunch, and my daughter expressed a wish to see a Roman Catholic priest. I thought this odd and expressed concern, but Daisy wouldn't say anything more about her request. We went in her carriage to the church off North Street. She found a priest was available in the rectory. I didn't go in but, when she came out with the priest, I heard them conversing. He seemed to be praying; then he blessed her and handed her some reading material. When we arrived back at her home, she told me that she wanted to see a friend in Kingston before leaving for Mandeville. Her driver came back at about 6:30 and said he had left Daisy at Cross Roads. She told him to tell me she would be late and not to wait up. This worried me, but there was nothing I could do."

At this point, Isabella could no longer hold back her tears. All eyes in the room were on her as she sobbed, and no one spoke for several minutes. Finally, the coroner quietly asked, "Mrs. Phillpotts, are you able to go on?"

Isabella looked at the coroner, nodded, blew her nose into a handkerchief, pulled herself up, and said, "Pardon me, your honor. Yes, I can go on." She inhaled deeply but continued to focus on her own hands as she continued. "I could hardly sleep that night, and at dawn on Saturday, when she hadn't come in, I called Daisy's brother, Laurence, and he called the police to report her missing. Later that day, he told me what happened. At first I refused to believe it, but he said he saw her body and her things . . . My heart was broken. I could only go to bed. I asked him to see about making arrangements. I couldn't face it."

As she ended she covered her eyes and bent forward. The room became quiet and every gaze was on the grieving mother. After a moment, the coroner addressed her. "I understand that there was a note."

"Yes. Later that day I opened the trunk Daisy had packed for our trip. On top was a bit of lined paper written in her handwriting."

"Please read the note to the court, Mrs. Phillpotts."

Isabella hesitated, then opened her purse on her lap and pulled out a small piece of paper folded once. When she began to read it, her voice cracked into sobs instead of words. She quickly put her left hand to her mouth in an attempt to hold back her gasps, but to no avail. She cried uncontrollably for a full two minutes; hers was the only sound in the room. As she slowly began to gather some composure, she looked up from the note and realized that the coroner was standing at her side. He said, "We know how difficult this is, madam. Perhaps I should read the note to the jury."

She said nothing but handed the paper to him. He returned to his seat, read the note in silence, and a scowl crossed his face.

"The note reads as follows:

'Goodbye Mama. Take care of little Jim for me. I am not insane, but every heart knows its own burden.'"

The coroner continued to look down at the paper. The room fell silent. Several of the jury and observers touched an eye or put a hand to mouth.

When the coroner looked up, Isabella's eyes met his. Then she scanned the room. Many were looking down, but, among those whose gaze she met, she found a mixture of sadness and dismay. Looking down again, she yielded to her grief and wept.

Finally, the coroner sat up and forward, as if to say that it was time to carry on. No one else moved; each was locked in the attitude created by the final words of the note.

The coroner cleared his throat and addressed the jurors. "Are there any further questions for this witness?"

Still, no one moved. "Then, Mrs. Phillpotts, again accept our condolences and gratitude for your willingness to assist us here. We know that this has been difficult. Thank you."

Isabella hesitated for a few seconds, placed the handkerchief in her purse, rose feeling a bit unsteady, and returned slowly to her seat. When she sat, she looked into her lap. *If only I had found that note earlier. Could I have done something? Oh Daisy, my darling child, could you really be gone?*

Doctor O. D. Robertson, a tall, handsome, erect, and elegantly dressed man of medium brown complexion rose and stepped to the witness chair. After being sworn, the coroner asked identifying information.

"Doctor of Medicine?"

"Yes."

"Practice specialty?"

"Neurology and psychiatry."

"Location of practice?"

"Primarily Kingston and surrounding area but across the island when called upon and available."

"Doctor Robertson," began the coroner, "we have heard in this inquiry thus far that Mrs. Turner was unwell for a period of time before her death. We further understand that you saw the deceased professionally. Please tell us what you can about her condition and its possible connection to her death."

"The deceased and her mother, Mrs. Phillpotts, came to my dispensary on the 10th of May of this year, referred to me by Dr. McCriedel. I examined Mrs. Turner—took her pulse and temperature, and asked her several questions. I also made inquiries of her mother, who reported a number of troubling things about her daughter's recent behavior. On the basis of this examination, I concluded that Mrs. Turner was suffering from neurasthenia."

The foreman held up an index finger, and the coroner nodded his assent. "Would you please explain what neurasthenia is, doctor?"

The doctor sat up a bit more erectly, pulled at his coat lapels, and responded in a lecture-like tone. "Neurasthenia is a nervous condition under which persons suffering are unable to apply themselves to their usual vocations. They frequently suffer a loss of appetite and insomnia."

"What is the cause of such a condition?"

"At this time, there is no agreed upon cause. Some assume that a malfunction of the brain is likely. Others speculate that some subtle infection, which cannot be detected, is the basis. Still others think in terms of a sickness of the soul. That is, they see the condition as arising out of a more spiritual, non-biological process. A person facing conflicts, guilt feelings, or overwhelming sense of loss may become desperate and confused."

"What is the treatment for this condition?" pursued the foreman, but went on without waiting for an answer. "Did you prescribe any treatment for Mrs. Turner?"

The doctor placed his hands on the chair arms, adjusted his position slightly, and responded. "I prescribed a sedative to help her relax and sleep. I also advised her mother to take her away for a rest and a change of air. There was nothing more I could do."

"And would you give it as your opinion, doctor," asked the coroner, "that this neurasthenia would have driven Mrs. Turner to take her own life?"

"It is possible."

Isabella felt her face warm and her heart pound. *You knew there was some danger? Was there nothing more you could have done to save her?*

Silence again fell on the room. The foreman turned toward the other jury members to invite further questions. Seeing only blank, somber faces, he turned and nodded in the direction of the coroner.

The coroner briefly consulted his notes. "We have now heard from all the witnesses scheduled to give testimony in this matter. Do the members of the jury wish to hear from Mr. Turner at this time?"

The jury members looked at one another and their eyes fell upon the foreman, who rose and asked, "May we have a moment to deliberate, your honor?"

"Of course."

The foreman stood in front of the other nine jury members, leaned into the center of them and whispered a question. He looked at each quickly, and the answers he received were mostly shrugs, grimaces, and slight head shakes. He moved closer to those who wanted to answer verbally, but there was only one barely audible " . . . off the island . . ."

After a moment the foreman returned to his seat and, addressing the coroner, said, "We see no need to hear from Mr. Turner, your honor."

"Very well. If there is no further evidence or testimony to be given, there remains only for the jury to render a finding in this inquiry. The first question is whether Mrs. Turner died by her own hand. The second is whether there is any person who can be held responsible for her death. Finally, the jury may wish to stipulate whether Mrs. Turner was insane at the time she took her own life. Please inform the bailiff, when you have reached a decision."

The jurors filed out. Within fifteen minutes the foreman called in the bailiff, who informed the coroner that the jury was prepared to give their finding. When the jurors were in their places and the room was again filled, the coroner turned to the jurors and asked, "Has the jury come to a finding in the case of the death of Mrs. Daisy Turner?"

"We have, your honor," responded the foreman.

"Please read your verdict."

"We unanimously find that the death of Mrs. Daisy Turner was a suicide by means of drowning. Two members of the jury voted to stipulate that Mrs. Turner was temporarily insane at the time of the suicide. The jury also unanimously finds that no other person was criminally responsible for Mrs. Turner's death. If it is permitted, the jury wishes to add the recommendation that a police constable be placed on duty at Brighton Beach and its vicinity at night."

"I will pass along your recommendation to the police authorities," said the coroner. "Thank you all for your careful consideration of the evidence in this case. I'll certify, for the record, that your finding was arrived at with attention to the evidence and with due deliberation. The inquiry is hereby concluded. Items used in evidence will be returned to their rightful owners."

The coroner collected the papers on the table. Without looking at anyone, he walked quickly from the room. Isabella didn't move.

CHAPTER 10:

Lies and Secrets

Isabella sat quietly, her eyes focused on her hands. Sadness enveloped her. She thought, *Daisy is gone.* She sighed deeply, rubbed her hands together, and tried to force herself to move. Her body didn't respond. She decided to wait until the hearing room cleared before trying to move again.

As she waited, she pictured her daughter on that last day. *Something happened that morning*, she thought. Daisy had been in a bad mood all week. For days, her bouts of crying had distressed Isabella enough that she considered putting off the Mandeville trip and taking her back to the psychiatrist, Dr. Robertson. On that morning, she recalled that Daisy had sat for hours staring out the window, and Isabella had braced herself for yet another day of distress. But in mid-morning, after Daisy finished her packing for the Mandeville trip, Isabella noticed a change in her. Her mood became tranquil, less agitated, and yet more detached from her surroundings.

Isabella remembered the note she found inside Daisy's trunk. *She must have written the note after she finished her packing. I was taking care of Little Jim in the next room. If only I had opened the trunk . . .*

Her reverie was interrupted by a deep voice. "Isabella?"

She turned to face James Turner, bending slightly at her right shoulder.

"I was wondering, Isabella, whether you would be up to meeting with me and Mr. Simpson for a few minutes."

"Of course. Just give me a moment."

James nodded and moved back and into the hall. Isabella turned and saw Aston Simpson, whose face was serious and whose posture was solicitous. The two men stood silently.

Gradually the hearing room emptied and the hallway fell silent. Isabella found the silence comforting as she continued to think back to the day Daisy left her. The change in her that morning must be the key to what Daisy had done. *Gone*, she said to herself again. Tears streamed down her face but she made no sound. She wiped the tears away, dabbed her eyes and took a deep breath.

She heard voices behind her. *They must be getting impatient*, she thought. She dabbed her cheeks and eyes once more. A deep breath propelled her body into an upright position. Another helped her rise from the chair.

As she approached the waiting men, her composure was nearly complete. Turner gestured toward a secluded area down the hall. When they stopped, Turner took her left hand with his right, and then held it with both his hands.

"Isabella, this has been a difficult time for all of us," he said. "I know you are grieving over the loss of Daisy. I hesitate to ask you to take on any additional burdens, but I feel I must."

She freed her hand and faced him squarely.

"Isabella, you may remember Mr. Simpson."

"I do," she responded and gave a slight nod and a pained smile. "You were at the funeral. I gather you're representing Mr. Turner in legal matters."

Simpson bowed slightly. "That is correct, madam. At present Mr. Turner and I have been discussing the care of the child James." Isabella was put off by this man—by his precise enunciation and heavy British accent, even by his deep baritone voice. His stiff self presentation seemed false.

"Poor baby," she said with a sigh, "losing his mother and just one year old. So sad . . ."

"Isabella, Mr. Simpson and I have been discussing a plan for the child. I'm concerned about his care—what would be the best arrangement. As you know, I regularly travel to the United States. Because of that, I worry about finding a way to have him raised in a stable environment—especially in his formative years. You have often cared for him over the last few months—before and after Daisy's death. I propose we come to some agreement that would place Little James in your care, at least for the time being."

Isabella didn't respond, but looked into Turner's face without knowing what she sought there. What she saw was such a mixture of painful emotions that it was all she could do to fight back the return of her tears. She looked at Mr. Simpson, her eyes full of inquiry. *Should I do this?* She felt sorry for the baby, but she didn't want his father to walk away from him, leaving her as his only support.

"James," she said, "you know I love Little Jim. He's my first grandchild. I would do anything to make sure he has a chance to grow up happy and healthy." She paused just long enough to know he had registered this preamble, and continued. "Of course I'll take care of him . . . for as long as you and he need me to—and as long as I'm able. But you must promise me that you will spend as much time with him as possible—and never be away from him more than three months at a time. He'll need the love of a parent, the guidance of his father."

"I make that promise without hesitation," he replied. "I only regret that business will take me off the island some part of every year. And you know my health is very uncertain in hot weather. I simply cannot tolerate the spring and summer months in Jamaica. Eventually, I hope my son will travel with me to the States. Perhaps the school terms could be spent here and the summers there."

"You have given this some thought. I'm glad."

"I also discussed with Mr. Simpson the best financial arrangement to make sure you and Little Jim have everything you need."

"I'll have to keep at least one servant to help with him. And another for housekeeping and cooking. We'll also have to stay on at your residence in Half-Way Tree . . . and we'll need Daisy's carriage and coachman . . ."

Aston Simpson broke in gently, "The particulars of the arrangement can be worked out later. If you will be so kind as to write a list, at your earliest opportunity, of everything you anticipate needing, I will send a messenger for it. I will draft an agreement specifying an estimated allowance. If adjustments need to be made, Mr. Turner has given me the authority to make them."

"When did you want me to move back to your residence?"

"I'm hoping to go for a week or more to the north coast to get away from the Kingston heat. I'll make those arrangements as soon as you tell me when it'll be convenient for you to move back."

"I believe I can arrange to be there a week from today," she said. "I'll require help from Daisy's coachman."

Speaking now to Simpson, he asked, "Is that sufficient time to draft the agreement?"

"Specify a day next week," he replied, "and I will have the documents for signing."

Taken aback, Isabella asked, "So formal? Must we sign a document? We're family. I'm the child's grandmother. Surely he can be left in my care without legal proceedings."

"You are, of course, correct, Mrs. Phillpotts," said Simpson, "but in order to be absolutely certain you'll be able to make decisions in the child's interest, if needed, a document signed by Mr. Turner would surely expedite matters. You will not be required to sign anything. This is entirely for the protection of the child and you."

"I see."

"Shall we say Thursday at one o'clock?" proposed Turner. "At my residence in Half-Way Tree?"

"Will you make arrangements for me to be transported that morning?"

"Of course," said Turner. Then, turning to Simpson, "I assume that suits you."

"I will be there."

"That's settled then," said James with a tone of finality and satisfaction. "May I drop you home, Isabella?"

"Thank you, no. The distance is less than two kilometers, and I need to stretch my stiff knees."

"Very well. Till next week then . . . I hope you know you're welcome to visit with Little Jim any time before that. I would be pleased to have you picked up and returned home."

"That's kind of you. It'll be a busy week, but I may take you up on that."

James Turner's rented house was a medium-size two-story Victorian, old but clearly well maintained. The large yard circling the house was interrupted only by the semi-circular driveway leading past the entry.

When Isabella arrived in the mid-morning on Thursday, James came out and greeted her warmly. He instructed Nathaniel to store her several suitcases and boxes in the large guest room near the rear of the house on the second floor. James guided Isabella into the modestly furnished parlor near the front door. Both walked in stiffly and sat tentatively on a curved overstuffed sofa with their backs to the window.

"Again, Isabella, I'm most grateful for your willingness to take on this responsibility."

She yielded a slight smile but didn't respond.

James continued. "After you have had a chance to unpack and settle a bit, you may want to visit with Little Jim. I believe Bertha is with him in the nursery. Now that he's beginning to walk, I see he'll be a handful."

"As you say, I'll surely want to spend a little time with him."

"I have ordered a simple lunch to be served around noon. Does that suit you?"

"That would be fine."

"As you remember, Mr. Simpson is scheduled to arrive at one o'clock."

"I do recall."

"He tells me that he has completed the document we spoke about. I assume it'll suffice for our limited purposes. His visit should be brief."

Isabella nodded slightly but her face registered no emotion.

These limited responses led James to pull at his coat lapels nervously, bring his palms down on his knees, and say, "Well then. I suppose I'll see you at lunch . . . which could be on the veranda, if you wish."

"Whatever suits you," she said as she rose and stepped toward the door.

During lunch Isabella was again minimally responsive to James's attempt at conversation. Her only interest was in getting medical information about the child: "When was he last seen by a doctor? . . . Any problems? . . . Is he scheduled for any appointments? . . ."

As she rose and left the dining room, she said, "Please send for me when your lawyer arrives. I'll be in my room or the nursery."

The agreement described in the document produced by Aston Simpson was brief and straightforward. It noted that Mrs. Isabella Phillpotts, the grandmother of James Julius Turner, son of James Julius

Turner Senior, whenever the latter was off the island or otherwise unavailable, would have primary responsibility for the care, including medical care, of the child.

A general statement of financial responsibility for Little Jim's care was included with the initial estimate of twenty pounds per month, which was to cover maintenance, salaries of servants and coachman as well as an allowance for Mrs. Phillpotts.

James asked, "Isabella, does this meet your approval?"

"I have no reason to question what is here. It covers what we talked about."

Turner retrieved the copy she held, stepped to a nearby table, and signed the agreement in triplicate. Simpson signed as witness, and each of them took a copy.

"I'm most grateful to you, Isabella," said James Turner, sitting and leaning back into the sofa. "I don't know what I would have done without your willingness to take on this responsibility. I know your suffering is no less than mine, after our tragic loss. I'm sure you agree that we must both do whatever we can to protect the child." He said this last with what she heard as a mild challenge.

Her response held its own bitter edge. "My only reason for agreeing to this is to make Little Jim's early life less traumatic. I'm not doing this for you—or for myself."

Aston Simpson, detecting the slight asperity in the tone of the exchange, excused himself "on account of pressing business," shook the hands of both, bowed slightly, and showed himself out.

Isabella and James sat in tense silence for a brief interval. Their eyes met, and both looked as if expecting the other to speak.

Turner finally began. "Isabella, is there something you want to say to me? Is there something we need to discuss?"

"What do *you* think?"

"I'm not sure. I simply have a feeling you want me to know something but without telling me what it is . . . Do you blame me for Daisy's death?" His agitation grew between the last two sentences.

"Blame?" she asked. "No one can be blamed for a person deciding to take her own life. All I know is that, before Daisy met you, she was a happy and healthy young woman. Something happened to her after she left Jamaica with you. Maybe you know what it was. Maybe you don't."

"I was as puzzled as anyone by her change after Little Jim was born," he began defensively, then went limp. "But I *do* blame myself." He looked away, then down, and finally back toward her. Their eyes met. She tried to discern the feeling behind what he was saying.

"More than anyone, I hold myself responsible." He looked away again. "Daisy and I had planned to tell you everything eventually—after things had been put right."

"I guessed there was some secret the two of you were holding." She sat back into her chair. "Please go on."

James stood up, looked at her, turned away, paced for thirty seconds, and said, "First, I want to apologize. I can't offer any reasons for my actions other than my own shame and cowardice." He returned to his seat. Isabella stared at him.

"Isabella," he began hesitantly, "when we returned to Jamaica after our first trip together to the United States, we told you . . . we told everyone here . . . we had been married in the States." He stopped, covered his face with both hands, as if to erase the emotions that were making him hesitate. "We were *not* married . . . Although I wanted us to marry on that trip, I could not . . . I was already married at the time."

She dropped her head and looked into her lap.

"Isabella," he began again, this time more agitated, "we *never* married."

He looked at her expectantly, but her only reaction was a gentle rubbing together of her palms. When she finally lifted her head and looked at him, she felt only sadness. "I want to hear it all, James. Tell me how this could have happened. Why?"

He leaned forward in his seat and looked pleadingly at her. "Please don't hate me, Isabella. We wanted to do the right thing, but it's difficult to act sensibly when you're in love. And we *were* in love from the beginning, within days of when we first met at your shop. You have to know we loved each other. You do know that, don't you, Isabella?"

She looked at him coldly. "What I *know* is that you took my seventeen year old daughter from me and from her home," she began, now showing her anger. "What I *know* is that she was seventeen and you were over forty—closer to my age than hers. What I *know* is that you lived as if married for three years. What I *know* is that you never married her, and she had your one-year-old baby. That's what I *know*, James. Don't talk to me about love. Tell me why it had to be like that."

He looked away before he answered. "There is no worthy excuse. I loved her so. That spring I had to return to the States but didn't want to leave Daisy. I persuaded her to come with me, told her we could be married there, but I didn't tell her I was a married man until we were already at sea. I told her I would get a divorce as soon as possible and we would get married immediately after that. Well, when I took steps to secure the divorce, it wasn't as simple as I thought. My wife wouldn't agree to any reasonable terms, and it was clear that we were to endure years of delay. Daisy and I were disappointed, but I promised her we would marry as soon as the divorce was finalized. When she wrote to you from the States, she said we were merely engaged. I thought we should delay our return until after we married, but Daisy missed her family and begged to come back in the fall of that same year. When we decided to return to Jamaica, we agreed that living together unmarried wouldn't be acceptable. We decided, for the sake of you and the family, we would have to say we were married. Everyone seemed to accept what we said without asking for details."

He paced again. "Daisy was very happy after Little Jim came . . . at least at first. Then she became more and more worried about being unmarried with a baby. I tried to reassure her that things would work out, and we were indeed getting closer to finally resolving the divorce. Daisy was getting very anxious about the situation when we celebrated Little Jim's first birthday in March. She began to have crying spells at night; then she accused me of not trying hard enough to get the divorce. I knew something had changed. I'm sure you did too. That's when I asked you to stay with us for a time."

He paused and looked at her. "Am I right about that?"

She gave a slight nod.

He continued. "I told Daisy I needed to go to the States at the beginning of May and hoped that, on that trip, the divorce would be settled. I promised to let her know, and if it was going to happen, I would send for her to come, and we would get married as soon as she arrived. I expected her to be pleased, but she didn't seem to understand what I was saying. By the time I left for the States I was really concerned about her. She was looking sad, crying more, and unwilling to talk at all. Still, I had to go . . . '*had* to go' . . . Now, that sounds foolish."

He passed his right hand over his face as if trying to wipe away his shame. "I even wrote her two letters while I was on the trip. You heard them read at the hearing. I hoped to assure her things would be resolved soon. In the last letter I even said things were looking good for my court hearing and she should plan to join me around the time things would be settled—probably late June. Then I received the telegram about what had happened. You can't imagine what I suffered on the trip back, just thinking that she was gone—that I wouldn't see her alive again. I felt like throwing myself into the ocean. I couldn't help thinking I was to blame. If only I had never met her? . . . not taken her away from Jamaica? . . . not lied to her about being married? . . . Could I have done more to secure the divorce sooner? . . . Should I have stayed on the island until she could go to the States with me?"

He leaned forward and pleaded. "Isabella, please forgive me. I need to know you don't hate me. You and I are all Little Jim has. We need to do what we can to make him safe and happy. I hope you agree."

She looked up and away, then answered slowly and somberly, "I need some time to absorb it all . . . What you told me doesn't affect how I feel about the baby or what I'm willing to do on his behalf . . . As far as forgiveness? I think you have to find a way to forgive yourself. If you need my forgiveness, it can be secured only by how well you care for your son. Let's leave it at that for now, James."

"I won't let him or you down, Isabella."

They rose and faced each other, both resolutely. James moved closer and took Isabella's hands into his own and said, "Thank you, Isabella."

Isabella felt somewhat relieved at their parting. For her, James' response to the confrontation and his expressions of shame and remorse tempered her resentment. She could see that the exchange had given him the opportunity he clearly yearned for to unburden himself of the guilty secrets he had been carrying.

They never again shared their feelings so openly about what had happened. The conversation established a hidden contract neither wished to reopen. Life would go on. They would dedicate themselves to Little Jim, and they hoped he would survive the loss of his mother and never know how she died.

On the three-and-a half-hour bus journey to Port Antonio, a resort town on the north coast, Daisy's death and the confrontation with her mother weighed heavily on James Turner's mind. Yet, he had *not* told

Isabella everything. How could he? He could hardly acknowledge it to himself. But then he remembered what he would have preferred to repress.

He found Daisy resting in the shade of a tree in the garden of Happy Retreat, where their son had been born and where she would rest for at least a week. As he approached, she greeted him with a broad smile, then put an index finger to her puckered lips to signal that the baby was asleep nearby. When he reached her, he bent over and kissed her forehead, then her lips. "I love you, Daisy." She responded with another smile and said, "I'm bursting with love and happiness. I have you and I have our son."

"How is Little Jim and the little mother this afternoon? You look comfortable. He's sleeping. The weather is delightful. What more could we want?"

"You know what I want, James." No response. Daisy closed her eyes and leaned back into the settee.

James did know what she wanted: to be married. A wave of anxiety passed through him as he remembered the year and half of wrangling about the divorce and the increasing pressure that Daisy put on him. He managed to calm himself and sat motionless admiring her beauty and serenity. If only this moment could go on forever, he thought.

Like Daisy's playful prodding about getting married, James sometimes enjoyed teasing her about their differences. Daisy usually accepted this in a light spirit of play. Her petite body, her long chestnut hair, her youth, even her "outrageous beauty" were all fair game. He usually knew when he had gone too far; she bristled and stared at him; he would make light of it, and assure her that he was only having a "little fun." On this occasion, his teasing and her response were different.

After a period of silence, James approached the bassinette to see the sleeping baby. He stood there for several minutes. Daisy, who had been dozing, opened her eyes and asked, "Having a little paternal visit? Is he still sleeping? He'll be due for nursing soon. He'll wake up when it's time." She let her head go back onto a pillow and closed her eyes again.

"Daisy, you are very fair and sometimes you're taken for white, but I'm dark. Don't you think it's odd that Little James is so white. Any stranger who saw him would say this is a white child. How is it we produced a white baby? Are you sure there wasn't some mix-up?"

Because he had meant to make a teasing joke, he expected her to be amused. He smiled and chuckled as he turned to see Daisy's reaction.

Daisy was sitting up straight, her eyes wide, her face crimson. She stared at him, anger and disbelief creating a face he had never seen. At first, she was speechless, but then she said with a gasp, "What are you talking about? . . . Is that supposed to be funny, James? That isn't something to make jokes about! Little Jim is our baby . . . our beautiful baby . . . You know he's our child! We've been saying for days how much he looks like us. He's got your hair and nose, my mouth and coloring. James, please never joke about something like that!"

James recovered from his shock and moved quickly to her. He knelt on one knee and held her hands. "Daisy. Daisy, please. I'm sorry. You have to know I was just teasing. Please forgive me, Daisy. I won't joke like that ever again. Of course he's our baby. It was foolish and thoughtless and . . ."

"Yes, very foolish." She freed her hands, stood, and moved to the bassinette. "The baby is still sleeping, but it's time for nursing. I'll ask one of the sisters to bring him to my room." As she turned and walked toward the house, he said, "Daisy, can we talk about it? I feel terrible. Please forgive me."

"Not now, James. Perhaps tomorrow."

James winced at the memory, and was left to wonder why he had been so insensitive—perhaps even cruel.

They didn't speak about the incident the next day. They never again spoke of it. For his part, James was afraid to bring up the matter and hoped Daisy's silence signified her willingness to forgive him.

But he also remembered how upset Daisy became when one of her aunts from the country near Mandeville came to see the baby three months later and expressed amazement at his light complexion. "Lawd, Lawd," she said. "De baby dem lyta dan de parents. In Jamaica so much mixin' no tellin' wha dey gittin'." Because the woman said this with a chuckle, a broad smile and infant-appropriate cooing, James's interpretation was that she thought she was giving a compliment. Daisy, red faced but otherwise composed, picked up the child and left the room saying, "He needs to be changed and nursed. Thank you for coming by." She didn't reappear until her aunt had left. This behavior worried James, but he was afraid to raise the matter with Daisy, and she returned to her usual demeanor and positive attitude the next day.

James wondered whether these two episodes might relate to Daisy's increasing unhappiness about not being married. Why would a tease about color cause her to react so angrily? He thought the emphasis Jamaicans put on skin shade as an indication of social standing was probably behind it somehow. Even before Little Jim was born, he had several times been present when her family spoke casually about color and assigned each other and acquaintances to categories. They all agreed that Daisy was the only one whose coloring, hair, and features made her sometimes taken for white. Once, when this came up at a family gathering, Daisy expressed displeasure with such a distinction, and looked at James for support. He didn't know what response she wanted, but he smiled and gave a wink. When they later discussed her uneasiness, she simply said, "I don't like that kind of talk." James also wondered whether his own dark complexion played some role in her feelings, although Daisy had insisted it did not.

On the long journey James also began to worry about his son's future. *I'm forty-six and in poor health,* he thought. *What will happen to Little Jim, if I die? The doctors keep carrying on as if I might be dead before my next visit. Doctors! Like everyone else, always worried about losing fee-paying customers.* A slight smile accompanied this last. Still, he knew he had to be concerned about his health and his son's future.

The resort where James stayed for the week overlooked SanSan Bay, just east of the town. For the first two days he did little more than rest, have his meals, walk the well tended grounds, and admire the flora. On the morning of the third day he decided to see the town. On one of the main streets he found an establishment with a prominent but simply lettered sign:

The Art Jewellery and Curio Shop.

S. J. Bonitto, Watchmaker and Jeweller,

No. 3 West Street,

Post Cards, Views & Jippi Jappa Hats

As he entered, he greeted the clerk, who was busy arranging pieces in a glass display case and gave a minimal acknowledgement to James's entrance. James perused the various displayed items—knick-knacks mostly, some with JAMAICA or PORT ANTONIO painted or embroidered in bright colors. After inspecting several cases of jewelry, he stopped at a shelf display of porcelain and wood figures of children in various attitudes of play. Without realizing it he became transfixed, staring at the objects for several minutes. He wondered whether his son would get to enjoy such play. He regained his focus on the objects only when the clerk offered assistance. Startled, he tried to cover his embarrassment with a simple enquiry. "Are these objects made by local artisans?"

"The wood carvings were done locally," said the clerk. "We buy the porcelain items from a supplier in Kingston. They come from all over the world."

James continued inspecting them while the clerk stood nearby. Then he noticed that the shop also had an area in the rear with a desk and two chairs. He asked, "Would it be possible for me to use the desk in the rear to write out some cards and a letter?"

"That's the purpose of the desk," the clerk said. "As you can see we have a large collection of cards with pictures of local and other island sites. There's a pen and inkwell available at the desk. You'll find there some sheets of our own stationary, if you wish to use them." James chose a few cards picturing local sites. When he sat at the desk, however, he immediately reached for the stationary. He reflected for a moment before he took up the pen and wrote.

June, 1909

My dear darling little son,

I leave this letter to tell you me and your loving mother loved you so much That God took her away from you and me.

I will live long as I can for your sake to look after you. Your grandmother is your best Friend. Be kind to her for my sake. See that she wants for nothing while you live.

Mr. Aston Simpson will look after your business until you become 21 years old. Then he will give you everything I leave for you. Wear my rings as I did in life. Be honest for God sake. Never gamble for money. Studie for to be a doctor, James Julius Turner.

Your father and mother loved you better than they did their own selves. Your mother's name was Daisy Maud Turner. I called your mother Doll because she was so pretty.

God will bless you for my sake.

Your loving father,
James Julius Turner

He placed the letter into an envelope but didn't seal it. He wouldn't take it out again until he was on his death-bed thirteen years later.

CHAPTER 11:

Jamaica Farewell

In late July of 1909 the elder James Turner returned to New York City, and his divorce was settled in mid-August. Although the memory of Daisy stayed with him over the thirteen years he survived her, he married another Jamaican woman, Annie, the following January. When they left for the States in the spring of 1910—for James's health and business—Annie was pregnant and gave birth to their first child, Merle, in September while visiting Chicago. Isabella Phillpotts, Daisy's mother, had agreed to care for Little Jim while James and his new wife were in the States. When they returned to Jamaica the following October, Annie insisted that she wasn't up to taking care of Little Jim—who came to be known as Jimmy—as well as her infant and persuaded James to ask Isabella to continue Jimmy's care. Isabella agreed to do so until the following April, when Merle would be seven months and Jimmy would be three years old. But James and Annie had two additional children—a son, Roy, and a daughter, Fern—within the following two years, and Annie never developed any maternal attachment to Jimmy. Throughout his preschool years, she took every opportunity to turn Jimmy over to Isabella, who was always willing to take him.

James knew he would have to find a way to earn a living in Jamaica. His investments and properties in the States weren't enough to support both an acceptable living standard in Jamaica and annual trips to the States, even though he usually took those alone. He had considerable success in buying and reselling Jamaican real estate, but money lending became his primary business. He gained a reputation for integrity, fairness, and good judgment, and his business flourished. Soon he needed an assistant to help with record keeping and collections, and he hired Sarah, the thirty-year-old relative of a Jewish business associate.

Within the year James began an affair with Sarah, who bore him a daughter, whom she named Fae. This added to the complexity of his already complicated life: he had an ex-wife in the States; a son, Jimmy, by his deceased wife, Daisy; a current wife, Annie, who bore him three additional children; and now Sarah and Fae.

Daisy's child, his son Jimmy, was a living reminder of his loss. James developed a particular closeness to Jimmy. His special fondness for Jimmy was subtly manifested, but at times it became a source of considerable tension in the family. After the spring school term of 1919, James took the eleven year old Jimmy with him to the States for the summer. He pointed out that Jimmy was the eldest and should have the first opportunity for such a trip, but Annie and her children still resented this show of favoritism. When James and Jimmy returned in the fall, Merle became still more jealous when Jimmy boasted of their visit to the Indian reservation in Indiana where James had been born. He made things worse by sporting an elegant feathered headdress, which he claimed made him a member of the Miami Indian tribe—an honor that did *not* extend to his half siblings. Merle never quite forgave Jimmy for this blow to her pride. Neither did Annie, who suspected that James favored Jimmy because he was so much lighter than her own children.

The elder James Turner's health gradually worsened over the thirteen years following Daisy's death, despite his continuing the routine of returning to the United States for the hottest Jamaican months. In March of 1922, however, an unseasonable heat wave enveloped the island, and James, who couldn't leave because of business, soon suffered from it. The family doctor diagnosed his condition as acute bronchitis, but a more serious problem was that the bronchitis and the heat exacerbated his chronic heart condition. His hacking cough, frequent asthmatic attacks, and ebbing strength worried all who saw him.

On March 10th Jimmy, who would soon turn fourteen, headed home from Kingston College Preparatory School to "Everton" at 6 Eureka Road, feeling apprehensive. The school term was half over and he was doing well, but he doubted his grades would satisfy his father, who had always insisted upon his achieving First Honors. But what weighed on his mind most were the many problems at home. His father had been ill and bedridden for a full week and showed no improvement. His stepmother remained distant and critical. His annoying step-sisters and step-brother frequently complained to her about his impatience with them.

As soon as he got home, he headed upstairs and found his father sitting up in his four-poster double bed and laboring for breath. He gestured for his son to come closer. Jimmy, unsure how to respond, grabbed a fan from the bedside table and began to wave it back and forth before his father's anguished face.

"Should I call the doctor?" Jimmy asked. "What should I do?" There was no response. He grew panicked as he fanned for several minutes with no sign of improvement in his father, so finally he turned and ran through the house screaming for help. No one answered, so he returned to his father's bedside and found, to his great relief, that his father's crisis had somewhat abated. His breathing was less labored and he had lain back, apparently more relaxed.

"What can I do, Daddy?" the boy asked again.

When his father pointed toward a pitcher on the side table, he quickly filled the nearby glass. With difficulty his father moved the glass toward his lips, but Jimmy saw that he needed assistance, so he held and tilted the glass. James swallowed a small amount of water and relaxed back onto his stack of pillows.

He finally said, "I think I'm all right now." After a few minutes, he looked directly at his son but paused to gather his strength. "Jimmy, I need to talk to you about something."

Jimmy replaced the glass and moved closer. "Yes, Daddy?"

"I worry about you, my boy. I'm afraid I won't be around much longer, so you must listen to me carefully."

James saw his son tense up but kept looking at him intently as he said, "What concerns me most is that you continue having trouble getting along with your mother."

"She's mean to me," Jimmy said quickly. After a brief hesitation, "Anyway, she's not my mother. My mother died."

James began again to struggle for breath. For him even to speak in a whisper required obvious effort. "Of course, but your mother isn't here. When I'm gone, your stepmother will be the one in charge of you. She's the only one who will be able to take care of your needs and see to your education. You will have to depend on her and get along with her. I know it may be difficult at times, but you have to try, son. I won't be around to help you. Please, son, do it for my sake. I need to know you'll be all right."

"Yes, Daddy," the son said without enthusiasm. "I'll try." Then he began to whimper and asked, "Why are you going to leave me, Daddy? You'll get well soon. Please don't leave me, Daddy."

James withdrew into the pillows. He closed his eyes, and tears began to roll down his cheeks.

Jimmy stood quietly by the bed for several minutes. When James opened his eyes, he looked at his son standing and made a weak gesture with his arm. "Open the top drawer of the night table and take out what's there."

Jimmy found there a single item: an unsealed envelope with his name "James Julius Turner Esquire." His father waived him closer and said, "I wrote this for you soon after your mother died—thirteen years ago in May. I want you to have it now, so you can know something about your dear mother and how I felt when she died. Read it now, son."

As soon as the youngster unfolded the letter, he noted the letter-head: *Jewellery and Curio Shop, Port Antonio*; then his attention was drawn to the date: June 1909. He read aloud but had to stop for a moment, fighting back tears, at "God took her from me and you." As Jimmy read the concluding "God will bless you for my sake" tears did well up, but he quickly wiped them away and returned the letter to the envelope. He moved to put it back in the drawer, but his father said, his voice a little clearer, "It's for you to keep, son, so you'll remember me and what your dear mother meant to me."

"Now," he continued, "I think it's time for you to call Dr. Robertson. The number is on the wall next to the telephone in the kitchen. Tell him to come soon."

Jimmy turned and ran downstairs and through the house, hoping his stepmother had come in with the other children, but she had not; getting help for his father was all up to him. The operator responded quickly to his urgent tone, and Dr. Robertson, their family doctor for as long as Jimmy could remember, promised to arrive within the hour.

"You have to come now, doctor," Jimmy yelled into the telephone box. "I think my father will die if you don't come right away."

"I will be there as soon as I can," the doctor responded. "Just keep him as comfortable as you can."

The youngster paced anxiously in the kitchen for a few minutes, afraid to go upstairs again. But the doctor had told him to make his father as comfortable as possible. He didn't know what he could do, but he went upstairs anyway. He kept his focus on his father's face as he quietly approached the bed. His father lay very still with his eyes closed, as if he had fallen into a restful sleep. Hoping that was so, Jimmy picked up the fan again and slowly passed it back and forth near his father's face. No response. He continued fanning for several minutes, then said softly, "Daddy, I called the doctor . . . he said he would come as soon as possible." There was no response, and Jimmy was afraid to say or do anything more. Fanning and staring at his father's face, he hoped for signs of movement or breathing. Finally, he stopped, put the fan down, and continued to stare for another minute. Then, very gently, he put a hand on his father's shoulder and gave a nudge. No response. He nudged again, this time a bit more firmly. Still, no response. Jimmy backed away from the bed slowly but kept his eyes on his father's motionless face. When he finally backed into a chair on the other side of the room, he stood staring.

Jimmy remained standing by the chair, immobile and unblinking, until the front door opened and closed. He went out and peered over the banister. Dr. Robertson had let himself in and was already coming up the stairs. When their eyes met, neither spoke. Jimmy followed the doctor back into his father's room. He stood next to the chair and kept his eyes on his father. The doctor approached the bed, placed his bag on the side table, and began to touch his patient—felt his hand, his forehead, his neck. He opened the bag and removed a stethoscope, then leaned over and slowly moved it across his chest. Finally he straightened up and very deliberately replaced the instrument before turning toward the youngster, who stood frozen-faced.

"I'm sorry, Jimmy. Your father is gone."

Jimmy slowly sat in the chair. He looked at the doctor, then at his father's face, and then back to the doctor. "What am I to do?" he murmured. Tears welled up and began rivulets down his face.

"Where is your mother?" the doctor inquired as he removed his suit coat.

"I don't know," said Jimmy.

When Jimmy asked to be excused from the dinner table, his stepmother, Annie, told him to meet her in the parlor after dinner. "I have something important to discuss with you," she said. Jimmy guessed that this meant trouble, but he arrived at the parlor door twenty minutes later.

He was tense as he walked into the spacious, over-furnished and dimly lit room. He tried to look as casual as he could, but when his stepmother stared at him and directed him to sit on the sofa facing her arm chair, he had difficulty maintaining eye contact.

Sitting back into her well padded chair, Annie began. "You seem to have no appreciation of our situation, Jimmy. Your father died a year ago, and since then you have never ceased walking around this house with a long face and surly manner. You have been barely civil to me and mean to your sisters and brother. I would say it's time for you to get over mourning and move on, young man. Don't you agree?"

Throughout this brief speech Jimmy stared at his hands. When she finished, he looked up and met her intense stare. He was anxious but determined not to show how scared he was. His response was more conciliatory than he wished. "I suppose."

"Well, if we can agree on that point at least, what I have to say may be somewhat easier." She hesitated. He looked down again. Pulling her body up and forward in the arm chair facing him, she continued. "I have a decision to make, Jimmy. It's the biggest decision I have had to make in a long time. It involves you and your future."

Jimmy felt his face warm and his body stiffen. *What now?* he thought.

She seemed to notice his reaction but went on. "Since your father was taken from us," she began again, looking at him sternly, "I have had to struggle alone to keep this family in this house, fed, and everything else. Believe me, it has been difficult. You children don't know what it takes to hold this family together without your father. You, in particular, are the oldest and should have enough sense to see how much I have to carry. But do you try to help me, support me, make my struggles easier? The answer is no. You act like you can go on sulking and keeping to yourself—as if everybody should feel sorry for you. Well, you're not the only one who misses your father. Have you considered my feelings and my situation? Four children and no husband, no regular income except the little coming from your father's real estate investments and money lending business. Believe me, I struggle to make it stretch. Just one example: Have you ever stopped to wonder how your school fees are being paid? Well I have had to squeeze them out of the little we have, and it hasn't been easy. Think about it: school fees for four children. How long do you think I can keep that up?" She stopped but he could feel her continuing to stare at his now bent head. "How long?" she insisted.

Jimmy didn't look up but said quietly: "I don't know."

"You don't know," she said with a tone of annoyance. "And you don't care either. Well, I care, and as I see things, it can't go on any longer. One way or the other things have to change. First of all, whatever happens, I refuse to pay for your school fees any longer. You are fifteen now. You're not my child, and your father didn't leave enough money for me to support you all your life. It's time you start thinking about how you'll survive in this world. I can't take responsibility for what happens to you."

Jimmy looked up with sudden real alarm: "What am I to do? If I don't finish school, I'll never get a good job. How can I live?"

"I'm not saying I'm just putting you out, Jimmy," she responded, "but it's clear you're unhappy here. You never speak to me unless I specifically ask about school or household matters. You're unhappy, and I'm unhappy, and I don't see why I should have to put up with it. As I see it, there are two options. You could find some kind of employment and remain here—assuming you can pay for your own maintenance. The only other possibility I can come up is for you to move to the United States, where you can find work or get training in some career or trade. Your father had business associates in New York City and Chicago. I could write them to see what might be possible. Maybe you could be taken on in some real estate company—as an apprentice or some such. Who knows? You might make a success in real estate like your father. How does that sound?"

Jimmy listened to these proposals with his head down, his head reeling. He knew his stepmother was unhappy with him, and even thought she might have reason to be, but this was far more drastic than anything he could have imagined. Now, looking up with tears in his eyes, he responded: "I don't know. I don't know what to say. If I went to the America, where would I live? I don't know anyone there. I would be alone."

"Not to worry," she said dismissively. "Some kind of arrangement could be made, I'm sure." She hesitated, then said, "The more I think about it, the more sensible the emigration idea sounds. Being in a new place could help you get over your sadness from losing your father. I could make our limited funds stretch further without the burden of your school fees and your maintenance here. Yes. I think I'll start to make inquiries. I'll begin by writing to some people in New York City I met when your father and I visited. They live in Harlem—mostly a colored section. Maybe you could stay with them, at least until you made more permanent arrangements. They are nice people. I think you would get along well with them." Stopping and focusing on him again, she asked, "What do you think?"

"I don't know," he said yet again, pinching the tears from his eyes and trying to grasp the enormity of what she had said.

"Neither do I," she said sharply, "but I'm going to start writing letters today."

Jimmy was filled with dread of the unknown—away from Jamaica, his family, and his friends; in a strange place, a huge, crowded city; knowing no one.

"When would I go?" he finally managed to ask.

"That depends on what I find out," she responded. "It would have to be after the school term, but certainly before the fall. If things work out, I would think you could leave by the end of August."

Looking down, he felt like screaming but instead asked quietly, "Do I have to go?"

He had offered no real resistance, but she didn't answer even this timid question, and he knew she would be determined not to give in to arguments anyway. Finally Annie said simply, "I think this is for the best." She paused and then went on with what seemed to be a new thought. "But you shouldn't think of this in terms of 'have to.' Think of it as a grand adventure, an opportunity to learn about the world off this island, a chance to make your fortune. I dare say you'll probably end up helping us out before too long. Your father was a good businessman.

I'm sure you'll be just like him. Don't fret about it now. We'll have plenty of time to talk about it and consider all your options."

His head still bent, Jimmy rose from the sofa and left the room without saying anything more. In his room he buried his face in a pillow to muffle the sobs, which went on until the room darkened. He changed into his night clothes but had difficulty falling asleep. The image of leaving Jamaica was a frightening one. The nagging questions went on for an hour: What job could he possibly get at the age of fifteen, not having finished high school, in a big city? Would people like him? Be kind to him? How could he survive? Would he ever return to Jamaica?

When Jimmy finally fell asleep, he dreamt first of being alone in a dark place, searching for his father, who appeared but only at a distance, and voiceless. He begged his father to return to help him, but his father's only response was his sad expression. Next he dreamt he was surrounded by large people who walked past him in all directions, but seemed not to notice him. He tried to grab their legs and called out for help, desperate for any response. As he struggled, he realized he was sinking into the ground; it appeared to be as hard as stone, but he sank into it and felt the helplessness of drowning. Finally, he was actually under water, yet floating. Above, there was a stream of light, but he couldn't move toward it, and he felt content to float. It was as if the water held him in a warm caress. It was strange that he had no trouble breathing, but he felt happy and safe, opening and closing his eyes slowly.

When Jimmy woke in the early morning, he was in the fetal position. He opened his eyes but lay quietly on his side looking at a sunny dawn and remembering the dream images in the same sequence as they had appeared. He hadn't forgotten what his stepmother told him, but he was surprised that he felt better than he had when he went to sleep. *Strange*, he thought. *I know I'm facing an unknown and frightening future. But maybe it's for the best. If I'm an orphan, so be it; I'll have to make my way alone.* Acceptance of his situation, his change in attitude made him feel somehow liberated. Still, he was sure that what was happening wasn't fair, that this was *not* what his father would have wanted. He fell back into the sadness that always arose when he thought of his missing father. It was only a momentary reversal, however; he caught himself and resolved to let go of any self pity and go on with making his life.

Jimmy felt tense and hesitated at the door of the parlor, where he was to join his stepmother after dinner. Her request at the end of a silent meal had come as a surprise. Many weeks had passed since they had first spoken of his planned emigration. Back then he had nearly resigned himself to the inevitable and simply tried to suppress the thought of it. But now, sure that this meeting would have something to do with those plans, he found that the prospect of further developments brought back the anxiety and sadness that had come from being confronted with the plan the first time. He tried to fight those feelings.

"You may enter," came the answer to his quiet knock. Sitting in her usual easy chair by a window, Annie beckoned Jimmy to sit on the sofa facing her. As usual he was intimidated but now he tried to hide it by keeping his head up and his eyes on hers.

"Good news, Jimmy," she began, with a self satisfied smile as she held up an unfolded letter and envelope. "This letter is from one of your father's old friends in New York. He says here that he and his wife would be pleased to have you stay with them for as long as you need to. He also has a real estate business in Harlem and thinks he could use you as an office boy. He's willing to consider your work payment for your room and board—with maybe even a little extra for spending money. This sounds like just what you need—room and board and employment until you're older and can find something more suitable. Isn't this good news?"

"What does it mean to be an office boy?" inquired Jimmy. "What would I have to do?"

"Gracious! I don't know. I suppose it means you would be asked to do anything around the office that needed to be done to help the office people do their jobs. You used to help your father sometimes with his business. What kind of things did you do for him? Organize papers? Stuff envelopes? Go to the Post Office? Make other deliveries? I don't know. It would certainly be things you would be capable of doing."

"Could I possibly go to school too?" he asked.

She was startled. In a stern voice she said, "You don't seem to understand your situation, Jimmy. You should consider yourself as having all the education you are likely to get. You have to earn a living.

You can't do that and go to school too. I think you should consider yourself very lucky indeed that we got this positive response from America."

"If I can't go to school," he pursued, "why can't I stay *here* and work for room and board?"

Her eyes narrowed and she stared at him with apparent annoyance. "I had hoped to avoid this kind of discussion to spare your feelings, but you are determined to push me to be more candid than I wished. Well then . . . First of all, as you are so often inclined to assert, I'm not your mother. As testament to that, you have never given me the respect a mother should be able to expect from a child. Since you have been unwilling to give me that respect, I don't see why I should bear responsibility for you—or give you the care and affection a child would expect from a parent. Secondly, we're both unhappy living under the same roof. Again, I see no reason I should have to endure a stressful situation. On the other hand, as long as you are on the island and still a minor, I carry legal responsibility for you. It would certainly be unseemly for you to be here on the island but not living in the house your father left for us. Finally, I sincerely believe you will be happier and also find many more opportunities in the United States than you could hope to find here. Working in an office might just be the beginning of a business career."

Throughout this speech their eyes were locked, but Jimmy finally broke in, "There are business offices in Jamaica."

"This is just the kind of response I'm talking about," she snapped. "No respect . . . always questioning . . . always wanting to argue . . . If you want to do things your way, young man, you might as well be on your own. I have had enough of you. And, I dare say, you seem to take no pleasure in my company. What is the point?"

"The point is," he responded slowly and calmly, "you are telling me I must give up my education, I must leave the only people and home I have ever known, I must go to a strange country where I'll know no one, and I must fend for myself from now on. You don't think I should question all that?"

Annie looked away. Jimmy looked away. Both remained silent for several minutes. Then, continuing to look away and taking a deep breath, Jimmy said, "Maybe I *would* be better off away from here. I haven't been happy since my father died."

Annie looked at him closely, as if trying to discern the spirit in which he was taking this new position. If she saw beyond his grim resignation, she didn't show it and seemed content with his grudging acceptance. Resignation was better than resistance, she must have thought, and she no doubt hoped this would be the last word on the matter.

"When will I be leaving?" he asked.

"The letter says they would be able to have you come any time after the end of June. They need to make some preparations. I can probably secure passage for you any time. There are ships going to New York City at least twice a week. You need not feel rushed, but there's no reason for delay, as far as I'm concerned. You would probably like some time to say your farewells to everyone—family, friends."

He rose and, as he went to the door, said, "Yes I would," then slammed it.

When Jimmy entered Grandmother Phillpotts's bedroom, she was resting but not sleeping. Her delight in seeing him was clear from the brightening of her eyes and the gentle smile she offered as he approached the bed, but she didn't otherwise stir.

"How are you, Grandma?" he said quietly. He moved a wicker chair close to the head of the bed.

She slid her left hand toward the edge of the bed, and he took it in both of his. "Not very well today, I'm sorry to say."

"What's the matter, Grandma?"

"Doctor tells me it's another flare-up of rheumatism. It feels to me like my whole body is being stretched on a rack. The medicine he gave me helps for a while, but then I can barely get out of bed or get around the house. He told me to rest but to move around whenever I can. Right now, that's not very often."

"I'm sorry you're not feeling well. Is there anything I can do for you?"

"No, no," she answered quickly. "Just seeing you is a blessing. I haven't seen many people lately—just your uncle Laurence and my helper Judith, who comes in for a few hours at a time. I appreciate your company—at least for a little while."

With considerable difficulty and obvious pain, she slowly pulled herself up so that her back was on her pillows and her head more upright. "I *am* a little thirsty," she said finally. "You could get me some water in the cup on the table."

Jimmy retrieved the cup and filled it from the pitcher nearby, then put a gentle hand behind her head and helped her take several sips. "Thank you, darlin'," she said and relaxed back into the pillows. The effort going into these simple movements seemed to tire her, and she closed her eyes.

Jimmy sat for half an hour simply being with her. A cloud of sadness enveloped him when his thoughts turned to his imminent departure from the island, and he feared he wouldn't see her again. He was also anxious about what he was about to ask, but he felt desperate. He held her hand again, and she opened her eyes.

"Grandma," he began, "you know I'm supposed to leave for the United States. It turns out I go next week . . . I wish there were a way I could stay in Jamaica. I don't really want to go. I feel like I have no choice."

"So soon? Seems like things have been moving so fast." Orienting her body ever so slightly to make sure of eye contact, she said, "I too wish you didn't have to go."

He hesitated but then stiffened with resolve, and asked, "Grandma, is there anything you can do to help me stay?"

She looked at him and her face fell. "I didn't tell you this before, but I already spoke with Mrs. Turner about the plans for you. I offered to take you in with me—even though I can barely take care of myself and don't have money for your school fees either."

Jimmy became animated at hearing of this intercession. "I could work, Grandma. I could help out . . . take care of you when you're sick."

"Hold on, Jimmy," she said, now trying to head off any unrealistic expectations. "It's not up to me. I offered, but that's all I can do. Your stepmother said she couldn't approve such a plan. She thinks it would be best for your future to be in the United States, and this is your chance. Lots of opportunities, she says. I told her I thought you were too young to be going off to a strange place by yourself. She disagreed; she thought it could be just the thing for a smart youngster like you. She is determined to have her way. I have no legal right to do anything about this. Even if there was a way to fight it, I don't have the funds it would take to hire a lawyer. I wish I did. I surely do."

Jimmy looked away, then down, and said, "I understand, Grandma. I just thought I would at least ask. I know you would help me, if you could. Please don't worry yourself about this anymore. I'm sure I'll be fine."

They were silent for a few minutes, he looking at their hands, she looking at him with a face full of sadness.

"I will miss you, my boy," she finally said. "I have faced a great deal of loss in my long life, but you have lost even more in your short one. Losing your mother when you were still an infant; losing your father last year really made you an orphan; now losing everyone and everything you grew up with . . . and your country. It's all too sad." After a brief hesitation she went on. "Still, you have to make the best of it. And I know you will—with God's help. Just work hard and take care of your health. God will take care of the rest."

"Yes, Grandma. I'll do my best . . . And I'll miss you too . . . and I'll come back to see you some day—as soon as I can. I know I will." Even as he said this last, he wondered whether he would ever be able to return. He stood by the bed quietly for several minutes while she dozed.

"More water, Grandma?" he asked finally.

She shook her head and said, "But give grandmother a kiss before you go. I doubt very much I'll be up to seeing you off."

Standing by the bed and continuing to hold her hand, he bent over, and, as she had often done to him, kissed her first on her forehead, then on both cheeks, and finally lightly on her lips. He had never known what this meant to her, but he wanted her to know she had given him something of herself that he would hold in his heart, because he feared he would never see her again.

Straightening and gently placing her hand on the blanket, he said: "I'll come back some day, Grandma. I promise."

"I will pray for the day," she said, "and I'll pray for you. Please write to me when you can . . . I love you, grandson." She closed her eyes when she couldn't blink back the hanging tears.

"Goodbye, Grandma," he said as he moved toward the door. "I love you."

Sarah's daughter Fae was now twelve years old. Over the years, James had taken Jimmy along on some visits to see Fae and Sarah, and

Jimmy preferred the company of Sarah and Fae to that of Annie and his other three half-siblings. Sarah had always been kind to him. When they were young, he and Fae played easily together, and by the time their father died, they had developed a warm friendship. Jimmy treated her as an equal, even though she was three years younger. Sometimes he even complained to her about the problems he faced at home with both his stepmother and the other children. For her part, Fae had made it clear she adored her father and looked up to her big brother. She acted as though she considered them her only real family other than her mother; she said her mother's family were less welcoming when they went to visit them from time to time. They weren't wealthy but, like most Jamaican Jews, solidly middle class or better—some professionals but mostly small businessmen and shop owners. For some of them, the unmarried Sarah and her child were an embarrassment. Jimmy wasn't sure how much of this Fae understood, but his father had dropped enough hints for him to figure it out—more or less.

Three days before his departure, Jimmy went to say goodbye to Sarah and Fae. At first the sadness of the occasion dominated their exchanges, but Jimmy tried to put a positive face on his departure.

"When I have made my fortune in America," he boasted, "I'll send for both of you to come and live with me. Who knows? I might be able to buy you your own house."

"Ga'n wi choo," said Sarah. Then to Fae standing near: "Dem bwoy hay no ha'penny kin roob but tawk'n bout dim houses! Wha fe do?"

Jimmy and Fae had to laugh at her island patois, her playful response to Jimmy's rash yet solemn promise. They all stood close in the kitchen sharing this bittersweet moment, and Sarah threw an arm over each child, pulling them together in a close embrace. Jimmy knew she felt as much as he did the sadness of this farewell, but he saw that she too wanted to avoid having it spoiled with too many tears. She released them and shooed them over to the table, where she laid out biscuits and cups of fruit juice, then sat facing Jimmy.

"So, what's the plan for you in the States?" she began. "I do hope it's something you can advance in. Will you be able to go to school?"

"I'll be staying with some people my father knew in New York City. They think I might work out as an office boy in their real estate business. I'll stay there until I'm old enough to get a real job. But school? That's not part of the plan. My stepmother thinks I should forget about more education. I need to make a living."

"I imagine your father would have had different plans for you, if he had lived," Sarah began. "I know he wanted you to get as much education as possible. He had great hopes for you—even thought you might become a doctor or some other professional. Your father, you know, never had much of a chance for education himself. He never went to high school. But he worked hard and made a success in everything he did. That could happen to you too."

After a brief pause, Sarah went on. "Did he tell you children about when he left home?"

She directed the question primarily at Jimmy, whose face had grown serious. "Not much. He said he was born and grew up on an Indian reservation in Indiana. When I was eleven, he took me with him to the United States. We visited lots of people there, but I never understood who they were or how I was related to them. Seemed like he never wanted to go into the details of his life."

"Well, first of all," she began, "your father's mother was an Indian. She had him just about at the end of the Civil War in America. I forget the name of her tribe—it sounded something like Miami. He never knew his real father, but the man he lived with most of his early life was also an Indian. His mother and stepfather had more children. I don't remember how many. Until he was older he always believed this was his real father, but gradually he realized the truth—from what he heard his parents say to each other and because he didn't look much like the other children or his stepfather.

Sarah looked at Jimmy, whose attention was so riveted on her words that it made her lose her train of thought.

"Anyway," she continued following a long pause, "after he turned around fourteen, he started to have more and more conflicts with his parents—the usual teenage problems, according to him. One thing led to another, and finally he had enough. As soon as he told them he was leaving, his stepfather said 'good riddance 'cause you're not my child anyway'."

Jimmy stared at her. "He told you that?" he asked insistently. "Are you sure that's what he told you?"

"Yes—at least close to it," she answered. "Why? Does it mean something to you?"

Jimmy looked away and grimaced. "That's something like what my stepmother said to me when she told me her plans for me—I'm not her child. It's true, but it still hurt to hear it said *that* way." As he said this, for the first time, he recognized the ambivalence he felt toward his stepmother. He had not only resented her because she replaced his own mother, but he had also yearned to be cared for and nurtured by her. Her distancing and coolness had caused him to reject her, which led her to be more distant and cold. Theirs was a terrible dance of mutual disappointments and growing resentments. The thought added a layer of guilt to his sadness.

Sarah interrupted his thoughts. "I'm sorry this is happening to you, Jimmy, I wish there was some way I could help."

"Don't worry. I'll be all right."

"I know you will," she said. "I know you will."

"Did he tell you anything more about his early life?" he asked.

"There's not much more I can tell you. Your father didn't often talk to me about his life in America either—I'd say he was on the secretive side. He did say that, from the time he left home, he worked in all types of jobs—farms, construction, any work he could get. Finally, he worked for a grain company in Chicago for a while and saved enough money to start his own business—something like middle man in the grain business. He had some ups and downs, but mostly he did all right and was able to invest in real estate. He travelled a lot, so he had properties from New York to Chicago."

Sarah paused, sipped her drink, and continued. "Your father first came to Jamaica just to get away from New York's winter weather. But he met your mother and decided to stay and make a home with her. You came along, and everything was fine at first. But within a year, though, your mother got sick and died."

"What did she die of?"

"I don't know. That was a few years before I met your father, and he never would say much about it. All I know is that she was much younger than your father. He said he was broken hearted at the loss and never really recovered. But then he met your stepmother. By the time I started working for your father, she was well underway with their second child. That's about all he ever told me."

Sarah didn't chronicle her own relationship with Jimmy's father, and Jimmy was satisfied to have her avoid what would have to be a complicated personal matter. He knew her as Aunt Sarah, as his father's assistant, and as Fae's mother. Her kindness was sufficient basis for a warm relationship. His father treated Fae as his daughter, and he had always thought of Fae as his little sister who didn't live with them.

"I never had much contact with your stepmother," Sarah went on. "I met her a few times before he died, but she wasn't involved in your father's business. Shortly after he died, though, she showed up at my door with a solicitor and demanded all the books from your father's business. She had an official court order, so I had to hand them over. I never had anything more to do with her."

The three of them passed another hour sharing more pleasant memories—and a few fantasies. As was traditional in Jamaica, Jimmy received small farewell gifts: stationery and pencils from Sarah, a St. Christopher medal from Fae. The goodbyes were warm and upbeat, but Jimmy walked away from the house in a cloud of sadness, fearing he would never see them again.

Jimmy had come to think of his leaving in positive terms—opportunity, challenge, freedom. He fought back tears, however, as he climbed the steep gangplank toward the vast bulk of the *La Estrella—Barcelona*. He felt a huge part of himself was being ripped away and left behind. But fear of what he was to face was no less powerful than the sadness. He didn't look back until he had reached the mouth of the boarding deck, where he handed over his ticket and other papers to a dour-looking man, formal and slightly forbidding in his crisp naval officer's attire. By the time Jimmy looked back, his stepmother, who brought him to the dock, had disappeared.

As if to add to his isolation, he was the only passenger boarding just then, so he and the one suitcase he carried had the full attention of the neatly dressed youth who escorted him to his tiny cabin. At least it had a porthole through which light streamed from the ocean side. When Jimmy asked about his other luggage and the departure time, the young man simply smiled, bowed slightly, and left. Jimmy concluded that the youth probably didn't speak English.

Standing at the porthole, he could see the bay and the sea beyond. He was pleased to have this amenity, but he soon felt uncomfortable in the close little room and went out on deck to find a better view. The spacious rear observation deck was amply supplied with deck chairs, but its occupants, about a dozen in all, stood at the rails either looking back to the dock or out toward the bay. Two couples stood together in animated conversation; the others were alone. Jimmy found a spot on the rail well away from everyone and fixed his eyes on the distant horizon.

After more than an hour, he began to hear the rumble of engines and could feel the ship shudder as it made ready to embark. As it moved away from the dock, he was pleased to have a good view of Kingston and the Blue Mountains in the distance.

With the ship halfway out of the bay, his eyes greedily roamed the shore; looking east of the city, a docking area seemed familiar. Small boats bobbed in the water and he counted three piers of various sizes jutting from the beaches. He said to himself, "That's Rockport and the Brighton Beach wharf." He wondered if he would ever see them again. He never did.

Nor did he ever learn that it was where his mother died.

CHAPTER 12:

The Day Before

A t 5 o'clock on Thursday, March 15, 1945, James Turner ended his shift at the Russell Glass Company. Nearly six feet tall and thin, he looked as if he could be blown away by a strong wind. On his way to the locker room his supervisor stopped him and complained that he was working too slowly. He even threatened to let him go. Later, as James stood before his locker, the residue of toilet smells combined with the mustiness of the locker room to turn his stomach. He was still reeling from the confrontation and he fell into the cloud that often accompanied the end of his work day—his energy waned, his pace slowed, and his vision blurred. Men from the production lines laughed and joked as they washed in the circular sink in the middle of the room.

Although his lowly status as a janitor relegated him to a locker in a little used area, the men from the line sometimes greeted him with a nod and even spoke to him once in a while about what was going on upstairs. One had even tried to get him to go to a union organizing meeting. For the most part, however, they ignored him.

Today the men were talking about sex. They told crude jokes, laughed, teased each other about their lack of sex appeal or sexual interest, and laughed more. When the talk turned to prostitutes, James's attention was caught and he felt immediately more anxious. He thought to himself, *That's where my troubles started. One prostitute and . . .*

"I really do like to have some nigger pussy once in a while," one of the men said as he pulled on his shirt. Some of the others hooted, some hissed, but they all laughed. "You've got to be real careful with those black whores, though. Half the time they have a switchblade hid in their garter, just waitin' to rob you." Uproarious laughter.

James cringed but said nothing. He had guessed that at the factory he was seen as white because of his light complexion and straight black hair, but this was the first time he knew it for sure. Still, until today the other workers hadn't tried to draw him into this kind of after-work banter, and he didn't challenge what was being said now, or otherwise get involved. As he dressed, he looked straight ahead and tried as usual to be as inconspicuous as possible; on most days this was signal enough that they should leave him alone. But this wasn't a typical day. One of the loudest men noticed his silence.

"Hey, James," he said. "You ever have any black pussy?" After a pause: "Come on," he continued. "Nobody's gunna tell." Finally James shook his head slightly. "I don't believe that," asserted the man. "Don't you live down near Jew Town? Nothin' but niggers, spics, and old Jews around there. I know you're not fuckin' old Jews, so you must get some nigger or spic ass."

The laughter was loud and long, but James said nothing and kept looking into his locker as he finished dressing.

When James walked out onto Desplaines Street, his focus returned and he took up his usual walking speed, but his mind was not at ease. He was filled with shame at not confronting the prejudice he had witnessed. *Am I such a coward? Just stood there like a weak nobody. Let them laugh at me and ridicule colored women.*

He searched out, ticked off, and dwelt on every reason for self hatred and despair: the demeaning janitorial job he had been forced to accept after he left the hospital; his wife, Loleet, whom he loved but who didn't understand what he was going through; his four children and the grinding poverty in which they were growing up. He dwelt on what the doctor had told him a month earlier about his illness: incurable brain disease caused by syphilis, which had lain dormant but non-contagious for as many as twenty years. Nothing could be done; his symptoms would gradually worsen. Finally, he pictured his stepmother Annie Turner and her three children living a life of luxury in Jamaica, while he and his family barely survived. The most painful stroke was that he was powerless to do anything about it. He had to live through this hell, and he had to live through it alone, caught in a tangle of mistakes and misfortune, with nowhere to turn.

As he approached the streetcar stop at Desplaines and Madison, he decided to walk home and save the ten cents. *Fifteen or twenty short blocks*, he thought. *A forty minute walk might do me good.*

But the walk offered no relief from his agonizing ruminations; instead, the emotions they set off—anger, fear, sadness, and despair—vied for his attention but went unresolved. He bumped into people on the sidewalk three times and, while crossing a street, came close to being hit by a car. Once he was forced to stop and hold onto a post to cope with the pain building in his head, until the brief seizure passed. *That was the second today*, he thought.

When he reached Halsted Street, James consoled himself by thinking it was a straight line now to 14th Street. He would be home in less than half an hour. He looked ahead resolutely and quickened his pace, but his breathing soon became labored, his heart raced, and he had to slow down. Then he remembered the doctor's warning not to exert himself. He pictured the examining room at the Cook County Hospital and remembered.

James hadn't wanted to believe the doctor's preliminary diagnosis when he first heard it some weeks earlier. This time the doctor had insisted that his wife come with him to the appointment. When the doctor confirmed the diagnosis, James looked at Loleet and found what he feared: her jaw dropping and tears forming.

The doctor said to James, "You need to realize the damage already done to your brain by the infection can't be reversed. We'll do everything we can, but the spells and other symptoms will gradually get worse."

He went on to explain that, although syphilis was the origin of the illness, in its current stage, James was not contagious and had not been for at least fifteen years—five years before he met Loleet. Because she had never shown symptoms of syphilis, it was very unlikely that she was ever infected. Loleet seemed to understand, looked at James, and appeared to relax.

Then the doctor began writing and said, "To be absolutely sure, we would like Mrs. Turner to have a blood test."

"You mean you're not really sure?" Loleet asked and put a hand across her mouth.

"I can understand how all of this would be upsetting," said the doctor, "but I assure you this is just standard procedure at the hospital for cases like yours. The Public Health Department requires it."

Loleet wiped the tears from her eyes, grimaced, and asked, "Can I take it today? When will we know the results?"

Later, as they left the examining room, without making eye contact with Loleet, James angrily dismissed what they had just been told. "That doctor doesn't know what he's talking about. I never had syphilis!—not that I know of."

Despite his protest, he could see that Loleet believed the doctor. When they reached the hospital lobby, she sat on a wooden bench off by herself and sobbed into her hands, then into a handkerchief. Gasping through her tears, she asked, "How could you do this to me? I was a clean woman. Why couldn't you find someone who was already diseased? Now, maybe I've got it and I'll get sick too." They had just learned that this was very unlikely, but he was hurt by what she said. He knew the doctor was right. He also felt his wife's pain and disappointment, but he was unable to comfort her.

When he reached the corner of Halsted and 14th Streets, a streetcar rolled up behind him and its loud clang startled him out of his reverie. He wondered how many streetcars had made it to this corner since he had started walking. *Maybe none*—he hadn't noticed any passing him, but he had been occupied with his own thoughts. He recognized no one at the corner; no one gave any sign of recognizing him. He felt alone and invisible.

As he turned the corner onto 14th Street, he tripped on the uneven sidewalk and fell forward. He caught himself before hitting the pavement full force, but the fall banged his left knee and left him briefly stunned. He got to his feet quickly, rubbed his knee, brushed some dirt from his pants, and walked on quickly, too embarrassed to look around to see whether anyone had noticed or moved to help him.

This wasn't the first time he had fallen recently. *Just tired from the long walk,* he told himself. But ever since he left Elgin State Hospital, his body had felt unbalanced and his gait awkward. His handwriting had gone from artistic to a scratchy scribble. *It's happening just like the doctor warned, and there's nothing I can do about it.*

The entry door of their four-story tenement had no lock and swung freely on bent and creaky hinges. As he entered the dark stairway, he could hear children's voices and footsteps coming down, but his weren't among the five he met at the second floor landing. He stepped aside to let them pass; they pushed each other, laughed, and generally behaved like kids having fun. *Could they actually be happy and enjoying life?*

It seemed a tremendous effort to reach the third floor. Looking up the stairs toward the window at the top, he wondered whether the illness was sapping his strength. He pushed himself. *One step at a time. No point in stopping now.*

At the top he leaned against the window sill and took several deep breaths. The upper section of the window retained its glass pane and provided a little light despite being caked with filth, but the bottom had been replaced with a sheet of tin from a *Shlitz* beer sign. *Must be after six o'clock,* he thought. *The hall lights should have been turned on by now.*

He reached into the pocket of his well-worn overcoat and found his single key attached to a piece of brown shoelace, dirty and frayed at both ends. Alone now in the quiet hallway, he hesitated, listening for sounds coming from the apartment. He heard children's voices, then the clatter of pots. He entered quietly.

In the entryway, boots and galoshes lay on the floor and coats and hats were hung on plain metal hooks and long nails. An inside door, usually kept closed in winter to preserve heat, let a bit of welcome light into the dark entryway as he opened it. In the center of the crowded dining room stood a pot-bellied stove, in the far corner a double bed, against the wall to the left of the entryway a mirrored dresser, and behind the door a small slant top desk. He hung his coat and stood by the stove. It was giving off little heat. *I may need to start it up again, if it gets colder tonight,* he thought, reclosing the door.

"Making dinner?" he asked when he reached the threshold of the kitchen. Loleet looked around but didn't answer. James entered the small bathroom off the kitchen.

When he emerged, he said, "I think I'll lie down for a while. I had a hard day. I'll put a few more pieces of coal in the stove."

He slept until nearly eight. The children were in the living room listening to the radio and preparing for bedtime. He helped the eldest, ten year old June, spread a sheet and blanket, sat between the two youngest and hugged them, and watched Jimmy fiddle with the radio knobs. This was the best he had felt all day. When he entered the kitchen, Loleet was washing the dishes. "You must be starving," she said, "I'll heat up the dinner—it's just beans and rice and bread."

"I'm not hungry," he said. "Maybe I'll have it a little later. I could use a cup of coffee, though."

"I could too. I'll make half a pot."

When she'd finished cleaning up, she noticed him staring into space. "The coffee's about ready," she said, hoping to bring him back from his ruminations.

As she poured his coffee, his worried expression didn't change. She said, "You *must* have had a hard day. What happened? Something at work?" She sat next to him with her own cup.

"Loleet, I don't know how much more I can take. I walk around all day feeling like I'm dragging myself from one place to another. The supervisor told me I was too slow. Threatened to fire me if I didn't work faster. Then, at the end of the day, in the locker room, a bunch of white guys were talking and laughing and making fun of colored women . . . of colored prostitutes. I just sat there and said nothing, afraid that something would happen if I said anything. I could've said I'm colored and let them know I didn't appreciate that kind of talk. I'm already the lowest of the low in that place, and most of the time I'm treated like a piece of furniture . . . That job! Forty cents an hour, cleaning wash basins and toilet bowls, sweeping and mopping floors. I never thought I'd end up in a job like that. And I can't stop thinking about what the doctor told us. I'm not going to get better, Loleet. I feel it happening every day. I'm already contributing next to nothing to this family, but if I lose this job . . . What's the point, Loleet?"

She reached out to his hand on the table, covered it with hers, and said, "Whatever happens, you have your family, Jim."

His eyes met hers, and he said, "I know, and that's the only thing keeping me going. I don't know what I would do if I didn't have you and the children. But I keep thinking you shouldn't have to suffer because of me. I feel like I'm dragging you all down into my misery."

"Oh, Jim, don't talk like that. We all love you. I love you. The children love their daddy."

"Have you forgiven me, Loleet? . . . Really forgiven me? I know the news from the doctor was hard to accept at first, but what's important is that the tests showed you're not infected and never were. You've been as loving a wife as any man could expect, Loleet—more than I deserve."

She squeezed his hand lightly, and both fell silent for several minutes.

They were still sitting silently when June came quietly to the threshold of the kitchen. In the background the other children were arguing about what program to listen to.

Loleet looked up at June but didn't speak. She rose, took her hand away from her husband's and said, "I'd better get the children to bed." She shooed June out ahead of her, leaving James sitting up but still looking grim. Loleet said, "There's some mail for you on the icebox. I forgot to tell you. It's from Jamaica."

Loleet was right—the airmail stamp was British. He stared at it for a minute, hesitating as if facing a feral animal that had to be dealt with. It was from his stepmother, Annie Turner, undoubtedly responding to his plea for money. In his letter he had described the family's financial distress, and he had also told her the bad news about his health. He had been out of touch for a few years, in part because of his mental health problems and his hospitalization at Elgin State Hospital the previous year. He hoped for a positive response but didn't really expect it. He'd wanted his stepmother to know the extent of his troubles and suffering, and had hinted once again that he held her primarily responsible for his problems. But only hinted, because she had always reacted defensively and angrily to his direct accusations, and he needed financial help. He was willing to beg.

The typed letter read as follows:

My dear Jimmy,

I was pleased to receive your letter after such a long time not hearing from you, but I was very sorry to hear about all your troubles and especially the latest news about how sick you are and have been for these last few years. No matter how serious it is, don't give up hoping for the best. These days there seem to be new cures being found for all kinds of illnesses. Please don't despair. Trust in the goodness of God, who will always come to the aid of those who look to him in times of distress.

I know you asked me to send some money as soon as possible, but that will not be possible at this time. First of all, the government here won't let any money leave the island for the duration of the war. God willing, the war might finally be over soon, the way things are going now. The other thing is—I don't have a single shilling to spare. I live with Merle or Roy when I am in Jamaica, and I have to pay them something and take care of all my own expenses too. Believe me, Jimmy, I know what it is to have to get by on little money. Everton is being rented, but after taxes and maintenance, I end up with very little.

Speaking of Everton, I want to remind you that you made it very difficult for me to sell it, because you would not accept what everyone here thought was a fair share of the proceeds. The last I heard from my solicitor you wanted to wait until the war was over. So you ended up with nothing and I get very little out of it. I wish you had taken the hundred pounds we offered you back then. I know it was not much, but maybe it would have made it easier on you and your family over these last few years. But all that is behind us now. We need to go on the best we can and leave it in God's hands.

Merle, Fern, and Roy send their love. We all look forward to seeing you and your family someday—perhaps in Jamaica or maybe in the States. Do keep us in your thoughts, and I will pray for you and your family.

Yours sincerely,
Annie R. Turner

"Damn hypocrite!" James said at the letter. "You and your God! You goddam bitch! I hope your God sends you to the lowest part of hell for what you did to me!"

He tore the letter and envelope into small pieces, then stacked them on the table. He took a box of matches from the stove shelf, struck one, and lit several places on the pile. As the flame took hold, James began to laugh quietly.

Loleet chose that moment to return to the kitchen. "Jim, what are you doin'? You'll burn the table top. You'll scare the children!"

She rushed to the table, brushed the burning paper onto the linoleum floor with her hands, and stepped on the few pieces still burning.

"What are you doin'?" she repeated. "Do you want us to burn up in here? What's the matter with you?"

He sat and continued to laugh. Loleet sat facing him and said, raising her voice above his laughter, "If you don't stop this, I'm gonna have to take you back to the doctor . . . back to the state hospital."

He suddenly stopped, looked searchingly into her eyes, then leaned forward with head in hands and elbows on knees. This wasn't the first time he had heard this threat. *She hasn't really forgiven me*, he thought. *Why should she? I can't forgive myself.*

"I'm sorry, dear, I didn't mean that. You were scarin' me, Jim. Please don't do that again." She placed an arm around his shoulder and rubbed his back.

After she cleaned up the ashes, they sat quietly for a few minutes. Then she remembered the children.

In the living room all four huddled around the beat up console radio. "Time for bed, past time," she said. "School tomorrow."

"Please, Ma," said June. "This program is almost over. Please."

"All right," she answered after a slight grimace, "but it goes off as soon as it's over. Your daddy's not feeling well."

Without looking up, June said, "We know."

"Okay, so I want you all to be quiet when you go to bed."

In the kitchens, James hadn't moved. Loleet sat next to him, again put an arm around his shoulders, and said, "I know it's hard, Jim, but everything is gonna be all right."

After a few minutes she rose and asked, "Would you like more coffee? Looks like you didn't drink but half. I'll just put what you left back in the pot and pour you a fresh cup."

He sat up straighter, pulled his chair closer to the table, and took a sip of the coffee. He stared without focus at his own reflection in the window, then through it into the dark night, across the alley, over the house tops on 14th Street, over the store roofs on Halsted Street, past the L Klein department store sign on the north-east corner of the intersection, to the blackness beyond.

"I don't know, Loleet," he said. "I don't know if everything will be all right. Right now I see nothing but misery. I think I might be let go tomorrow. The supervisor warned me today about doing a better job and keeping up with the work, but I don't know how I can do any more. As it is, I've been pushing myself. I'm not feeling right. I can feel myself going down a little every day. The sickness in my brain is taking me away more and more, and it's making me crazy, Loleet. You can see that yourself. I'm not myself . . . not the same Jim I was."

Minutes of silence; both occasionally took sips of coffee.

"When I came in, you were burning the letter you got from Jamaica. Something in it must have upset you. What was it?"

"I wrote to my stepmother," he said, "told her I was sick, hardly able to work, barely putting food on the table for my family. I pleaded for some kind of financial help. I didn't hold back, plainly told her how badly off we are and have been for years. I begged."

"And?"

"She was so very sorry for my misfortune. God will take care of everything, she says. Don't give up no matter what, she says. I told her a long time ago I didn't believe in her God. What kind of God would let so many people in the world live in misery? I told her, people need food and shelter, not a God who ignores their suffering. After her sympathy and God talk, she tells me, 'Sorry, can't help you out with money; government restrictions; and, anyway, I don't have a cent to spare.' That bitch! After all she stole from me, she claims she's poor!"

"So, that's it I suppose," Loleet said with a sigh. "You tried. We'll get through somehow. We can go back to the relief office and ask for more help, if you can't keep working. We'll find a way." She hesitated, then said, "But don't use foul language. The kids are just gettin' to bed. They'll hear you."

"Wait, wait," he went on, now quietly but more agitated, "that's not all. Then she needles me about how I held up the sale of Everton and implies that, if I had gone along with her scheme, we would have had a hundred pounds . . . from a house and estate worth thousands. She stuck it in good, pointed out that, instead, we got nothing."

"Please, Jim, don't upset yourself thinking any more about that."

But now he felt compelled to finish with the last exasperating detail from the letter. "What made me crazy, Loleet, was how the letter ended. They send their love . . . hope to see you and the family in Jamaica someday . . . Sincerely yours. Can you beat that? Sincerely! The insincerity, the hypocrisy, is all so unbelievable! I had to do something. That's why I tore up the letter and burned it. So unbelievable!"

He took both her hands in his and said, "I'm sorry I scared you, Loleet. I just couldn't help myself. Please forgive me."

"Nothing to forgive, my dear, dear Jim. I can't even imagine what you must be going through. I only wish I could help."

They sat for half an hour, quietly drinking coffee, occasionally looking up and making eye contact, holding hands, more at ease with each other than they had been for some time. Then he looked down into his lap and said, "I feel as sorry for you as for myself. You don't deserve the trouble I've put you through . . . and probably will continue to put you through. I wish there was some way I could make it up to you, but I know I can't. At this point I'm less than useless to you and the children."

"Please, Jim, don't say things like that. You've been a wonderful husband, and you've done the best you could. I love you no matter what . . . And you're a great father. The kids love their daddy. You're so good with them. You're a good man, Jim. Believe me, I don't have any regrets. We've just been unlucky and times have been hard for so long."

"I really feel sorry for the children," he said, "for what they have had to go through because of me. I know it must frighten them when I have one of my spells. I can only hope they'll be all right."

"I better go make sure they're settled," she said and left the kitchen.

When she returned and saw him sitting slumped across the table, she said, "You must be tired too, Jim. You had a hard day . . . and that letter didn't help any. Let's go to bed. It's almost nine-thirty."

"You go ahead. I'm really not so tired . . . Must be all the coffee and the long nap. I'm going to stay up for a while. I have some thinking to do."

"Please don't make it long, Jim. You'll be startin' out for work tired, and that's not gonna help you do the work either . . . Oh, I forgot.

You never did have any dinner. You want me to heat up the beans and rice?"

"No thanks. I won't be up much longer . . . just want to think over a few things."

While others slept, he paced the kitchen floor. His agitation intensified after Loleet went to bed, his grievances tumbling through his mind one after another, like boulders into a cavernous, echoing valley. The litany of all the events and people that had caused his problems felt like blows to his head and chest. He tortured himself in this way for over an hour.

He had become accustomed to having seizures—"spells"—several times a week. The doctor had warned him that they would come and gradually become more frequent and intense. Now, as he sat at the table, a seizure came. He knew its warning signs and its course: seeing stars, uncontrollable shaking, sharp pain in various parts of his head, temporary paralysis, and finally the rapid receding of all these symptoms. It was over in three minutes.

He sat for another half hour staring into space. When exhaustion finally overtook him, he crossed his arms on the table to pillow his head, and fell asleep.

CHAPTER 13:

"Sweet Repose"

The ceiling light was still on when James opened his eyes. He straightened his back, felt the stiffness in his neck and arms, and pushed away from the table. With his eyes closed, he slowly swiveled his head around in all direction as far as it would go. He stretch both arms away from his body, then up, and finally rested them in his lap and opened his eyes. The sliver of sky above the *L Klein* building was reddish but still dawn grey. *Sun just coming up over Lake Michigan. Must be around six.*

He listened for sounds from the rest of the apartment. Nothing. Sitting up straight in the chair, he remembered that he had just been dreaming and, closing his eyes again, he tried to retrieve some image. *Something about the children . . .* but it was gone. *Lost it.*

He washed his face in the kitchen sink, rubbing his eyes and then his whole face, trying to wake up completely. He stepped into the bathroom. When he came out, the kitchen was a little brighter, but he thought it would be a while before he could turn off the light. He decided against warming the half cup of coffee remaining from the night before. As he rinsed the pot, he recalled some of what had happened the previous night.

I'm really losing my mind. What was that? Out of control laughing and burning that letter on the table! Scaring my family! This is too much. What can I do?

When the coffee stopped percolating, he filled a cup. Without thinking he took a mouthful then instinctively sent the steaming liquid back into the cup. He quickly rinsed his mouth with cold water and thought, *Now I can't even think straight. What's next?*

The sky had brightened considerably since he first woke. He stared blankly through the window. He knew it was his stepmother's letter that had pushed him over the edge. But he also knew it was only part of his problem. She and her letter didn't cause his illness, the spells of shaking, his problem with balance and his awkward movements. She and her letter didn't cause him to end up stuck cleaning toilets and mopping floors.

But it all began with her sending me here to scuffle on my own. One thing after another, and here I am. Yes, that's where it all began. Everything happens because of something that happened before it. If my real mother had lived, she would have loved me and taken care of me, and my father would never have married that witch . . . My father knew what was going to happen . . . he knew she wouldn't treat me right. Even though he warned me, I can't believe he could ever have imagined she would be so cruel as to send a fifteen year old away from his home, family, and friends. If only my father had lived . . . he would never have sent me away. Even if all of my problems can't be traced to her and what she did to me, I can still do one thing. I can answer her letter and let her know she is responsible for some of those problems. Even if she denies it or gives excuses, I need to let her know straight out how I feel.

He went quickly to the slant top desk behind the entry door and took out a fountain pen and several sheets of paper, along with a pencil, so he could make a draft copy to keep. At the kitchen table he arranged the sheets of paper with the pen and pencil above them, placed his unfinished cup of coffee an arm's length away at the upper right corner of the table, and wrote the date, March 16, 1945.

Dear Mrs. Turner,

I received your letter of March 10. I thank you for such a prompt response.

I am very disappointed that you cannot send any financial help at this time. I wish to point out that you failed, for many years, to provide funds for my "support, maintenance and education," as provided for in my father's will. Years ago, when you sought my signature for the sale of the Providence property, you said "you know that if you were sick and in need and let me know—I'd divide my last dollar and give you half." I am sick and in need now.

You seem to believe I am to blame for my present situation. I admit that I made mistakes, as a youth will, but how much better off I would have been in health and happiness had I been allowed to remain in Jamaica? Why did you not send me to some children's institution, to someone who would have shown me love?

I noticed that you again talked about God. Well, I am indeed sorry to say there is no God. And I believe that you are cognizant of this fact too. If there was a God he would not stay up in heaven and see innocent, honest, decent people suffer in poverty, sickness, worry and absolute misery while devils on the earth are enjoying the fat of the land. In comparison to this kind of life, death is not so bad as people may think. In fact, it seems to me a thing of beauty. It is sweet repose after the miseries of life, where mankind has become so inhumane towards each other and genuine love and friendship are becoming things of the past. The people do not need any God. They need bread, clothes, and shelter.

> Yours very very sincerely,
> James Julius Turner

He read through the letter several times. Each time he stopped at the section about death. He had not intended to write anything like that when he began the letter. He'd just wanted her to know he didn't believe that she couldn't send financial help and that he held her responsible for much of his misfortunes. But the sentences about death seem to have written themselves. He saw no way out of his misery, but how could he think such things? *Is the situation so completely hopeless?* He began grinding his clinched teeth.

What's the point? This letter won't make any difference. She knows what she did to me. She's known all along, but she did nothing but act like I was an annoyance. That's how she treated me before Daddy died, and that's how she treated me after he died. She did everything she could to let me know how much she resented me. Even my school fees—she did nothing but complain about them, wanted me to drop out. The more she mistreated and criticized me, the more I hated her and tried to show her how much I despised her. She tried to ignore me, and I tried to ignore her. Nothing's changed. Why should I expect her to respond with help now . . . or even feel anything like pity for me . . . or even care whether I lived or died?

Despair enveloped him. His arms fell to his side, and his head to his chest. He was like a balloon deflating—its final bounce gone, gasping out its last breath. Troubling images came rushing in—his dying father; his stepmother's angry face; the gradually fading view of Kingston Harbor and the Blue Mountains from the ship bringing him to New York City; the doctor giving his diagnosis; and now, his failing body.

He came out of his daze when he heard Loleet moving in their bedroom. She'd be dressed and coming into the kitchen momentarily. For reasons he didn't understand, he couldn't face her. He quickly gathered up his work, placed what he had written into a solid storage box containing his correspondence, and returned everything else to the desk. As quietly as he could, he slipped into the entryway, took his overcoat and hat, and left.

When James stepped out onto the sidewalk, he felt the chill in the early morning air and was glad he had a warm coat. When he reached Halsted Street, the big clock under the L Klein sign said ten before seven. The morning traffic was picking up. He automatically looked south down Halsted Street to see whether a streetcar was in sight. But he decided he would walk, since he would have no trouble reaching work by eight o'clock,.

As he crossed Maxwell Street, the store fronts and hotdog stands appeared flattened and distorted. As he passed under the sidewalk canopy of the Irving Theatre, he recognized only the words "Now Playing" and "Coming Soon" over blurry pictures on the front displays.

He was in a daze. *Lack of sleep? Spell coming on? Can I really make it all the way?*

Then he regained his resolve, shook off some of the fog that had settled onto his mind and vision, and pushed on. With hands in the coat pockets and teeth clinched, he quickened his pace. For a few blocks he walked looking mostly at the sidewalk and felt secure in a bubble of oblivion. That changed when he crossed Roosevelt Road and passed the 12th Street Store on the corner.

As always, he could feel the spell coming and knew he would have to stop to give it time to pass. He held onto an accordion security gate of a grocery store that had not yet opened. He stared into the distance, felt the wave of low level jerky shakes of the head begin and intensify. Within minutes each element slowly receded, until he felt back in control. These seizures, with their frozen time and head tics, had become frequent over the last week. When he had described them to the doctor at the Cook County Hospital, the doctor told him such seizures were common with his condition and that he should expect them to become more frequent. They had.

After he recovered his balance and his perception cleared, he continued north on Halsted Street, now somewhat slower but with his eyes focused straight ahead and resolute. The cold wind picked up, and the ache in his legs told him the pants he was wearing were no match for its bite. But he couldn't stop—now that he had lost time.

As soon as he got into a rhythm of steps, his thoughts returned to what had happened the previous night. He recalled how out of control he felt, how he seemed to have fallen out of contact with himself. He had recovered his senses, but the utter despair that had led to his bizarre behavior was unchanged when he woke in the morning. He began to enumerate again the many reasons for his despair. He remembered the time following his father's death, when his life was made miserable by the feeling that he wasn't wanted in his stepmother's domain. He never knew his biological mother, and the death of his father made him fully aware that he was an orphan. At his father's graveside, his stepmother gathered the other children around her. Only his grandmother Phillpotts had approached him, put an arm around him, and comforted him with an acknowledgment of his special sources of grief.

The depression that held him for a year after the funeral was interrupted only by his periods of sullen rage at his stepmother. He took every opportunity to be away from home and stayed away as long as he could. When at home, he usually stayed in his own small room. He couldn't avoid being present for meals, but he spoke only when spoken to. Although he was allowed to take this withdrawn stance most of the time, whenever his stepmother addressed him directly, he felt assaulted, even when the matter addressed was routine. He took every question as an intrusion, every suggestion as a criticism, and every reminder of his parentless status as a threat. She let him know that she was offended by his apparent lack of sensitivity to her loss and his refusal to thank her for her generosity to him. That was their standoff.

He remembered his other reasons for despising her. She had failed to live up to the terms of his father's will, which had stipulated that the latter's legacy should pay for his support, maintenance and education until his 21st birthday. Instead, when he had just turned fifteen and the spring term at Jamaica College Preparatory School had ended, she gave him a one-way ticket to New York City and didn't bother to communicate with him for seven years. She wrote him only to request his agreement to the sale of property.

Twice she had asked him to sign away his rights in her selling of real estate—in Rhode Island and in Jamaica. She had managed to sell the Rhode Island property without his consent and gave him not a cent of the proceeds. The Jamaica property had not been sold because he had again refused to sign away his rights. This time he decided to wait until the end of the war to settle the matter.

At the corner of Madison and Halsted he turned east and knew he was only ten minutes away from work. He wasn't looking forward to being there, but he had to be there—he needed that job. The thought of being unemployed made him tense. As it was, they could barely pay the rent and buy food. What would he do if he lost this job? The thought threw him into a state of anxiety. He tried to calm himself and suppress the thought, but he could once again feel the beginning of a seizure.

When he regained his control and focus, he thought, *That was the second time within an hour. This is what I have to look forward to—a life of increasing spells that turn me into a near zombie and no hope of getting better. No one should have to live in such misery.*

As he approached the factory his anxiety increased; he saw by the small number entering that it was close to eight o'clock. He picked up his pace. When he punched his timecard, he was five minutes late. He hadn't seen his supervisor as he entered, so he relaxed and proceeded to the locker room. There he found a few straggling line workers changing in silence, except for an occasional grunted greeting. Because he hadn't changed his clothes since leaving the day before, he now regretted having left home so rapidly. Then he watched himself slowing down, lingering at every piece of clothing he took off, examining and carefully hanging them. He knew something was wrong, but he felt unable to do anything about it. This went on for several minutes, and his control seemed to be slipping away.

"James!" yelled the short heavy-set man who had silently entered the locker room. "What the hell do you think you're doin'?" As he approached James, he saw that there was something unusual happening and moderated his tone and the anger behind it. "You sick again? Got one of your spells?"

"No, no," said James, hardly moving. "I don't know. Maybe it was . . . I don't feel like myself."

"I told you yesterday, we just can't have this sorta thing," said the man, returning to his gruffness. "If you're sick, that's one thing, but I can't let you just hang around here workin' at a snail's pace. We need to get the toilets cleaned. You should have started one by now."

"I know," said James. "I'll get it all done today. I just need a few minutes to . . ."

"A few minutes like hell!" snarled the man. "You get to the first floor toilets now or get your sorry ass out of here. I need you to be done with all the toilets in the building before noon. I have a special project that needs to get done on the fifth floor before the end of the day."

No response. James sat there, half dressed, staring into the locker, but not moving. He felt both paralyzed and distant from what was happening. He knew he had to respond, but he felt dragged down by the huge boulder sitting in the center of his chest. Finally, he looked up and made eye contact with the man.

"Dammit, James!" the man yelled. "I'm not playin' with you. Either you get yourself movin' or go to the office and pick up what's owed you and get the hell out."

James said nothing but stood up and resumed the process of changing into his overalls and work boots. The man stood looking at him for a moment, then said, "All right, now listen to me. I'll be back in about an hour. When I get back, I want to see you're getting it done." As he watched James trying to respond, he softened his tone somewhat. "You know, James, I don't want to have to let you go. But I have my responsibilities, and some things gotta get done around here, or it's my neck. So, come on, give me a break . . . and yourself a break. Let's just get the job done. Okay?" The man didn't wait for a response; he turned and left the room.

James was ready for work in a matter of minutes. Thinking about the prospect of being without a job, he pushed himself to move quickly. He tried concentrating on one task at a time and not allowing his problems to interrupt what he had to do. This worked until he had finished both toilets on the first floor. He hadn't been watching the time, so he wasn't sure when to expect the supervisor to return to check on him. When the service elevator opened and the supervisor stepped out, both were surprised.

"James," said the man, "I was just comin' to see how you were doin'. I sure hope you finished this floor by now."

"All done," said James, pushing the cleaning and trash collection cart into the elevator. "I'm heading for the second floor now."

"Be done with the first four floors before lunch time," said the man and hesitated. "I might as well tell you now what the project is on the fifth floor. You've seen for yourself the fifth floor has been mostly empty and unused for as long as you've been here. The bosses are considerin' using that floor for a new contract with the government. They wanna do a walk through inspection of the whole space up there on Monday—and with the owners. The floors up there will look all right after a good sweep, but the windows need cleaning bad." He looked at James squarely, as if trying to make sure he was getting his message across. "Now, James, can I count on you?"

James felt his energy draining away as the man spoke, but said, "I'll do my best."

"Your best? Well your best better be good enough to get those windows cleaned. This is it, James. I'm not puttin' up with any more of your bullshit. Get it done or I look for a replacement on Monday." Turning and walking away, he said over his shoulder, "I'll be back to check on you around noon. Don't stop for lunch 'til I find you."

As the elevator door closed, James felt as if gripped in a vise, needing to muster the energy to do the job even as the enormity of it rendered him hopeless. He began to feel again that there was no way out for him. If he lost this job, which he had gotten with the help of the relief office, it would take time for him to get another and, in the meantime, he would have to ask for more relief help, which itself would take time to come through. *Even if I got another job*, he thought, *why wouldn't the same thing happen?* This job wasn't difficult; still, he found it almost impossible to do.

The elevator began to rise, and James realized he hadn't pushed the button for the second floor. *Someone else must have called for it*, he thought. Hoping he could get the elevator to stop at the second floor before it went any higher, he quickly pressed the button. The elevator suddenly stopped, but the door didn't open, and he realized it had stopped between the first and second floors. Had he done something to cause this? Whether he did or not wasn't as important as how he could get the elevator moving and get out.

This crisis pushed him out of his semi-stupor and into action. First, he pulled the emergency stop button, which led to a loud clanging alarm. He pushed the button back in, and the alarm stopped, but there was no movement. He pulled the emergency and pressed all the floor buttons several times with no effect. He decided to leave the alarm on and hoped that whoever had called for the elevator would get help. The alarm was so loud he had to cover his ears. After a few minutes of bearing this, he could stand it no longer and turned the alarm off. The elevator didn't move. He panicked, knowing that, if he didn't get out soon, he would be unable to finish all the toilets on the remaining floors before noon.

He wasn't surprised when he felt the first signs of another seizure coming. *Hold on*, he thought. *Get through this and get out. Can't stay here.* Holding the handle of the cart, he let himself go with what was happening. Again, he felt the spasms gradually increase and bore the worst of it by focusing on a spot in the corner of the elevator. As the spell receded, he could hear voices coming from above. He hoped he would be back in control and able to act normally by the time anyone reached him.

Suddenly the elevator jerked back into motion and rose. When the door opened at the second floor, three men were standing in front of it. "You all right?" asked one of them. James couldn't muster the will to respond. Finally, his eyes came into focus on the man who asked the question. "Are you all right, James?" the man asked again. James recognized the man as one of the foremen he had often seen pacing the second floor assembly line and was pleased his rescuer was someone he knew well enough to exchange greetings.

Because James didn't respond immediately, all three stepped into the elevator with an attitude of concern. One of them took charge of the cart, pulling it and placing it well away from the elevator. The foreman could see something wasn't right and guided James out and toward a plain wooden bench nearby. The third man had gotten a paper cup of water from a nearby cooler; offering it, he appeared to be as concerned as the other two.

"Thanks," said James, carefully taking the cup and sipping. He was grateful for the help, but he was afraid to let them know what was really happening. "I'm fine now," he said. "I guess it was pretty scary being stuck in there. Shook me up a bit . . . I'll be all right now. Thanks a lot."

"Are you sure?" asked the foreman. "You don't look so good. Maybe you should take it easy for a while."

"I'll be fine. I just need a few minutes to pull myself together. Really, I'll be okay. I appreciate the help, but I'm okay."

"All right, then," answered the foreman, "but, when you see your supervisor, tell him what happened. He might want you to get some medical attention."

"As soon as I see him," said James, "I'll let him know what happened." He had no intention of bringing this incident to his supervisor's attention. That, he thought, would be the end of this job for him. He knew he had to get himself together and back on schedule, if he had any hope of being done with the toilets by noon. The seizure had passed, he was feeling better and more in control, but the elevator confinement had made it clear how tightly stress was now tied to the onset of his seizures. He also feared that having three attacks in one morning was a sign his condition was worsening fast. The thought brought him to his feet, but then he decided that he had to keep himself from getting upset and sat. He took a deep breath and tried to relax.

One of the toilets on the second floor was near the elevator. *Keep concentrating on what you're doing,* he thought. *One thing at a time.* As soon as he said this, his mind flooded with all that he wished to keep out. First, he reminded himself that his condition had gotten worse and would likely end in death. The thought of being dead didn't frighten him. What he had said in his letter to his stepmother about death being "sweet repose" must be true. Surely nothing could be as bad as the life he was enduring. He imagined quiet sleep, painless oblivion; he yearned for such a state. But then he thought about his family. What would happen to them? How could they survive without him? Loleet had gone to the third grade and had few skills. *How could they survive without me?*

Then, with a start, he thought, *How are they surviving with me? A sick and dying man is no help.* He had stopped breathing but now released the air in a rush. *Everyone would be better off if I died sooner rather than later. I'm just dragging them all down into my misery.*

After a moment of standing by the cart, without much thought, he pushed it toward the toilet. Although he was moving slowly, he thought he would be all right, if he kept moving. He was feeling somewhat more relaxed and in control by the time he reached the second toilet on the floor. *Yes*, he thought, *this is working. All I have to do is keep moving and I'll be all right.*

When he finished the second floor toilets, James stood waiting for the elevator. As he leaned against the cart, two men approached and stood waiting with him. They were talking about baseball, the approaching start of a new season, the training camps starting that day. He felt a powerful sense of estrangement from them. Did he and they live in the same world? While he experienced misery and saw misery everywhere, they saw the signs of spring. They seemed content. How could such contentment exist in the same world as the devastation of war and widespread suffering? On this same planet, people were dying of starvation and disease by the millions, people were slaughtering one another by the thousands for reasons they didn't understand, *and* people were betting the Cubs would finally make it to the World Series again. *This is insane*, he thought.

When the elevator arrived, the two men entered; one held the elevator for him to push in the cart. James stood paralyzed by the thoughts that had just flashed before him. After a few seconds, the two men looked at each other; then the holder let the elevator door close.

I live in that world, James thought. *Should I simply accept this as the reality of human existence: suffer and witness suffering on a gigantic scale?*

His ruminations ended when the elevator opened. It was empty. *Those men must have sent it back*, he thought. *Must have realized I would still be waiting here.*

When he reached the third floor, he felt in control. The strategy of steadily moving had worked. On the wall above the elevator there was a large clock. *Ten fifteen. I can do this. Just keep moving. I'll be on the fourth floor in no time.*

The pattern continued, however, with periods of being stopped by thoughts about his life, the suffering world, and the futility of it all. After finishing the third floor, he felt tired and figured he had made up some time, so he sat on the bench near the elevator. He hadn't eaten anything since lunch the day before, but he didn't feel hungry. He wondered why. *Too tense, I suppose. I need to relax.*

The fourth floor was quieter than the floors below. There were fewer workers and no large machines, which were the source of much of the noise on the other floors. Glass-enclosed offices occupied opposite corners, and there were several areas of people working at desks and drafting tables. Otherwise, it was a large empty space with tile floors and fluorescent lights. As on other floors, one of the two toilets on the floor was near the elevator. Looking at the clock above the elevator, he thought, *Forty minutes to finish two toilets. Just keep focused.*

The toilets on this floor weren't used as much as those on other floors. The smell of urine was not as overwhelming. The floors were relatively free of debris. He rarely had to face un-flushed toilet bowls. He had no difficulty finishing them with ten minutes to spare. Tired again, he sat on the bench near the elevator to wait for the supervisor. The prospect of cleaning windows made him cringe. *I hope there aren't too many up there*, he thought.

When the supervisor arrived, a little before noon, he said without giving James more than a glance, "Let's go upstairs, so I can show you what needs to be done. You'll need your cleaners, so bring the cart." Waiting together by the elevator, the supervisor said offhandedly, "So I guess you managed to pull yourself together well enough to finish the toilets. I checked them all. I knew you could do it. You just need a little push sometimes." His giggle seemed forced, and James didn't respond.

Standing at the elevator facing the large open space of the fifth floor, James counted the windows. "Twelve windows?" he asked. "They are large windows. I'll need a ladder . . . All this afternoon?"

"After lunch, you'll have four hours," said the supervisor. "I figure three an hour should be about right . . . C'mon, you can do it . . . This has to be done today. It won't wait until Monday."

"I don't know. I'm feeling very tired from doing the toilets. How about I do the bottom panes of all of them and as many of the top panes as I can before the end of the day? Most people would look at the bottom panes first. When I do the top panes, I could start on the ones closest to the elevator. I could also pull the shades down far enough to cover the top panes I can't finish. I could come in a little earlier on Monday."

"Look, James," said the supervisor, "I'm not bargaining with you. The bosses could arrive first thing in the morning on Monday. I was told this place needs to be cleaned up. You best not leave today without finishing all the windows—top and bottom panels. If I come in on Monday and find dirty windows, you might as well not come in to work."

James wilted slightly in the face of this onslaught, and the supervisor again noticed and softened his tone. "I know you have your problems, James, and I've tried to take that into account. But I have my own problems, and nobody upstairs cares two cents about them. I take care of my job or I lose it . . . just like you and your job. Understand?"

"OK. I've got it."

As he walked away toward the elevator, the supervisor looked back and said, "I'll be back to see how you're doin' aroun' four."

For a few minutes after the supervisor left, James stood in the room alone, frozen, surveying the lines of windows on each side of the room. Spirit seemed to flow out of him as he considered what he had to do. *I better forget about stopping for lunch.* he thought. *I would have to go out, and that takes time. I'm not really hungry.*

Pushing the cart slowly toward the first window, his legs felt heavy and unresponsive. He thought a seizure was on its way, stopped, and braced himself. But then the sharpest pain he had ever experienced cut across his head and seemed to lodge at the top of his skull. He grabbed his head with both hands, knelt on the floor in front of the window, and groaned as the pain intensified. He was in such breathless agony that he thought he would lose consciousness. Then, as quickly as the pain began, it abated; but his body remained rigid as he tried to return to a regular pattern of breathing. When he felt able to stop moaning, he realized his body was sprawled across the floor like a rag doll. With great effort, he straightened his legs, turned his body to face the tiled floor, and cradled his forehead with his left hand. He was afraid to open his eyes lest that cause the pain to return. He lay there motionless for ten minutes.

This is the illness getting worse, he thought. *Can't bear this.*

"Loleet," he said in a whisper, "I'm sorry . . . I wish I had the strength to go on, but I don't . . . Forgive me . . . I don't know why I have been made to suffer so."

Lying still, memories began to roll out. His life in Jamaica seemed now to have been like yesterday. Until his father died, he had felt special. But he regretted that his father hadn't spoken of his mother until the very end, and then only with the brief letter he had written when she died. If only she had lived, life would have been very different . . . very different . . . and if only his father had lived . . . very different. After he died, everything changed. Grieving the loss of his father and alienated from his stepmother, he withdrew as much as possible from everyone.

The years in the New York City flashed quickly before him: boarding with strangers; being alone and lonely; accompanying a neighbor to a prostitute; working as an office boy for next to nothing in a real estate agency; educating himself by reading; eloping with Loleet; and leaving for California but never getting past Chicago.

He thought about the long years of the Depression in Chicago: the children; no work; no money; bread lines; government relief; hunger; evictions; nowhere to turn; utter misery and despair.

Why? What could this all be about? Am I being punished? Now my brain and body are being ravaged by this illness, which I brought on myself.

He tried to move his arms, but he was able to move only the left, which he moved under his body, with difficulty, toward the right arm. When he reached it, there was no feeling. Determined now to reach the window, he pushed his body up and leaned his upper body on his left elbow. Then he could see his limp, unresponsive right arm. Holding still and catching his breath now, he could see what it would take to reach the sill and a chance to open the window. He realized he wouldn't be able to do it. There would be only one way. He rested and thought, *Please! I have suffered enough.*

Then there was a shot of pain across his head even worse than the earlier one. He let out a scream heard on the fourth floor. With all the strength he had remaining, he pulled himself onto the sill, turned away from the window, and pushed back and through. "Loleet, forgive me," he said, as he fell to the concrete alley below.

EPILOGUE:

"Life goes on"

In the early 1960s my mother and siblings moved from Chicago to Los Angeles. Mary June, the eldest, began this migration with her husband and three young children. A few years later, days after Barbara and I married, my mother and Precious followed. Precious, who soon had the steady income of a teacher in the Los Angeles school system, secured a mortgage and bought a house, "Ma's house." Jim joined them a few years later, after his first marriage ended.

When Barbara and I moved from Chicago to Massachusetts for our first academic positions in 1968, we added considerably to the geographic and emotional distance between my family and us. After that, face-to-face contact with them became a matter of an occasional summer vacation, during which my mother now and then hinted that we ought to move to Los Angeles to be nearer the family. Subsequently I also learned, from the remarks of others, that my mother was upset that we had chosen to spend our first sabbatical in Jamaica instead of California. This undoubtedly influenced the choice for our next sabbatical.

Partly because we wanted to give Adam and Shomari an opportunity to know their African-American extended family better, and partly because I wanted to reconnect with my mother and siblings, we decided to take our next sabbatical leave, 1981-82, in the Los Angeles area.

The year was very successful. We received visiting appointments at UCLA and had a productive year writing research articles. We lived in a blue-collar suburb, a walking distance away from the Pacific and the south beaches, which we all enjoyed. The children made friends easily and did well at their school, which was a three-minute walk across a small park abutting our apartment building. My siblings and their families included us in outings to amusement parks, beach parties, picnics, and social events. Adam and Shomari did get to know their family better, and I felt more involved with my family of origin than I had for many years.

The high point of our eleven-month stay, however, was the party for our mother's 80th birthday in June, 1982. My siblings and I began planning the party in the fall of 1981, soon after we arrived in California. We shared the costs, but Precious took the lead in finding a venue and making final arrangements for a sit-down dinner and music. It was a wonderfully joyous occasion. All our relatives living within driving distance were there, as were our family's friends who had joined the great migration from Chicago to Los Angeles, and all of my mother's church friends. It even happened that Barbara's mother, whose birthday was the same day as my mother's, was visiting us at the time. The parish priest gave an invocation, and several family members and friends gave toasts and speeches. But the highlight of the evening was when my mother led a traditional New Orleans line dance and sang "When the Saints Go Marching in." I had never seen my mother so radiantly happy. Her smile beamed ever more brightly as she lightly stepped and bounced in time with the tune while holding an open black umbrella, which she moved up and down over her head in time with the music and her step. I thought, *Is this my eighty-year-old mother?* But the pleasure I felt far exceeded my surprise. What I found most baffling, though, is that this tradition is associated with New Orleans jazz funeral celebrations.

The party was a high point for our mother and for the whole Turner family—a long way from the tragedy of 1945 and poverty at 812 West 14th Street in Chicago. But in retrospect, it also marked the beginning of a downward spiral. Before Thanksgiving of that year, my mother fell and broke her hip. She never completely recovered. Six weeks later, in January of 1983, June, age 48, suffered a massive hemorrhagic stroke. The attending doctors at Daniel Freeman Hospital held little hope for her survival. But she did live. Over the next year, she was given physical therapy and speech therapy, but she remained partially paralyzed, wheelchair-bound, and unable to speak or swallow.

The three women, each with serious health problems, now lived together in Ma's house. By the time our mother's and June's health stabilized, Medicare and Medi-Cal were paying for home-health aides to provide them daytime care while Precious worked as a fifth-grade teacher, but during the evenings, overnights, and weekends she was the primary caregiver. This arrangement continued until January 1989, when Precious's struggle against cancer came to a climax.

My meeting with Dr. Montz following Precious's surgery was the last time I saw him. After that, Jim was the major source of support for our mother and sisters, and he was the one who met with Montz and other healthcare providers whenever the family needed to be involved. As expected, Precious's recovery was slow and difficult, but she returned home to primary responsibility for the management of the household, including arrangements for medical services and homecare services for herself, our mother, and June.

In February of 1989, while she was still recovering at UCLA Medical Center, Precious wrote a will which two nurses signed as witnesses. In it she expressed the wish that any residue of her estate be placed into a trust fund to be used for the education of her mother's descendents. It further stipulated that the funds would be used for ninth grade onward. She named me the trustee and Jim as contingent trustee. When she first showed me this document, I believe she wanted to know my reaction to another specific stipulation—none of her siblings were to receive anything, on the grounds that they were all financially secure. I thought this a reasonable decision, but I didn't know whether she had shared the document with Jim.

It became clear that Precious was unable to continue taking care of her own health while managing and providing care for both our mother and June at home. We would have to make arrangements for our mother's institutional placement, since she would soon need twenty-four hour care. In August of 1989, after visiting several nursing homes in Los Angeles, I recommended one to Precious. After our mother recovered from pneumonia in Daniel Freeman Hospital, Precious arranged for her to be moved to St. John's Catholic nursing home, which was meant primarily for priests and nuns of the Los Angeles diocese. Our mother suffered several episodes of pneumonia and acute infections and was each time returned to the hospital. When I arrived from Massachusetts in response to one such episode, Jim and I agreed on the advisability of having a DNR order in place. I agreed to communicate the family's wishes to the hospital staff, since I was soon going to visit.

When I spoke to the charge nurse, I became tongue-tied and could get out only " . . . no Spartan efforts.," but she understood. After that I skulked away to another ward and cried in a public telephone alcove. My mother slept through my visit, and I never saw her again. She died at Daniel Freeman Hospital on January 24, 1990 at age 87.

At the funeral Mass, I had an overwhelming sense that I would see my mother again. In retrospect that epiphany was the first step toward my eventual return to religious faith.

Over the next eighteen months I made several visits to see Precious and June; the latter had been moved to a nursing facility in Garden Grove, in Orange County, close to her two daughters. During the spring of 1991 the UCLA oncology group informed Precious that there was nothing more they could do for her. After the City of Hope did an assessment and said they wouldn't accept her into experimental trials, she began making arrangements for death. Jim and I accompanied her to the Angelus Funeral Home, where she made "pre-need" arrangements. We also accompanied her to see an estate lawyer.

The three of us met twice with an attorney in Beverly Hills. In the first meeting Precious described what she had previously told me she wanted: an education trust fund in the name of our mother. The purpose of the trust would be to provide financial support for the education of Loretta Turner's descendents. The lawyer advised against such a plan because the estate was relatively small and the expense of administering a trust fund substantial. Precious was disappointed and asked whether money could be left to nieces and nephews with the requirement that the funds be used for educational purposes only. Again, the lawyer said such stipulations would be difficult to enforce without considerable administrative cost. An executor would have to hold the funds in trust and make decisions on every request for funds. Again disappointed, Precious agreed to the idea that the estate's funds would be split equally among all her nieces and nephews. But she wanted her *wish* that the money be used for education be part of the bequests. As in her earlier written will, no provisions were to be included for her siblings.

During the meeting Precious made the unexpected announcement that she wanted to include Jim's son born to a woman back in Chicago. Jim and I were speechless at first. Jim was surprised that she had known anything about that child. Finally he expressed appreciation for the gesture, but he didn't know his son's whereabouts or situation. He agreed to find him and determine whether he was likely to make good use of the legacy.

The lawyer proposed a second meeting to settle the details. In particular, he wanted a complete list of the names and mailing addresses of all nieces and nephews to be included.

I was staying with Jim on that visit. During the night Jim's pacing around the apartment woke me several times, but I didn't question him about the reason for his agitation. I assumed that the arrangements we had been party to were upsetting him. At the next meeting with the lawyer Jim made clear why he was troubled: he felt it unfair for her brothers and sister to be left out of the will. Precious then explained her thinking about excluding us: Since she wanted me to be the executor, she assumed that I could not also be named as a beneficiary of the estate. Because I could not benefit, she thought it unfair for Jim and June to be included. The lawyer promptly said that there was no such legal restriction; an executor could also be included as a legatee. Given that, Precious agreed that her brothers and sister would receive equal shares. I felt ambivalent about this outcome. I had earlier told Precious that I had no expectation of being included; but, once the decision was made, I was grateful, and promised myself that my share would be added to those of my two children for their education expenses.

Precious also wished to exclude one of June's children. Because of his history of struggling with substance abuse, she thought he would make poor use of any money left to him. The lawyer suggested he be left a token amount, which would make clear that he wasn't overlooked but wasn't to be considered on the same basis as the other legatees.

Between the two meetings Jim found his son's mother in Chicago; he found that his son was a college graduate, married with children, and living and working in Illinois. Precious responded with a broad smile; he would receive an equal share of the legacy.

In the fall of 1989, after our sabbatical at UCSF, Barbara and I moved from the University of Massachusetts at Amherst to the Boston campus. Jim called within weeks of the beginning of the fall semester 1991.

"You should probably come," he said. "Precious has taken a turn for the worse. We were told she may go very soon."

My throat tightened and I sat.

"I'll make arrangements to be there as soon as I can," I said. "Did something happen?"

"She has been losing weight and the cancer has been spreading. When she was moved from UCLA, she asked to be placed in the nursing facility where June was. That worked out well . . . She knew this was her last move . . . They had a chance to see each other when Precious arrived . . . Now Precious is on a system where she manages the flow of her pain medication, so she is sleeping most of the time. But she talks to visitors when she's awake."

"I should be able to get a flight in the morning," I said. "How are *you* doing? Does June realize what's going on?"

"I'm okay. June did recognize Precious, but I don't know what she thought was happening. Everyone else seems to be holding up . . . but it's hard."

"I know . . . So I'll see you soon. I'll rent a car at the airport so I can go see them as soon as I get there. I remember seeing June there, so I have a pretty good idea how to get out to the nursing care place. I'll call you when I get in. If I don't see you out there, we could meet at your place or at Ma's later."

When I arrived the following afternoon at the Hallmark Nursing Center, a plain one-story multi-wing building facing a wide boulevard, the receptionist gave me direction to find both Precious and June. They were in different wings, but I had no difficulty locating either. I looked in on Precious first. I hesitated at the door, took a deep breath, and entered. At the first sight of Precious, I was so shaken that I reached for something to hold onto—possibly the door itself. I have never fainted, but I felt myself reeling for a few seconds. *This cannot be my sister*, I thought. *This is a dead person.* Her head was slightly propped by pillows, but her skeletal face, ashen skin and widely gaping mouth looked like a death mask. Standing at the foot of the bed for a minute, I fought back the impulse to alert the staff that my sister must have died since the last time someone had checked on her.

When I finally approached on the left, I saw two small devices near her left hand and knew one must be for calling an attendant and the other for administering pain medication. On the right, two plastic bags with clear liquids hung on a metal tree; their tubes led to her taped left arm. I stood looking at her for several minutes.

When I took her right hand, it was limp and cold. Her eyes opened but she seemed unable to focus.

"Precious," I said softly and hesitantly, "it's Castie. I'm here."

"Castie?" she asked weakly, as she strained to focus.

"Yes," I answered, moving in closer. "I'm here."

"Have you seen June?" she asked.

"Not yet, but I will."

"I had a short visit with her the day I came here," she said with difficulty, "but I haven't seen her very much. Jim has wheeled her in a few times."

"I'm sorry to take you away from your family," she said. "How are Barbara and the children?"

"Everyone's fine," I answered. "They send their love."

"That's nice." She closed her eyes and didn't open them during the hour I remained by her bed.

When I visited with June, I found her much as she had been for many years. She recognized me and responded with a smile and sounds of glee. I kissed her and said I had seen Precious. She held my hand, looked searchingly into my face for a minute, then turned to the TV set facing her bed. I kept saying how good it was to see her looking so well. As usual, I commented on the pictures of her children and grandchildren tacked to the board next to her bed. She made happy guttural sounds and raised her functioning arm in a weak power salute as I named everyone I recognized. When someone was unfamiliar to me, I said so, but she still made her sounds and gestures. Following these routines, I felt my usual discomfort with trying to communicate without knowing what difference it made to her. Finally, I stopped talking, but she continued to hold my hand even as we both looked silently at the TV set.

When I returned to Precious's room, her eyes remained closed for the next hour. When she stirred, I told her I would see her in the morning and left. For several days I stayed in a motel nearby.

Sitting by her for much of the week, I waited—mostly in silence. Sometimes she was awake for short periods and we exchanged a few words. Nursing staff came to check or change the drips keeping her hydrated and pain-free. Meal trays were regularly brought in and placed where she could have reached them; later they were taken away untouched. When she was bathed or the bed changed, I stepped away or left the room, because even then I imagined that her modesty would be offended by my seeing her naked. For my part, I was ambivalent; on the one hand, the desire to fully witness and participate in her suffering was strong; on the other, I felt repelled by the thought of seeing her trunk bloated by cancer.

On one occasion Precious asked me to assist her in cleaning her mouth and lips, which were so chapped that the cracks in the skin became inflamed. She pointed to a sterile packet on the bedside table; it included a small brush and swabs, some dry and some moistened with what I soon discovered was citrus flavoring, presumably meant to freshen the mouth. I tried my best to be gentle as I brushed, but as I touched her lips with a moistened swab, Precious immediately grimaced, turned away and said with difficulty: "No. No. Stop. That hurts." I felt awful. I had added to her discomfort.

"I'm so sorry," I said, feeling that I had failed her.

"A little water, please," she said. "Would you hold the bottle?"

She carefully wrapped her lips around the straw and, with exertion, drew in a small amount of water. She again closed her eyes and slept.

On Saturday morning, because no one could say how long Precious would hold on, I made reservations for a Sunday morning flight. I had already been away from my teaching and administrative responsibilities for a week, so I felt obliged to return home. On Saturday afternoon, Jim received a call from the nursing facility saying they didn't expect Precious to live through the day. Jim and I sped to Garden Grove—in separate cars in case we needed to leave at different times. When we walked into her room, we were pleased to see her awake and alert. She had apparently rallied. We spent a wonderful afternoon reading scripture and singing hymns. In the late afternoon Tony, June's oldest child, arrived with his wife and newborn daughter. At one point, Tony held the child up so that Precious could have a full view of her. Precious was clearly very weak, but she managed a smile as the baby gurgled. We all beamed when Precious extended her right arm, as if to touch the child at a distance, and said softly: "Life goes on."

After Tony and his family left, I told Jim I intended to make my flight back to Massachusetts the next morning, even though I would likely be returning to Los Angeles very soon. After Jim left, I spent another hour saying goodbye to my sister.

"Precious," I began quietly, leaning toward her from a chair, "I'm planning to leave in the morning. I have to get back to work."

She looked at me squarely and said: "I understand. It was good having you here for such a long time. I'm sure your family misses you."

Tears were held back as I continued: "This is probably the last time I'll see you." I held her right hand as gently as I could.

"I know," she said, looking away. "It's time . . . I never thought it would take so long to starve to death."

This statement surprised me. I had assumed that she had neither appetite nor strength to respond to the food brought to her all week. Doubtless, cancer took her life, but it hadn't occurred to me that she thought of herself as actively letting go.

"Precious," I began again, "I've been thinking all week about when we were kids growing up in Chicago—all those days we walked back and forth to St. Joseph's; the times we went on Saturday or Sunday to the movies; the time you and Jimmy and I threw all our Quaker Oatmeal-boxes-full of marble winnings down into the alley at neighborhood kids, who scooped them up and filled their pockets?"

"Yes," she said, "I remember how we laughed and had a gay old time. It was funny how we never thought about how we played all spring to win those marbles. Just kids having fun, I guess . . ."

"Sounds like you thought about it," I said. "As I remember, you won most of those marbles. They were more yours than ours."

"Yes," she said, "I was a good shooter . . . I also liked winning marbles from the boys." She managed the slightest of smiles, though it ended with a grimace of pain. She closed her eyes, and after a minute, I thought she had fallen asleep. Then she opened her eyes and asked, "Do you remember the Saturdays when Ma used to take us downtown shopping?"

"Sure," I said. "We would walk through Sears & Roebuck and maybe some other stores, but we always ended the trip at Hellman's Foods.

She would situate us at some strategic spot, and then go shopping from one counter to the next, each time bringing packages for us to hold, until we each had a shopping bag for the streetcar ride home."

"Yes. Seems like yesterday." She closed her eyes again.

Opening her eyes just enough to look at me, she said: "I bet you remember when I broke one of your front teeth."

"Oh, yes," I answered. "I sure do."

"You were teasing me about something—I don't remember what—and I flipped a shoe at your face. I didn't throw it hard, just with my wrist, but it hit that tooth just right and broke it in half. One in a million shot."

"I was sprawled across Ma's double bed with my head hanging a bit over the side," I said. "I can picture it clearly. After I realized what happened, I didn't move . . . just lay there astonished. I wasn't even angry or upset. Maybe I figured I deserved it for teasing you."

"I never told you how bad I felt about it," she said. "You had that broken tooth for years, and every time I faced your smile, I had a reminder of what I did."

"I really never thought about it being your fault," I said. "It just became part of my identity—who I was—like the gaps we all had between our two front teeth . . . but then I had a little extra something."

She turned slightly toward me and managed a weak smile. "I'm glad."

Her eyes were closed for less than two minutes. I said, "Precious." She opened her eyes. I wanted to share one more thing with her. "Precious, do you remember when you asked me to take you to UCLA? I never told you this, but when the first surgeon told me how bad it was, I immediately cried and wrote out a vivid flashback of the day our father died."

"Oh?" she said. "That's interesting. What was that like?"

"Well," I began, "part of the memory included you. The evening of the day he died, I remember Ma was distraught and crying uncontrollably in bed. You knelt next to her, cried, and pleaded with her not to cry. Then I joined you, and eventually Ma pulled us into bed with her . . . Do you have any memory of that day or that evening?"

"No," she said, "I can't say I do. My memory is fuzzy. But it sounds like you remember it pretty well . . . What do you make of it?"

"Well," I began, "two things: first, you taught me, that night, about compassion—feeling deeply the pain of another person and letting them know that's where you want to be—with them—for whatever comfort that might give."

"Seeing you *has* been a comfort," she said. "I do hope you know that."

After a brief pause, I went on. "The other thing the flashback is telling me is that, at a deep level, I experienced a connection between that day and your illness. I think you were victimized, even more than the rest of us, by our father's early death. You've never been the type to complain, so I don't know how you felt about many things—staying with Ma and being the major provider all your life; never getting married and having your own family; working hard to keep June's family from falling into dysfunction. I don't know all the burdens and stresses you've had over the years, but I know the ones I've witnessed were enough to wear down most people's body and spirit."

"I tried not to think about things like that. I love my family and tried to be there for them, when they needed me."

"You were," I said. "I wonder how many understood how important you've been to the family all these years. It took a long time before *I* understood. Sometimes I felt guilty about not carrying more of the burden—leaving you to cope with Ma, with June's children, with June after her stroke, and with a fulltime job as a teacher. In a way, being so far away from the family allowed me to escape all the problems you were dealing with."

"I don't think there was much you could do," she said. "I'm sure you had your own problems. We all have to make our own choices in life. I made mine, and most of the time I was happy enough. I have no complaints." Then, closing her eyes, she said: "Now I'm tired."

"Is there a prayer we could say together?" I asked.

Without opening her eyes, she said, "Just pray for me . . . and Ma . . . and June. Just pray for us.

"Precious," I said, "I know we will all be together again."

With head bent near her hand, I prayed the Our Father. Then I asked: "Is there anything you want to say to God?"

When our eyes met, there was a question in hers. Then she looked away and said: "Dear Lord, I am ready . . . I am ready to enter." Her eyes closed. They didn't open again while I was there. After several minutes, I released her cold hand, kissed her on the forehead, and left her for the last time.

The next morning, when I presented my ticket at the airline check-in counter, the agent said there was an emergency phone call for me. When I heard Jim's voice, I knew Precious was gone.

"The nursing home called this morning," Jim began. "Precious died around five o'clock."

After a few seconds, I said: "Not a surprise . . . I'll cancel my flight."

"I'll pick you up," Jim said. "Just stand outside. Won't be long."

In the car on the way to UCLA Medical Center, I felt drained of energy and feeling. Looking straight ahead, I could barely attend to Jim as he described a remarkable early morning scene, before he received the news from the nursing home: after days of dreary weather, the sun uncharacteristically brightened LA's early morning sky. "It was like Easter Morning, the sun coming up bright in the clear morning air, as if to announce a new beginning . . . like an omen. I knew it meant something."

The memory of Precious the night before rushed in, and I wondered whether she had known she would die so soon. *Did she finally let go? Had she prayed to be released from her suffering? Did she believe that God would take her when she declared that she was ready?*

Gone, I thought.

When we arrived in Westwood, Jim wanted to pick up some flowers for the nurses at UCLA Medical Center who had cared for Precious. As expected, finding a parking spot on the street near a florist close to UCLA was impossible. Double-parking in front of a florist on one of the streets of elegant shops, Jim asked me to sit in the driver's seat while he went in. Although I sat there, my mind and my attention wandered back to Precious the night before, and I stared into the distance.

The scene came abruptly into focus: "License and registration," demanded a policeman standing at the driver's side of the car. I said nothing but reached for my license and searched for the registration.

The policeman said gruffly as he walked away toward his motorcycle: "You people need to learn you can't treat the streets of Westwood like a parking lot."

I thought, *You people? Parking lot?* I felt like a foreigner mistaken for a member of one of the local notorious gangs. The police were out to teach someone a lesson. My muteness solidified.

When Jim came out of the florist shop, he placed a potted plant on the floor of the back seat. I got out, walked to the passenger side and sat. Just as Jim sat in the driver's seat, the policeman approached with the ticket. The change in the seating confused him. Who should get the ticket? Our eyes met, and I could see the officer wanted me to have it; I imagined, however, he realized what had happened. Jim took it, and we drove away in silence and neither ever mentioned the incident or the ticket.

As we walked into the hospital ward where Precious had been before her transfer to the nursing home, Jim saw some familiar faces at the nurse's station, placed the flowers on the counter and announced that Precious had died. He thanked the nursing staff for the care they had given Precious. They responded with condolences. One nurse in the hall, upon recognizing Jim, embraced him. We were there for less than five minutes.

As we left the nurses, I realized that Jim had been there for Precious while I had missed most of the final months of her gradually worsening condition. I spoke with her a few times during that period; each time we talked, I heard the growing pain and the fading spirit in her voice. I had cried after those conversations, but now my grief was mixed with guilt. The previous night I had been grateful for the opportunity to apologize for being so distant from the problems she faced all those years; I had been even more grateful for her forgiveness. But as we drove away from UCLA Medical Center for the last time, I knew that my sorrow would be with me for a long time—and that it would be laced with regret.

The Angelus Funeral Home took care of most of the arrangements. My major role in the funeral program was to speak at the wake on Thursday evening at St. Brigid's Church. Earlier that day, I made some notes for what I wanted to say. I remembered a line from the farewell message our grandmother had left for her mother in 1909: "Every heart knows its own burden." *How fitting*, I thought. *That could be Precious speaking those words to me now. The only one who can judge a life is the one who lives it. Only that person knows what their own life means, the pains, the sorrows, the joys.* Soon I realized it was a poem that would begin my eulogy:

Elegy For a Sister:
In Memory of Preciosa Lolita Turner
October 17, 1991

"Every heart knows its own burdens."
Every heart knows its own joys.
This precious spirit, this strong heart
Rarely spoke of her burdens.
She freely spread her joy.
She labored in love without complaint.
She gave joyously of herself all her life.

Most of us live lives of quiet desperation.
She lived a life of quiet dedication—
To God, to her mother, to her sister,
To all in our family, and to untold numbers
Of children whom she taught and loved.
May she and her mother live forever in the
Peace and presence of God.